UNUSUAL AND UNEXPECTED TALES BY CAPTAIN FREDERICK MARRYAT, HERMAN MELVILLE, JACK LONDON, W. CLARK RUSSELL, JOSEPH CONRAD, JOHN MASEFIELD, C. S. FORESTER, RUDYARD KIPLING, ARTHUR CONAN DOYLE, RICHARD SALE, WILLIAM HOPE HODGSON, H. G. WELLS, EDGAR ALLAN POE, AND RAY BRADBURY

"These, then, are your means of transport to mystery on the high seas—if, like me, you would prefer to voyage safe and warm in the comfort of your armchair. For those watery places where spirits haunt the upper deck and monstrous creatures tear at the ship's bowels are not for the landlubber or the faint-hearted."

—William Pattrick,
from the Introduction

MYSTERIOUS SEA STORIES

Compiled and Edited by
WILLIAM PATTRICK

A DELL BOOK

Published by
Dell Publishing Co., Inc.
1 Dag Hammarskjold Plaza
New York, New York 10017

This work was first published in Great Britain by W. H. Allen & Co.,
PLC.

Dell ® TM 681510, Dell Publishing Co., Inc.

ISBN: 0-440-16088-X

Reprinted by arrangement with W. H. Allen & Co., PLC

Printed in the United States of America

First U.S.A. Printing

September 1987

10 9 8 7 6 5 4 3 2 1

WFH

CONTENTS

INTRODUCTION

NOT LONG BEFORE his death that great British seaman, Lord Nelson, remarked, 'At sea, nothing is impossible and nothing improbable.' Although he put it splendidly, what he said was really nothing new, even then – for almost since the first man pushed himself gingerly away from the safety of the shore and cast himself and his frail craft to the mercy of the waves and the elements, sailors have come to appreciate the mysterious powers of the sea. Even today when shipping has all the sophisticated equipment provided by modern technology at its disposal, there is still the element of the unknown lurking just across the horizon – and it is a foolish seaman who would choose to ignore such a fact.

Of course, in the early days of sail, mariners believed if they went too far from land their ships might fall off the edge of the world; and even in later ages seafarers clung tenaciously to the most amazing superstitions which gave the sea and all things above and below it quite extraordinary powers. The discoveries of the early explorers may well have removed fears about a flat earth, but there are still many of these old superstitions being religiously observed. Their influence is as powerful and mysterious and timeless as the very sea itself.

Because of the uncertainty of life at sea and the temperamental nature of the wind and weather – not forgetting the unusual conditions that can exist far from land – sailors have always been coming home with stories of strange, inexplicable happenings. Of ships beset by phantoms, of deep sea creatures unlike any seen before, and of places where none but the most foolhardy would go. These have provided the raw material for storytellers and have ultimately developed into what we now know as the sea mystery story.

Although the mysterious incidents which have given rise to these stories can be traced back many, many years, it is in fact only in the last couple of hundred years that they have become a literary genre in their own right. To be sure, there are whole libraries of books of ancient sea voyages in which are recorded encounters with strange people, sea serpents and ghostly vessels. But it is primarily with the work of Edgar Allan Poe at the beginning of the last century that such tales emerged and took on the form now so recognisable and widely read.

In this collection I have tried to assemble some of the best and most representative of the short sea mystery stories, taking a tale by Poe as my starting point. As the reader will discover, the tales range across many years and most of the great oceans of the world. They have for their themes some of the best known mysteries of the sea, and convey us as often by sail as by steam. They also happen to be written by some of the most popular authors of maritime fiction – although I have tried as much as possible to avoid frequently anthologised works by these people.

Consequently, you will find some rather unusual and, I trust, unexpected tales by authors such as Captain Frederick Marryat, Herman Melville, Jack London, W. Clark Russell, Joseph Conrad, John Masefield, and C. S. Forester. All of these keep happy company with some other familiar figures who were fascinated by mysteries of the sea and put pen to paper in a most imaginative way. There is Rudyard Kipling on sea monsters, Sir Arthur Conan Doyle cleverly trying to solve the mystery of the *Marie Celeste*, Richard Sale doing the same for *The Flying Dutchman*, William Hope Hodgson exploring the legendary Sargasso Sea, H. G. Wells taking us into the depths of the ocean, and Ray Bradbury with a grim little fantasy about war at sea.

These, then, are your means of transport to mystery on the high seas – if, like me, you would prefer to voyage safe and warm in the comfort of your armchair. For those watery places where spirits haunt the upper deck and monstrous creatures tear at the ship's bowels are not for the landlubber or the faint-hearted. All the stories will, I believe, intrigue, chill and entertain you, and in leaving you to your pleasures I am reminded of those lines by Shakespeare: 'There are more things in Heaven and Earth . . ./ Than are dreamt of in your philosophy.' When you have finished reading *Mysterious Sea Stories*, I have more than a suspicion you will want to add 'and in the Sea' to that perceptive phrase . . .

WILLIAM PATTRICK
Suffolk, 1984

MS. FOUND IN A BOTTLE

Edgar Allan Poe

Although sailors of all nations had been telling stories for many centuries about the strange and bizarre things that could be experienced at sea, the first writer to produce a group of tales that could be categorised as sea mysteries was that tormented American genius, Edgar Allan Poe (1809–1849). Poe's interests were widespread, and amongst his work can be found some of the very first stories of detection, pioneer science fiction, and also some outstanding horror stories.

But the sea also exerted a special fascination for this remarkable man. Apart from using it as the theme of several short stories, it also formed the basis of his only novel The Mystery of Arthur Gordon Pym, *which he left incomplete at the time of his death in 1849. However, the novel was finished in 1897 by the famous French fantasy writer, Jules Verne, under the title of* An Antarctic Mystery.

In his work, Poe gave clear evidence that he sensed all the terrors and strangeness that lurked in the vastness of the world's oceans, using this knowledge to brilliant effect. The very first of his sea mysteries was MS. Found In A Bottle *which appeared in 1833, and which has since proved a model for many later similar stories. Apart from its vivid description of a storm at sea, it also deals with an ancient superstition that the earth was hollow and that there were entrances to this 'inner world' in the sea near the poles which could suck in the unwary vessel. It therefore makes a most suitable story with which to begin our voyage into the realms of mystery . . .*

> 'Qui n'a plus qu'un moment à vivre
> N'a plus rien à dissimuler.' — *Quinault – Atys*

OF MY COUNTRY and of my family I have little to say. Ill-usage and length of years have driven me from the one, and estranged me from the other. Hereditary wealth afforded me an education of no common order, and a contemplative turn of mind enabled me to methodise the stores which early study very diligently garnered up. Beyond all things, the works of the German moralists gave me great delight; not from any ill-advised admiration of their eloquent madness, but from the ease with which my habits of rigid thought enabled me to detect their falsities. I have often been reproached with the aridity of my genius; a deficiency of imagination has been imputed to me as a crime; and the Pyrrhonism of my opinions has at all times rendered me notorious. Indeed, a strong relish for physical philosophy has, I fear, tinctured my mind with a very common error of this age – I mean the habit of referring occurrences, even the least susceptible of such reference, to the principles of that science. Upon the whole, no person could be less liable than myself to be led away from the severe precincts of truth by the *ignes fatui* of superstition. I have thought proper to premise thus much, lest the incredible tale I have to tell should be considered rather the raving of a crude imagination than the positive experience of a mind to which the reveries of fantasy have been a dead letter and a nullity.

7

After many years spent in foreign travel, I sailed in the year 18— from the port of Batavia, in the rich and populous island of Java, on a voyage to the Archipelago of the Sunda Islands. I went as passenger – having no other inducement than a kind of nervous restlessness which haunted me as a fiend.

Our vessel was a beautiful ship of about four hundred tons, copper-fastened, and built at Bombay of Malabar teak. She was freighted with cotton-wool and oil, from the Lachadive islands. We had also on board coir, jaggeree, ghee, cocoa-nuts, and a few cases of opium. The stowage was clumsily done, and the vessel consequently crank.

We got under way with a mere breath of wind, and for many days stood along the eastern coast of Java, without any other incident to beguile the monotony of our course than the occasional meeting with some of the small grabs of the Archipelago to which we were bound.

One evening, leaning over the taffrail, I observed a very singular isolated cloud to the N.W. It was remarkable, as well for its colour as from its being the first we had seen since our departure from Batavia. I watched it attentively until sunset, when it spread all at once to the eastward and westward, girting in the horizon with a narrow strip of vapour, and looking like a long line of low beach. My notice was soon afterwards attracted by the dusky-red appearance of the moon, and the peculiar character of the sea. The latter was undergoing a rapid change, and the water seemed more than usually transparent. Although I could distinctly see the bottom, yet, heaving the lead, I found the ship in fifteen fathoms. The air now became intolerably hot, and was loaded with spiral exhalations similar to those arising from heated iron. As night came on, every breath of wind died away, and a more entire calm it is impossible to conceive. The flame of a candle burned upon the poop without the least perceptible motion, and a long hair, held between the finger and thumb, hung without the possibility of detecting a vibration. However, as the captain said he could perceive no indication of danger, and as we were drifting in bodily to shore, he ordered the sails to be furled, and the anchor let go. No watch was set, and the crew, consisting principally of Malays, stretched themselves deliberately upon deck. I went below – not without a full presentiment of evil. Indeed, every appearance warranted me in apprehending a simoom. I told the captain my fears; but he paid no attention to what I said, and left me without deigning to give a reply. My uneasiness, however, prevented me from sleeping, and about midnight I went upon deck. As I placed my foot upon the upper step of the companion-ladder, I was startled by a loud, humming noise, like that occasioned by the rapid revolution of a mill-wheel, and before I could ascertain its meaning, I found the ship quivering to its centre. In the next instant, a wilderness of foam hurled us upon our beam-ends, and, rushing over us fore and aft, swept the entire decks from stem to stern.

The extreme fury of the blast proved, in a great measure, the salvation of the ship. Although completely water-logged, yet, as her masts had gone by the board, she rose, after a minute, heavily from the sea, and, staggering awhile beneath the immense pressure of the tempest, finally righted.

By what miracle I escaped destruction it is impossible to say. Stunned by the shock of the water, I found myself, upon recovery, jammed in between the stern-post and rudder. With great difficulty I gained my feet, and, looking dizzily around, was at first struck with the idea of our being among breakers; so terrific, beyond the wildest imagination, was the whirlpool of mountainous and foaming ocean within which we were engulfed. After a while, I heard the voice of an old Swede, who had shipped with us at the moment of our leaving port. I hallooed to him with all my strength, and presently he came reeling aft. We soon discovered that we were the sole survivors of the accident. All on deck, with the exception of ourselves, had been swept overboard; the captain and mates must have perished as they slept, for the cabins were deluged with water. Without assistance we could expect to do little for the security of the ship, and our exertions were at first paralysed by the momentary expectation of going down. Our cable had, of course, parted like pack-thread, at the first breath of the hurricane, or we should have been instantaneously overwhelmed. We scudded with frightful velocity before the sea, and the water made clear breaches over us. The framework of our stern was shattered excessively, and in almost every respect we had received considerable injury; but to our extreme joy we found the pumps unchoked, and that we had made no great shifting of our ballast. The main fury of the blast had already blown over, and we apprehended little danger from the violence of the wind; but we looked forward to its total cessation with dismay; well believing, that in our shattered condition, we should inevitably perish in the tremendous swell which would ensue. But this very just apprehension seemed by no means likely to be soon verified. For five entire days and nights – during which our only subsistence was a small quantity of jaggeree, procured with great difficulty from the forecastle – the hulk flew at a rate defying computation, before rapidly succeeding flaws of wind, which, without equalling the first violence of the simoom, were still more terrific than any tempest I had before encountered. Our course for the first four days was, with trifling variations S.E. and by S.; and we must have run down the coast of New Holland. On the fifth day the cold became extreme, although the wind had hauled round a point more to the northward. The sun arose with a sickly yellow lustre, and clambered a very few degrees above the horizon — emitting no decisive light. There were no clouds apparent, yet the wind was upon the increase, and blew with a fitful and unsteady fury. About noon, as nearly as we could guess, our attention was again arrested by the appearance of the sun. It gave out no light, properly so called, but a dull and sullen glow without reflection, as if all its rays were polarised. Just before sinking within the turgid sea, its central fires suddenly went out, as if hurriedly extinguished by some unaccountable power. It was a dim, silver-like rim, alone, as it rushed down the unfathomable ocean.

We waited in vain for the arrival of the sixth day – that day to me has not arrived – to the Swede never did arrive. Thenceforward we were enshrouded in pitchy darkness, so that we could not have seen an object at twenty paces from the ship. Eternal night continued to envelop us, all unrelieved by the phosphoric sea-brilliancy to which we had been accustomed in the tropics. We observed too, that, although the tempest continued to rage with unabated violence, there was no longer to be discovered the usual appearance of surf, ⌐ foam, which had hitherto attended us. All around were horror, and thick gloom, and a black sweltering desert of ebony. Superstitious terror crept by degrees into the spirit of the old Swede, and my own soul was wrapped up in silent wonder. We neglected all care of the ship as worse than useless, and securing ourselves, as well as possible, to the stump of the mizen-mast, looked out bitterly into the world of ocean. We had no means of calculating time, nor could we form any guess of our situation. We were, however, well aware of having made farther to the southward than any previous navigators, and felt great amazement at not meeting with the usual impediments of ice. In the meantime every moment threatened to be our last – every mountainous billow hurried to overwhelm us. The swell surpassed anything I had imagined possible, and that we were not instantly buried is a miracle. My companion spoke of the lightness of our cargo, and reminded me of the excellent qualities of our ship; but I could not help feeling the utter hopelessness of hope itself, and prepared myself gloomily for that death which I thought nothing could defer beyond an hour, as, with every knot of way the ship made, the swelling of the black stupendous seas became more dismally appalling. At times we gasped for breath at an elevation beyond the albatross – at times became dizzy with the velocity of our descent into some watery hell, where the air grew stagnant, and no sound disturbed the slumbers of the kraken.

We were at the bottom of one of the abysses, when a quick scream from my companion broke fearfully upon the night. 'See! See!' cried he, shrieking in my ears, 'Almighty God! See! See!' As he spoke, I became aware of a dull, sullen glare of red light which streamed down the sides of the vast chasm where we lay, and threw a fitful brilliancy upon our deck. Casting my eyes upwards, I beheld a spectacle which froze the current of my blood. At a terrific height directly above us, and upon the very verge of the precipitous descent, hovered a gigantic ship, of perhaps four thousand tons. Although upreared upon the summit of a wave more than a hundred times her own altitude, her apparent size still exceeded that of any ship of the line or East Indiaman in existence. Her huge hull was a deep dingy black, unrelieved by any of the customary carvings of a ship. A single row of brass cannon protruded from her open ports, and dashed from their polished surfaces the fires of innumerable battle-lanterns, which swung to and fro about her rigging. But what mainly inspired us with horror and astonishment, was, that she bore up under a press of sail in the very teeth of that supernatural sea, and of that ungovernable hurricane. When we first discovered her, her bows were alone to be seen, as she rose slowly from the dim and horrible gulf beyond her. For a moment of intense terror she paused upon the giddy pinnacle, as if in contemplation of her own sublimity, then trembled and tottered, and – came down.

At this instant I know not what sudden self-possession came over my spirit. Staggering as far aft as I could, I awaited fearlessly the ruin that was to overwhelm. Our own vessel was at length ceasing from her struggles, and sinking with her head to the sea. The shock of the descending mass struck her, consequently, in that portion of her frame which was already under water, and the inevitable result was to hurl me, with irresistible violence, upon the rigging of the stranger.

As I fell, the shop hove in stays, and went about; and to the confusion ensuing I attributed my escape from the notice of the crew. With little difficulty I made my way, unperceived, to the main hatchway, which was partially open, and soon found an opportunity of secreting myself in the hold. Why I did so I can hardly tell. An indefinite sense of awe, which at first sight of the navigators of the ship had taken hold of my mind, was perhaps the principle of my concealment. I was unwilling to trust myself with a race of people who had offered, to the cursory glance I had taken, so many points of vague novelty, doubt, and apprehension. I therefore thought proper to contrive a hiding-place in the hold. This I did by removing a small portion of the shifting-boards, in such a manner as to afford me a convenient retreat between the huge timbers of the ship.

I had scarcely completed my work, when a footstep in the hold forced me to make use of it. A man passed by my place of concealment with a feeble and unsteady gait. I could not see his face, but had an opportunity of observing his general appearance. There was about it an evidence of great age and infirmity. His knees tottered beneath a load of years, and his entire frame quivered under the burden. He muttered to himself, in a low, broken tone, some words of a language which I could not understand, and groped in a corner among a pile of singular-looking instruments, and decayed charts of navigation. His manner was a wild mixture of the peevishness of second childhood and the solemn dignity of a God. He at length went on deck, and I saw him no more.

A feeling, for which I have no name, has taken possession of my soul – a sensation which will admit of no analysis, to which the lessons of bygone times are inadequate, and for which I fear futurity itself will offer me no key. To a mind constituted like my own, the latter consideration is an evil. I shall never – I know that I shall never – be satisfied with regard to the nature of my conceptions. Yet it is not wonderful that these conceptions are indefinite, since they have their origin in sources so utterly novel. A new sense – a new entity is added to my soul.

It is long since I first trod the deck of this terrible ship, and the rays of my destiny are, I think, gathering to a focus. Incomprehensible men! Wrapped up in meditations of a kind which I cannot divine, they pass me by unnoticed. Concealment is utter folly on my part, for the people *will not* see. It was but just now that I passed directly before the eyes of the mate; it was no long while ago that I ventured into the captain's own private cabin, and took thence the materials with which I write, and have written. I shall from time to time continue this journal. It is true that I may not find an opportunity of transmitting it to the world, but I will not fail to make the endeavour. At the last moment I will enclose the MS. in a bottle and cast it within the sea.

An incident has occurred which has given me new room for meditation. Are such things the operation of ungoverned chance? I had ventured upon deck and thrown myself down, without attracting any notice, among a pile of ratline-stuff and old sails, in the bottom of the yawl. While musing upon the singularity of my fate, I unwittingly daubed with a tar-brush the edges of a neatly-folded studding-sail which lay near me on a barrel. The studding-sail is now bent upon the ship, and the thoughtless touches of the brush are spread out into the word DISCOVERY.

I have made many observations lately upon the structure of the vessel. Although well armed, she is not, I think, a ship of war. Her rigging, build, and general equipment, all negative a supposition of this kind. What she *is not*, I can easily perceive; what she *is*, I fear it is impossible to say. I know not how it is, but in scrutinising her strange model and singular cast of spars, her huge size and overgrown suits of canvas, her severely simple bow and antiquated stern, there will occasionally flash across my mind a sensation of familiar things, and there is always mixed up with such indistinct shadows of recollection an unaccountable memory of old foreign chronicles and ages long ago.

I have been looking at the timbers of the ship. She is built of a material to which I am a stranger. There is a peculiar character about the wood which strikes me as rendering it unfit for the purpose to which it has been applied. I mean its extreme *porousness*, considered independently of the worm-eaten condition which is a consequence of navigation in these seas, and apart from the rottenness attendant upon age. It will appear perhaps an observation somewhat over-curious, but this wood would have every characteristic of Spanish oak, if Spanish oak were distended by any unnatural means.

In reading the above sentence, a curious apothegm of an old weather-beaten Dutch navigator comes full upon my recollection. 'It is as sure,' he was wont to say, when any doubt was entertained of his veracity, 'as sure as there is a sea where the ship itself will grow in bulk like the living body of the seaman.'

About an hour ago, I made bold to thrust myself among a group of the crew. They paid me no manner of attention, and, although I stood in the very midst of them all, seemed utterly unconscious of my presence. Like the one I had first seen in the hold, they all bore about them the marks of a hoary old age. Their knees trembled with infirmity; their shoulders were bent double with decrepitude; their shrivelled skins rattled in the wind; their voices were low, tremulous, and broken; their eyes glistened with the rheum of years; and their grey hairs streamed terribly in the tempest. Around them, on every part of the deck, lay scattered mathematical instruments of the most quaint and obsolete construction.

I mentioned some time ago the bending of a studding-sail. From that period the ship, being thrown dead off the wind, has continued her terrific course due south, with every rag of canvas packed upon her, from her trucks to her lower studding-sail booms, and rolling every moment her top-gallant yard-arms into the most appalling hell of water which it can enter into the mind of man to imagine. I have just left the deck, where I find it impossible to maintain a footing, although the crew seem to experience little inconvenience. It appears to me a miracle of miracles that our enormous bulk is not swallowed up at once and for ever. We are surely doomed to hover continually upon the brink of eternity, without taking a final plunge into the abyss. From billows a thousand times more stupendous than I have ever seen, we glide away with the facility of the arrowy sea-gull; and the colossal waters rear their heads above us like demons of the deep, but like demons confined to simple threats, and forbidden to destroy. I am led to attribute these frequent escapes to the only natural cause which can account for such effect. I must suppose the ship to be within the influence of some strong current, or impetuous under-tow.

I have seen the captain face to face, and in his own cabin – but, as I expected, he paid me no attention. Although in his appearance there is, to a casual observer, nothing which might bespeak him more or less than man, still, a feeling of irrepressible reverence and awe mingled with the sensation of wonder with which I regarded him. In stature, he is nearly my own height; that is, about five feet eight inches. He is of a well-knit and compact frame of body, neither robust nor remarkable otherwise. But it is the singularity of the expression which reigns upon the face – it is the intense, the wonderful, the thrilling evidence of old age, so utter, so extreme, which excites within my spirit a sense – a sentiment ineffable. His forehead, although little wrinkled, seems to bear upon it the stamp of a myriad of years. His grey hairs are records of the past, and his greyer eyes are sybils of the future. The cabin floor was thickly strewn with strange, iron-clasped folios, and mouldering instruments of science, and obsolete long-forgotten charts. His head was bowed down upon his hands, and he pored with a fiery, unquiet eye over a paper which I took to be a commission, and which, at all events, bore the signature of a monarch. He muttered to himself – as did the first seaman whom I saw in the hold – some low, peevish syllables of a foreign tongue; and although the speaker was close at my elbow, his voice seemed to reach my ears from the distance of a mile.

The ship and all in it are imbued with the spirit of Eld. The crew glide to and fro like the ghosts of buried centuries; their eyes have an eager and uneasy meaning; and when their figures fall athwart my path in the wild glare of the battle-lanterns, I feel as I have never felt before, although I have been all my life a dealer in antiquities, and have imbibed the shadows of fallen columns at Balbec, and Tadmor, and Persepolis, until my very soul has become a ruin.

When I look around me I feel ashamed of my former apprehensions. If I trembled at the blast which has hitherto attended us, shall I not stand aghast at a warring of wind and ocean, to convey any idea of which the words tornado and simoom are trivial and ineffective? All in the immediate vicinity of the ship is the blackness of eternal night, and a chaos of foamless water; but, about a league on either side of us, may be seen, indistinctly and at intervals, stupendous ramparts of ice towering away into the desolate sky, and looking like the walls of the universe.

As I imagined, the ship proves to be in a current – if that

appellation can properly be given to a tide which, howling and shrieking by the white ice, thunders on to the southward with a velocity like the headlong dashing of a cataract.

To conceive the horror of my sensations is, I presume, utterly impossible; yet a curiosity to penetrate the mysteries of those awful regions predominates even over my despair, and will reconcile me to the most hideous aspect of death. It is evident that we are hurrying onwards to some exciting knowledge – some never-to-be-imparted secret, whose attainment is destruction. Perhaps this current leads us to the southern pole itself. It must be confessed that a supposition apparently so wild has every probability in its favour.

The crew pace the deck with unquiet and tremulous step; but there is upon their countenances an expression more of the eagerness of hope than of the apathy of despair.

In the meantime the wind is still in our poop, and as we carry a crowd of canvas the ship is at times lifted bodily from out the sea! Oh, horror upon horror! – the ice opens suddenly to the right, and to the left, and we are whirling dizzily, in immense concentric circles, round and round the borders of a gigantic amphitheatre, the summit of whose walls is lost in the darkness and the distance. But little time will be left me to ponder upon my destiny! The circles rapidly grow small – we are plunging madly within the grasp of the whirlpool – and amid a roaring, and bellowing, and thundering of ocean and of tempest, the ship is quivering – Oh God! and – going down!

NOTE.—The 'MS. Found in a Bottle' was originally published in 1831, and it was not until many years afterwards that I became acquainted with the maps of Mercator, in which the ocean is represented as rushing, by four mouths, into the (northern) Polar Gulf, to be absorbed into the bowels of the earth; the Pole itself being represented by a black rock towering to a prodigious height. [E.A.P.]

THE LEGEND
OF THE BELL ROCK

Captain Frederick Marryat

Poe may have written the first short sea mystery story, but it was an English contemporary, Captain Frederick Marryat (1792–1848) who earned the distinction of the title 'Father of the Sea Story'. Such, in fact, is Captain Marryat's fame among lovers of nautical fiction that he scarcely needs an introduction, and there is no disputing that the most famous of his books have been enormously influential on all later works in the genre. Titles such as Peter Simple *(1833),* Mr Midshipman Easy *(1834) and* Masterman Ready *(1843) are familiar all over the world and still read and enjoyed today.*

As a writer of sea stories, Marryat has no peer, and his descriptions of seamen braving the elements and fighting naval actions are written with an incredible gusto. The fact that he had spent many years at sea before becoming a writer doubtless added to the authenticity of his work. After serving in the West Indies as a young man, he was made the commander of a sloop which cruised off St. Helena to guard against the escape of Napoleon; and he then saw combat off the Burmese coast before returning to home waters to wage war on the smugglers in the English Channel. His reward was a C.B. and an even more important command; but in 1830 he decided to resign his commission and follow a life-long ambition to write about the sea. The resulting books can be counted among the most enduring and exciting maritime tales ever written.

Strangely, Captain Marryat wrote very few short stories, and 'The Legend of the Bell Rock' (1836) is his only short sea mystery. It is a fascinating portrait of a doomed seaman, and has clear parallels with the tale of the legendary Flying Dutchman *which Marryat helped to immortalise in his later novel,* The Phantom Ship *(1839). The inclusion of 'The Legend of the Bell Rock' in this anthology marks the story's first reappearance in print for over one hundred years.*

THERE WAS A grand procession through the streets of the two towns of Perth and Dundee. The holy abbots, in their robes, walked under gilded canopies, the monks chanted, the censers were thrown, flags and banners were carried by seamen, lighted tapers by penitents; St Antonio, the patron of those who trust to the stormy ocean, was carried in all pomp through the streets; and, as the procession passed, coins of various value were thrown down by those who watched it from the windows, and, as fast as thrown, were collected by little boys dressed as angels, and holding silver vessels to receive the largesses. During the whole day did the procession continue, and large was the treasure collected in the two towns. Everyone gave freely, for there were few, indeed none, who, if not in their own circle, at least among their acquaintances, had not to deplore the loss of some one dear to them, or to those they visited, from the dangerous rock which lay in the very track of all the vessels entering the Firth of Tay.

These processions had been arranged, that a sufficient sum of money might be collected to enable them to put in execution a plan proposed by an adventurous and bold young seaman, in a council held for the purpose, of fixing a bell on the rock, which could be so arranged that the slightest breath of wind would cause the hammer of it to sound, and thus, by its tolling, warn the mariner of his danger; and the sums given were more than sufficient. A meeting was then held, and it was unanimously agreed that Andrew M'Clise should be charged with the

21

commission to go over to Amsterdam, and purchase the bell of a merchant residing there, whom Andrew stated to have one in his possession, which, from its fine tone and size, was exactly calculated for the purpose to which it was to be appointed.

Andrew M'Clise embarked with the money, and made a prosperous voyage. He had often been at Amsterdam, and had lived with the merchant, whose name was Vandermaclin; and the attention to his affairs, the dexterity and the rapidity of the movements of Andrew M'Clise, had often elicited the warmest encomiums of Master Vandermaclin; and many evenings had Andrew M'Clise passed with him, drinking in moderation their favourite scheedam, and indulging in the meditative meerschaum. Vandermaclin had often wished that he had a son like Andrew M'Clise, to whom he could leave his property, with the full assurance that the heap would not be scattered, but greatly added to.

Vandermaclin was a widower. He had but one daughter, who was now just arrived at an age to return from the pension to her father's house, and take upon herself the domestic duties. M'Clise had never yet seen the beautiful Katerina.

'And so, Mynheer M'Clise,' said Vandermaclin, who was sitting in the warehouse on the ground-floor of his tenement, 'you come to purchase the famous bell of Utrecht; with the intention of fixing it upon that rock, the danger of which we have so often talked over after the work of the day has been done? I, too, have suffered from that same rock, as you well know; but still I have been fortunate. The price will be heavy; and so it ought to be, for the bell itself is of no small weight.'

'We are prepared to pay it, Mynheer Vandermaclin.'

'Nevertheless, in so good a cause, and for so good a purpose, you shall not be overcharged. I will say nothing of the beauty of the workmanship, or even of the mere manufacture. You shall pay but its value in metal; the same price which the Jew Isaacs offered me for it but four months ago. I will not ask what a Jew would ask, but what a Jew would give, which makes no small difference. Have you ten thousand guilders?'

'I have, and more.'

'That is my price, Mynheer M'Clise, and I wish for no more;

for I, too, will contribute my share to the good work. Are you content, and is it a bargain?'

'It is; and the holy abbots will thank you on vellum, Mynheer Vandermaclin, for your generosity.'

'I prefer the thanks of the bold seamen to those of the idle churchmen; but, never mind, it is a bargain. Now, we will go in; it is time to close the doors. We will take our pipes, and you shall make the acquaintance of my fair daughter, Katerina.'

At the time we are speaking of, M'Clise was about six and twenty years of age; he was above the middle size, elegant in person, and with a frankness and almost nobility in his countenance, which won all who saw him.

His manners were like those of most seamen, bold, but not offensively so. His eye was piercing as an eagle's; and it seemed as if his very soul spoke from it. At the very first meeting between him and the daughter of Vandermaclin, it appeared to both as if their destinies were to unite them.

They loved not as others love, but with an intensity which it would be impossible to portray; yet they hardly exchanged a word. Again and again they met; their eyes spoke, but nothing more. The bell was put on board the vessel, the money had been paid down, and M'Clise could no longer delay. He felt as if his heartstrings were severed as he tore himself away from the land where all remained that he coveted upon earth. And Katerina, she too felt as if her existence was a blank; and as the vessel sailed from the port, she breathed short; and when not even her white and lofty top-gallant sail could be discovered as a speck, she threw herself on her couch and wept. And M'Clise, as he sailed away, remained for hours leaning his cheek on his hand, thinking of, over and over again, every lineament and feature of the peerless Katerina.

Two months passed away, during which M'Clise was busied every ebb of the tide in superintending the work on the rock. At last, all was ready; and once more was to be beheld a gay procession; but this time it was on the water. It was on a calm and lovely summer's morn that the abbots and the monks, attended by a large company of the authorities and others who were so much interested in the work in hand, started from the shore of

Aberbrothwick in a long line of boats, decorated with sacred and with other various banners and devices. The music floated along the water, and the solemn chants of the monks were once heard where never yet they had been heard before, or ever will again. M'Clise was at the rock, in a small vessel purposely constructed to carry the bell, and with sheers to hang it on the supports imbedded in the solid rock. The bell was in its place, and the abbot blessed the bell; and holy water was sprinkled on the metal, which was for the future to be lashed by the waves of the salt sea. And the music and the chants were renewed; and as they continued, the wind gradually rose, and with the rising of the wind the bell tolled loud and deep. The tolling of the bell was the signal for return, for it was a warning that the weather was about to change, and the procession pulled back to Aberbrothwick, and landed in good time; for in one hour more, and the rocky coast was again lashed by the waves, and the bell tolled loud and quick, although there were none there but the sea-gull, who screamed with fright as he wheeled in the air at this unusual noise upon the rock, which, at the ebb, he had so often made his resting-place.

M'Clise had done his work; the bell was fixed; and once more he hastened with his vessel to Amsterdam. Once more was he an inmate of Vandermaclin's house; once more in the presence of the idol of his soul. This time they spoke: this time their vows were exchanged for life and death. But Vandermaclin saw not the state of their hearts. He looked upon the young seaman as too low, too poor, to be a match for his daughter; and as such an idea never entered his head, so did he never imagine that he would have dared to love. But he was soon undeceived; for M'Clise frankly stated his attachment, and demanded the hand of Katerina; and, at the demand, Vandermaclin's face was flushed with anger.

'Mynheer M'Clise,' said he, after a pause, as if to control his feelings, 'when a man marries, he is bound to show that he has wherewithal to support his wife; to support her in that rank, and to afford her those luxuries to which she has been accustomed in her father's house. Show me that you can do so, and I will not refuse you the hand of Katerina.'

'As yet, I have not,' replied M'Clise; 'but I am young and can work; I have money, and will gain more. Tell me, what sum do you think that I should possess to warrant my demanding the hand of your daughter?'

'Produce twelve thousand guilders, and she is yours,' replied the merchant.

'I have but three thousand,' replied M'Clise.

'Then think no more of Katerina. It is a foolish passion, and you must forget it. And, Mynheer M'Clise, I must not have my daughter's affections tampered with. She must forget you; and that can only be effected by your not meeting again. I wish you well, Mynheer M'Clise, but I must request your absence.'

M'Clise departed from the presence of the merchant, bowed down with grief and disappointment. He contrived that a letter, containing the result of his application, should be put in the hands of Katerina. But Vandermaclin was informed of this breach of observance, and Katerina was sent to a convent, there to remain until the departure of her lover; and Vandermaclin wrote to his correspondent at Dundee, requesting that the goods forwarded to him might not be sent by the vessel commanded by M'Clise.

Of this our young captain received information. All hope was nearly gone; still he lingered, and delayed his departure. He was no longer the active, energetic seaman; he neglected all, even his attire.

M'Clise knew in which convent his fair Katerina had been immured; and often would he walk round its precincts, with the hope of seeing her, if it were but for a moment, but in vain. His vessel was now laden, and he could delay no longer. He was to sail the next morning; and once more did the unhappy young man take his usual walk to look at those walls which contained all that was dear to him on earth. His reverie was broken by a stone falling down at his feet; he took it up; there was a small piece of paper attached to it with a silken thread. He opened it; it was the handwriting of Katerina, and contained but two words – *The Bell*.

The Bell! M'Clise started; for he immediately comprehended what was meant. The whole plan came like electricity through his brain. Yes; then there was a promise of happiness. The bell was worth ten thousand guilders; that sum had been offered, and would now be given by Isaacs, the Jew. He would be happy with his Katerina; and he blessed her ingenuity for devising the means. For a minute or two he was transported; but the re-action soon took place. What was he about to attempt: Sacrilege – cruelty. The bell had been blessed by the holy church; it had been purchased by holy and devout alms. It had been placed on the rock to save the lives of his brother seamen; and were he to remove it, would he not be responsible for all the lives lost? Would not the wail of the widow, and the tears of the orphan, be crying out to Heaven against him? No, no! Never! The crime was too horrible; and M'Clise stamped upon the paper, thinking he was tempted by Satan in the shape of woman; but when woman tempts, man is lost. He recalled the charms of Katerina; all his repugnance was overcome; and he resolved that the deed should be accomplished, and that Katerina should be gained, even if he lost his soul.

Andrew M'Clise sailed away from Amsterdam, and Katerina recovered her liberty. Vandermaclin was anxious that she should marry: and many were the suitors for her hand, but in vain. She reminded her father that he had pledged himself, if M'Clise counted down twelve thousand guilders, that she should be his wife; and to that pledge she insisted that he was bound fast. And Vandermaclin, after reasoning with her, and pointing out to her that twelve thousand guilders was a sum so large that M'Clise might not procure until his old age, even if he were fortunate, acknowledged that such was his promise, and that he would, like an honest man, abide by it, provided that M'Clise should fulfil his part of the agreement in the space of two years; after which he should delay her settlement no longer. And Katerina raised her eyes to heaven, and whispered, as she clasped her hands, 'The Bell.' Alas! that we should invoke Heaven when we would wish to do wrong: but mortals are blind, and none so blind as those who are impelled by passion.

It was in the summer of that year that M'Clise had made his arrangements: having procured the assistance of some lawless hands, he had taken the advantage of a smooth and glassy sea and a high tide to remove the bell on board his own vessel; a work of little difficulty to him, as he had placed it there, and knew well the fastenings. He sailed away for Amsterdam, and was permitted by Heaven to arrive safe with his sacrilegious freight. He did not, as before, enter the canal opposite the house of Vandermaclin, but one that ran behind the habitation of the Jew Isaacs. At night, he went into the house, and reported to the Jew what he had for sale; and the keen grey eyes of the bent-double little Israelite sparkled with delight, for he knew that his profit would be great. At midnight the bell was made fast to the crane, and safely deposited in the warehouse of the Jew, who counted out the ten thousand guilders to the enraptured M'Clise, whose thoughts were wholly upon the possession of his Katerina, and not upon the crime he had committed.

But alas! to conceal one crime we are too often obliged to be guilty of even deeper; and thus it was with Andrew M'Clise. The people who had assisted, upon the promise of a thousand guilders being divided among them, now murmured at their share, and insisted upon an equal division of the spoils, or threatened with an immediate confession of the black deed.

M'Clise raved, and cursed, and tore his hair; promised to give them the money as soon as he had wedded Katerina; but they would not consent. Again the devil came to his assistance, and whispered how he was to act: he consented. The next night the division was to be made. They met in his cabin; he gave them wine and they drank plentifully; but the wine was poisoned, and they all died before the morning. M'Clise tied weights to their bodies, and sank them in the deep canal; broke open his hatches, to make it appear that his vessel had been plundered; and then went to the authorities denouncing his crew as having plundered him and escaped. Immediate search was made, but they were not to be found; and it was supposed that they had escaped in a boat.

Once more M'Clise, whose conscience was seared, went to the house of Vandermaclin, counted down his twelve thousand guilders, and claimed his bride; and Vandermaclin, who felt that his daughter's happiness was at stake, now gave his consent. As M'Clise stated that he was anxious to return to England, and arrange with the merchants whose goods had been plundered, in a few days the marriage took place; and Katerina clasped the murderer in her arms. All was apparent joy and revelry; but there was anguish in the heart of M'Clise, who, now that he had gained his object, felt that it had cost him much too dear, for his peace of mind was gone for ever. But Katerina cared not; every spark of feeling was absorbed in her passion, and the very guilt of M'Clise but rendered him more dear; for was it not for her that he had done all this? M'Clise received her portion, and hastened to sail away; for the bodies were still in the canal, and he trembled every hour lest his crime should be discovered. And Vandermaclin bade farewell to his daughter: and, he knew not why, but there was a feeling he could not suppress, that they never should meet again.

'Down – down below, Katerina! this is no place for you,' cried M'Clise, as he stood at the helm of the vessel. 'Down, dearest, down or you will be washed overboard. Every sea threatens to pour onto our decks; already have we lost two men. Down, Katerina! down, I tell you.'

'I fear not; let me remain with you.'

'I tell you, down!' cried M'Clise, in wrath, and Katerina cast upon him a reproachful look, and obeyed.

The storm was at its height; the sun had set, black and monstrous billows chased each other, and the dismasted vessel was hurried on towards the land. The wind howled, and whistled sharply at each chink in the bulwarks of the vessel. For three days had they fought the gale, but in vain. Now, if it continued, all chance was over; for the shore was on their lee, distant not many miles. Nothing could save them but gaining the mouth of the Frith of Tay, and then they could bear up for Dundee. And there was a boiling surge, and a dark night, and roaring seas, and their masts were floating far away; and M'Clise stood at the helm, keeping her broadside to the sea: his heart was full of bitterness, and his guilty conscience bore him down, and he looked for death, and he dreaded it; for was he not a sacrilegious murderer, and was there not an avenging God above?

Once more Katerina appeared on deck, clinging for support to Andrew.

'I cannot stay below. Tell me, will it soon be over?'

'Yes,' replied M'Clise, gloomily; 'it will soon be over with all of us.'

'How mean you? You told me there was no danger.'

'I told you falsely; there is death soon, and damnation afterwards; for you I have lost my soul!'

'Oh! say not so.'

'I say it. Leave me, leave me, woman, or I curse thee.'

'Curse me, Andrew? Oh, no! Kiss me, Andrew; and if we are to perish, let us expire in each other's arms.'

''Tis as well; you have dragged me to perdition. Leave me, I say, for you have my bitter curse.'

Thus was his guilty love turned to hate, now that death was staring him in the face.

Katerina made no reply. She threw herself on the deck, and abandoned herself to her feeling of bitter anguish. And as she lay there, and M'Clise stood at the helm, the wind abated; the vessel was no longer borne down as before, although the waves were still mountains high. The seamen on board rallied; some fragments of sail were set on the remnants of the masts, and there was a chance of safety. M'Clise spoke not, but watched the helm. The wind shifted in their favour; and hope rose in every heart. The Frith of Tay was now open, and they were saved! Light was the heart of M'Clise when he kept away the vessel, and gave the helm up to the mate. He hastened to Katerina, who still remained on the deck, raised her up, whispered comfort and returning love: but she heard not – she could not forget – and she wept bitterly.

'We are saved, dear Katerina!'

'Better that we had been lost!' replied she, mournfully.

'No, no! say not so, with your own Andrew pressing you to his bosom.'

'Your bitter curse!'

''Twas madness – nothing – I knew not what I said.'

But the iron had entered into her soul. Her heart was broken.

'You had better give orders for them to look out for the Bell Rock,' observed the man at the helm to M'Clise.

The Bell Rock! M'Clise shuddered, and made no reply. Onward went the vessel, impelled by the sea and wind: one moment raised aloft, and towering over the surge; at another, deep in the hollow trough, and walled in by the convulsed element. M'Clise still held his Katerina in his arms, who responded not to his endearments, when a sudden shock threw them on the deck. The crashing of the timbers, the pouring of the waves over the stern, the heeling and settling of the vessel, were but the work of a few seconds. One more furious shock – she separates, falls on her beam ends, and the raging seas swept over her.

M'Clise threw from him her whom he had so madly loved, and plunged into the wave. Katerina shrieked, as she dashed after him, and all was over.

When the storm rises, and the screaming sea-gull seeks the land, and the fisherman hastens his bark towards the beach, there is to be seen, descending from the dark clouds with the rapidity of lightning, the form of Andrew M'Clise, the heavy bell to which he is attached by the neck, bearing him down to his doom.

And when all is smooth and calm, when at the ebbing tide the wave but gently kisses the rock, then by the light of the silver moon the occupants of the vessels which sail from the Frith of Tay have often beheld the form of the beautiful Katerina, waving her white scarf as a signal that they should approach, and take her off from the rock on which she is seated. At times, she offers a letter for her father, Vandermaclin; and she mourns and weeps as the wary mariners, with their eyes fixed on her, and with folded arms, pursue their course in silence and in dread.

HOOD'S ISLE
AND THE HERMIT
OBERLUS

Herman Melville

Captain Marryat has the distinction of being the 'Father of the Sea Story', but Herman Melville (1819–1891) is surely the most famous sea story writer, and his book, Moby Dick *(1851), the greatest maritime novel as well as being one of the masterpieces of world literature.*

Melville's life was almost as exciting as his stories. Born in New York, he first became a bank clerk, but tiring of the drudgery of the job, he joined a whaling ship and sailed for the South Seas. In the Marquesas he deserted ship and for a time lived with a tribe of savages. Next, he joined an Australian whaling ship, but on reaching Tahiti he was flung into jail for having taken part in a mutiny. Managing to escape, he lived precariously for a while on the island before going to sea once more on a man-o'-war which ultimately returned him to New York.

Having packed more adventures into a few years than most men experience in a lifetime, Melville decided to turn them into novels. Typee *(1846),* Omoo *(1847) and* White Jacket *(1849) made his name, but it was* Moby Dick *which assured him of immortality. This story of the whaling industry and one man's obsessive quest for the great white whale is told with such extraordinary detail and colour, and contains such remarkable philosophical reflections on the nature of evil, that it has earned a place among the classics.*

Like Captain Marryat, Herman Melville wrote very few short stories, yet a collection of sea stories without a contribution from him would be, quite simply, incomplete. I have been fortunate, therefore, to unearth the following short tale which is one of a series he wrote based on the time he spent in the Galapagos Islands in 1841. He found the islands very strange, and collected a number of stories and legends from the whaling seamen he met there. The strangest of all these tales concerned an Irishman named Patrick Watkins, who had been shipwrecked on Hood's Island. From the bare bones of the legend he wove the adventure of the Hermit Oberlus which was published in Putnam's Magazine *of May 1854 and now makes what I think will be greeted as a welcome reappearance.*

That darkesome glen they enter, where they find
That cursed man, low sitting on the ground,
Musing full sadly in his sullein mind;
His griesie lockes, long growen and unbound,
Disordered hong about his shoulders round,
And hid his face; through which his hollow eyne
Lookt deadly dull, and stared as astound;
His raw-bone cheekes, through penurie and pine,
Were shronke into his jawes, as he did never dine.
His garment nought but many ragged clouts,
With thornes together pind and patched was,
The which his naked sides he wrapt abouts.

SOUTHEAST OF CROSSMAN'S Isle lies Hood's Isle, or McCain's Beclouded Isle; and upon its south side is a vitreous cove with a wide strand of dark pounded black lava, called Black Beach, or Oberlus's Landing. It might fitly have been styled Charon's.

It received its name from a wild white creature who spent many years here; in the person of a European bringing into this savage region qualities more diabolical than are to be found among any of the surrounding cannibals.

About half a century ago, Oberlus deserted at the above-named island, then, as now, a solitude. He built himself a den of lava and clinkers, about a mile from the Landing, subsequently called after him, in a vale, or expanded gulch, containing here and there among the rocks about two acres of soil capable of rude cultivation; the only place on the isle not too blasted for that purpose. Here he succeeded in raising a sort of degenerate potatoes and pumpkins, which from time to time he exchanged with needy whalemen passing, for spirits or dollars.

His appearance, from all accounts, was that of the victim of some malignant sorceress; he seemed to have drunk of Circe's cup; beast-like; rags insufficient to hide his nakedness; his befreckled skin blistered by continual exposure to the sun; nose flat; countenance contorted, heavy, earthy; hair and beard unshorn, profuse, and of fiery red. He struck strangers much as if he were a volcanic creature thrown up by the same convulsion which exploded into sight the isle. All bepatched and coiled asleep in his lonely lava den among the mountains, he looked, they say, as a heaped drift of withered leaves, torn from autumn trees, and so left in some hidden nook by the whirling halt for an instant of a fierce night-wind, which then ruthlessly sweeps on, somewhere else to repeat the capricious act. It is also reported to have been the strangest sight, this same Oberlus, of a sultry, cloudy morning, hidden under his shocking old black tarpaulin hat, hoeing potatoes among the lava. So warped and crooked was his strange nature, that the very handle of his hoe seemed gradually to have shrunk and twisted in his grasp, being a wretched bent stick, elbowed more like a savage's war-sickle than a civilized hoe-handle. It was his mysterious custom upon a first encounter with a stranger ever to present his back; possibly, because that was his better side, since it revealed the least. If the encounter chanced in his garden, as it sometimes did — the new-landed strangers going from the sea-side straight through the gorge, to hunt up the queer greengrocer reported doing business here – Oberlus for a time hoed on, unmindful of all greeting, jovial or bland; as the curious stranger would turn to face him, the recluse, hoe in hand, as diligently would avert himself; bowed over, and sullenly revolving round his murphy hill. Thus far for hoeing. When planting, his whole aspect and all his gestures were so malevolently and uselessly sinister and secret, that he seemed rather in act of dropping poison into wells than potatoes into soil. But among his lesser and more harmless marvels was an idea he ever had, that his visitors came equally as well led by longings to behold the mighty hermit Oberlus in his

royal state of solitude, as simply to obtain potatoes, or find
whatever company might be upon a barren isle. It seems
incredible that such a being should possess such vanity; a
misanthrope be conceited; but he really had his notion; and
upon the strength of it, often gave himself amusing airs to
captains. But after all, this is somewhat of a piece with the well-
known eccentricity of some convicts, proud of that very
hatefulness which makes them notorious. At other times,
another unaccountable whim would seize him, and he would
long dodge advancing strangers round the clinkered corners of
his hut; sometimes like a stealthy bear, he would slink through
the withered thickets up the mountains, and refuse to see the
human face.

Except his occasional visitors from the sea, for a long period,
the only companions of Oberlus were the crawling tortoises; and
he seemed more than degraded to their level, having no desires
for a time beyond theirs, unless it were for the stupor brought on
by drunkenness. But sufficiently debased as he appeared, there
yet lurked in him, only awaiting occasion for discovery, a still
further proneness. Indeed, the sole superiority of Oberlus over
the tortoises was his possession of a larger capacity of
degradation; and along with that, something like an intelligent
will to it. Moreover, what is about to be revealed, perhaps will
show, that selfish ambition, or the love of rule for its own sake,
far from being the peculiar infirmity of noble minds, is shared by
beings which have no mind at all. No creatures are so selfishly
tyrannical as some brutes; as any one who has observed the
tenants of the pasture must occasionally have observed.

'This island's mine by Sycorax my mother,' said Oberlus to
himself, glaring round upon his haggard solitude. By some
means, barter or theft – for in those days ships at intervals still
kept touching at his Landing – he obtained an old musket, with a
few charges of powder and ball. Possessed of arms, he was
stimulated to enterprise, as a tiger that first feels the coming of its
claws. The long habit of sole dominion over every object round
him, his almost unbroken solitude, his never encountering
humanity except on terms of misanthropic independence, or
mercantile craftiness, and even such encounters being

comparatively but rare; all this must have gradually nourished in him a vast idea of his own importance, together with a pure animal sort of scorn for all the rest of the universe.

The unfortunate Creole, who enjoyed his brief term of royalty at Charles's Isle was perhaps in some degree influenced by not unworthy motives; such as prompt other adventurous spirits to lead colonists into distant regions and assume political pre-eminence over them. His summary execution of many of his Peruvians is quite pardonable, considering the desperate characters he had to deal with; while his offering canine battle to the banded rebels seems under the circumstances altogether just. But for this King Oberlus and what shortly follows, no shade of palliation can be given. He acted out of mere delight in tyranny and cruelty, by virtue of a quality in him inherited from Sycorax his mother. Armed now with that shocking blunderbuss, strong in the thought of being master of that horrid isle, he panted for a chance to prove his potency upon the first specimen of humanity which should fall unbefriended into his hands.

Nor was he long without it. One day he spied a boat upon the beach, with one man, a negro, standing by it. Some distance off was a ship, and Oberlus immediately knew how matters stood. The vessel had put in for wood, and the boat's crew had gone into the thickets for it. From a convenient spot he kept watch of the boat, till presently a straggling company appeared loaded with billets. Throwing these on the beach, they again went into the thickets, while the negro proceeded to load the boat.

Oberlus now makes all haste and accosts the negro, who, aghast at seeing any living being inhabiting such a solitude, and especially so horrific a one, immediately falls into a panic, not at all lessened by the ursine suavity of Oberlus, who begs the favour of assisting him in his labours. The negro stands with several billets on his shoulder, in act of shouldering others; and Oberlus, with a short cord concealed in his bosom, kindly proceeds to lift those other billets to their place. In so doing, he persists in keeping behind the negro, who, rightly suspicious of this, in vain dodges about to gain the front of Oberlus; but Oberlus dodges also; till at last, weary of this bootless attempt at treachery, or fearful of being surprised by the remainder of the party, Oberlus runs off a little space to a bush, and fetching his blunderbuss, savagely commands the negro to desist work and follow him. He refuses. Whereupon, presenting his piece, Oberlus snaps at him. Luckily the blunderbuss misses fire; but by this time, frightened out of his wits, the negro, upon a second intrepid summons, drops his billets, surrenders at discretion, and follows on. By a narrow defile familiar to him, Oberlus speedily removes out of sight of the water.

On their way up the mountains, he exultingly informs the negro that henceforth he is to work for him, and be his slave, and that his treatment would entirely depend on his future conduct. But Oberlus, deceived by the first impulsive cowardice of the black, in an evil moment slackens his vigilance. Passing through a narrow way, and perceiving his leader quite off his guard, the negro, a powerful fellow, suddenly grasps him in his arms, throws him down, wrests his musketoon from him, ties his hands with the monster's own cord, shoulders him, and returns with him down to the boat. When the rest of the party arrive, Oberlus is carried on board the ship. This proved an Englishman, and a smuggler; a sort of craft not apt to be over-charitable. Oberlus is severely whipped, then handcuffed, taken ashore, and compelled to make known his habitation and produce his property. His potatoes, pumpkins, and tortoises, with a pile of dollars he had hoarded from his mercantile operation were secured on the spot. But while the too vindictive smugglers were busy destroying his hut and garden, Oberlus makes his escape into the mountains, and conceals himself there in impenetrable recesses, only known to himself, till the ship sails, when he ventures back, and by means of an old file which he sticks in a tree, contrives to free himself from his handcuffs.

Brooding among the ruins of his hut, and the desolate clinkers and extinct volcanoes of this outcast isle, the insulted misanthrope now meditates a signal revenge upon humanity, but conceals his purposes. Vessels still touch the Landing at times; and by and by Oberlus is enabled to supply them with some vegetables.

Warned by his former failure in kidnapping strangers, he now pursues a different plan. When seamen come ashore, he makes up to them like a free-and-easy comrade, invites them to his hut, and with whatever affability his red-haired grimness may assume, entreats them to drink his liquor and be merry. But his guests need little pressing; and so, soon as rendered insensible, are tied hand and foot, and pitched among the clinkers, are there concealed till the ship departs, when, finding themselves entirely dependent upon Oberlus, alarmed at his changed demeanor, his savage threats, and above all, that shocking blunderbuss, they willingly enlist under him, becoming his humble slaves, and Oberlus the most incredible of tyrants. So much so, that two or three perish beneath his initiating process. He sets the remainder – four of them – to breaking the caked soil; transporting upon their backs loads of loamy earth, scooped up in moist clefts among the mountains; keeps them on the roughest fare; presents his piece at the slightest hint of insurrection; and in all respects converts them into reptiles at his feet – plebeian garter-snakes to this Lord Anaconda.

At last, Oberlus contrives to stock his arsenal with four rusty cutlasses, and an added supply of powder and ball intended for his blunderbuss. Remitting in good part the labour of his slaves, he now approves himself a man, or rather devil, of great abilities in the way of cajoling or coercing others into acquiescence with his own ulterior designs, however at first abhorrent to them. But indeed, prepared for almost any eventual evil by their previous lawless life, as a sort of ranging Cow-Boys of the sea, which had dissolved within them the whole moral man, so that they were ready to concrete in the first offered mould of baseness now; rotted down from manhood by their hopeless misery on the isle; wonted to cringe in all things to their lord, himself the worst of slaves; these wretches were now become wholly corrupted to his hands. He used them as creatures of an inferior race; in short, he gaffles his four animals, and makes murderers of them; out of cowards fitly manufacturing bravoes.

Now, sword or dagger, human arms are but artificial claws and fangs, tied on like false spurs to the fighting cock. So, we repeat, Oberlus, czar of the isle, gaffles his four subjects, that is, with intent of glory, puts four rusty cutlasses into their hands.

Like any other autocrat, he had a noble army now.

It might be thought a servile war would hereupon ensue. Arms in the hands of trodden slaves? how indiscreet of Emperor Oberlus! Nay, they had but cutlasses – sad old scythes enough – he a blunderbuss, which by its blind scatterings of all sorts of boulders, clinkers, and other scoria would annihilate all four mutineers, like four pigeons at one shot. Besides, at first he did not sleep in his accustomed hut; every lurid sunset, for a time, he might have been seen wending his way among the riven mountains, there to secrete himself till dawn in some sulphurous pitfall, undiscoverable to his gang; but finding this at last too troublesome, he now each evening tied his slaves hand and foot, hid the cutlasses, and thrusting them into his barracks, shut to the door, and lying down before it, beneath a rude shed lately added, slept out the night, blunderbuss in hand.

It is supposed that not content with daily parading over a cindery solitude at the head of his fine army, Oberlus now meditated the most active mischief; his probable object being to surprise some passing ship touching at his dominions, massacre the crew, and run away with her to parts unknown. While these plans were simmering in his head, two ships touch in company at the isle, on the opposite side to his; when his designs undergo a sudden change.

The ships are in want of vegetables, which Oberlus promises in great abundance, provided they send their boats round to his Landing, so that the crews may bring the vegetables from his garden; informing the two captains, at the same time, that his rascals – slaves and soldiers – had become so abominably lazy and good-for-nothing of late, that he could not make them work by ordinary inducements, and did not have the heart to be severe with them.

The arrangement was agreed to, and the boats were sent and hauled upon the beach. The crews went to the lava hut; but to their surprise nobody was there. After waiting till their patience was exhausted, they returned to the shore, when lo, some stranger – not the Good Samaritan either – seems to have very recently passed that way. Three of the boats were broken in a thousand pieces, and the fourth was missing. By hard toil over the mountains and through the clinkers, some of the strangers succeeded in returning to that side of the isle where the ships lay, when fresh boats are sent to the relief of the rest of the hapless party.

However amazed at the treachery of Oberlus, the two captains, afraid of new and still more mysterious atrocities – and indeed, half imputing such strange events to the enchantments associated with these isles – perceive no security but in instant flight; leaving Oberlus and his army in quiet possession of the stolen boat.

On the eve of sailing they put a letter in a keg, giving the Pacific Ocean intelligence of the affair, and moored the keg in the bay. Some time subsequent, the keg was opened by another captain chancing to anchor there, but not until after he had dispatched a boat round to Oberlus's Landing. As may be readily surmised, he felt no little inquietude till the boat's return; when another letter was handed him, giving Oberlus's version of the affair. This precious document had been found pinned half-mildewed to the clinker wall of the sulphurous and deserted hut. It ran as follows: showing that Oberlus was at least an accomplished writer, and no mere boor; and what is more, was capable of the most tristful eloquence.

Sir: I am the most unfortunate ill-treated gentleman that lives. I am a patriot, exiled from my country by the cruel hand of tyranny.

Banished to these Enchanted Isles, I have again and again besought captains of ships to sell me a boat, but always have been refused, though I offered the handsomest prices in Mexican dollars. At length an opportunity presented of possessing myself of one, and I did not let it slip.

I have been long endeavouring, by hard labour and much solitary suffering, to accumulate something to make myself comfortable in a virtuous though unhappy old age; but at various times have been robbed and beaten by men professing to be Christians.

To-day I sail from the Enchanted group in the good boat Charity bound to the Feejee Isles.

FATHERLESS OBERLUS

P.S.—*Behind the clinkers, nigh the oven, you will find the old fowl. Do not kill it; be patient; I leave it setting; if it shall have any chicks, I hereby bequeath them to you, whoever you may be. But don't count your chicks before they are hatched.*

The fowl proved a starveling rooster, reduced to a sitting posture by sheer debility.

Oberlus declares that he was bound to the Feejee Isles; but this was only to throw pursuers on a false scent. For, after a long time, he arrived, alone in his open boat, at Guayaquil. As his miscreants were never again beheld on Hood's Isle, it is supposed, either that they perished for want of water on the passage to Guayaquil, or, what is quite as probable, were thrown overboard by Oberlus, when he found the water growing scarce.

From Guayaquil Oberlus proceeded to Payta; and there, with that nameless witchery peculiar to some of the ugliest animals, wound himself into the affections of a tawny damsel; prevailing upon her to accompany him back to his Enchanted Isle; which doubtless he painted as a Paradise of flowers, not a Tartarus of clinkers.

But unfortunately for the colonization of Hood's Isle with a choice variety of animated nature, the extraordinary and devilish aspect of Oberlus made him to be regarded in Payta as a highly suspicious character. So that being found concealed one night, with matches in his pocket, under the hull of a small vessel just ready to be launched, he was seized and thrown into jail.

The jails in most South American towns are generally of the least wholesome sort. Built of huge cakes of sunburnt brick, and containing but one room, without windows or yard, and but one door heavily grated with wooden bars, they present both within and without the grimmest aspect. As public edifices they conspicuously stand upon the hot and dusty Plaza, offering to view, through the gratings, their villainous and hopeless inmates, burrowing in all sorts of tragic squalor. And here, for a long time, Oberlus was seen; the central figure of a mongrel and assassin band; a creature who it is religion to detest, since it is philanthropy to hate a misanthrope.

NOTE.—They who may be disposed to question the possibility of the character above depicted, are referred to the 2nd vol. of Porter's *Voyage into the Pacific*, where they will recognize many sentences, for expedition's sake derived verbatim from thence, and incorporated here; the main difference – save a few passing reflections – between the two accounts being, that the present writer has added to Porter's facts accessory ones picked up in the Pacific from reliable sources; and where facts conflict, has naturally preferred his own authorities to Porter's. As, for instance, *his* authorities place Oberlus on Hood's Isle: Porter's, on Charles's Isle. The letter found in the hut is also somewhat different; for while at the Encantadas he was informed that, not only did it evince a certain clerkliness, but was full of the strangest satiric effrontery which does not adequately appear in Porter's version. I accordingly altered it to suit the general character of its author. [H.M.]

A BEWITCHED
SHIP

W. Clark Russell

The most prolific of all writers of sea mysteries was William Clark Russell (1844–1911), who contributed his first such yarn in 1874 and was still going strong over eighty books and hundreds of articles and essays later when he died in 1911. Like Captain Marryat and Herman Melville he served his apprenticeship at sea, but gave up the life to earn his living as an author. He was later described by Algernon Swinburne as 'the greatest master of the sea, living or dead', and another critic called him 'the prose Homer of the great ocean'. Such praise may have been a little overblown, although there is no doubt that his work was enormously popular with Victorian readers. (Clark Russell's father, Henry Russell, was incidentally also deeply fascinated by the sea, and wrote a number of popular songs about it including 'A Life On The Ocean Wave'.)

Like Marryat, Clark Russell was intrigued all his life by the legend of the Flying Dutchman. *In 1888 he wrote* The Death Ship: An Account of a Cruise in 'The Flying Dutchman', *although this was not as popular as his bizarre tale* The Frozen Pirate *(1887) about a French buccaneer who, after being frozen solid for years, is resuscitated to reveal where a horde of buried treasure is hidden.*

From the large number of Clark Russell tales which would suit this collection, I have picked one of my favourites, 'A Bewitched Ship' (1884) which gives a nicely atmospheric picture of the supernatural at sea.

'ABOUT TEN YEARS ago,' began my friend, Captain Green, 'I went as second mate of a ship named the *Ocean King*. She'd been an old Indiaman in her time, and had a poop and topgallant forecastle, though alterations had knocked some of the dignity out of her. Her channels had been changed into plates with dead-eyes above the rail, and the eye missed the spread of the lower rigging that it naturally sought in looking at a craft with a square stern and windows in it, and chequered sides rounding out into curves that made a complete tub of the old hooker. Yet, spite of changes, the old-fashioned grace would break through. She looked like a lady who has seen better days, who has got to do work which servants did for her in the times when she was well off, but who, let her set her hand to what she will, makes you see that the breeding and the instincts are still there, and that she's as little to be vulgarized by poverty and its coarse struggles as she could be made a truer lady than she is by money. Ships, like human beings, have their careers, and the close of some of them is strange, and sometimes hard, I think.

'The *Ocean King* had been turned into a collier, and I went second mate of her when she was full up with coal for a South African port. Yet this ship, that was now carrying one of the dirtiest cargoes you could name, barring phosphate manure, had been reckoned in her day a fine passenger vessel, a noble Indiaman, indeed – her tonnage was something over eleven hundred – with a cuddy fitted up royally. Many a freight of soldiers had she carried round the Cape, many an old nabob had she conveyed – aye, and Indian potentates, who smoked out of jewelled hookahs, and who were waited upon by crowds of black servants in turbans and slippers. I used to moralize over her, just as I would over a tomb, when I had the watch, and was alone, and could let my thoughts run loose. The sumptuous cabin trappings were all gone, and I seemed to smell coal in the wind, even when my head was over the weather side, and when the breeze that blew along came fresh across a thousand miles of sea; but there was a good deal of the fittings left – fittings which, I don't doubt, made the newspapers give a long account of this "fine great ship" when she was launched, quite enough of them to enable a man to reconstruct a picture of the cuddy of the *Ocean King* as it was in the days of her glory, when the soft oil lamps shone bright on the draped tables and sparkled on silver and glass, when the old skipper, sitting with the mizzenmast behind him, would look, with his red face and white hair, down the rows of ladies and gentlemen eating and drinking, stewards running about, trays hanging from the deck above, and globes full of gold fish swinging to the roll of the vessel as she swung stately, with her stunsails hanging out, over the long blue swell wrinkled by the wind. The ship is still afloat. Where are the people she carried? The crews who have worked her? The captains who have commanded her? There is nothing that should be fuller of ghosts than an old ship; and I very well remember that when I first visited the *Victory*, at Portsmouth, and descended into her cockpit, what I saw was not a well-preserved and cleanly length of massive deck, but groups of wounded and bleeding and dying men littering the dark floor, and the hatchway shadowed by groaning figures handed below, whilst the smell of English, French and Spanish gunpowder, even down there, was so strong – phew! I could have spat the flavour out.

'Well, the old *Ocean King* had once upon a time been said to be haunted. She had certainly been long enough afloat to own a hundred stories, and she was so staunch and true that if ever a superstition got into her there was no chance of its getting out again. I only remember one of these yarns; it was told to me by the dockmaster, who had been at sea for many years, was an old man, and knew the history of all such craft as the *Ocean King*. He said that, in '51, I think it was, there had been a row among the crew: an Italian sailor stabbed an Englishman, who bled to death. To avenge the Englishman's death, the rest of the crew, who were chiefly English, thrust the Italian into the forepeak and let him lie there in darkness. When he was asked for, they reported that he had fallen overboard, and this seems to have been believed. Whether the crew meant to starve him or not is not certain; but after he had been in the forepeak for three or four days, a fellow going behind the galley out of the way of the wind to light his pipe – it being then four bells in the first watch – came running into the forecastle with his hair on end, and the sweat pouring off his face, swearing he had seen the Italian's ghost. This frightened the men prettily; some of them went down into the forepeak, and found the Italian lying there dead, with a score of rats upon him, which scampered off when the men dropped below. During all the rest of the voyage his ghost was constantly seen, sometimes at the lee wheel, sometimes astride of the flying jibboom. What was the end of it – I mean, whether the men confessed the murder, and if so what became of them – the dockmaster said he didn't know. But be this as it may, I discovered shortly after we had begun our voyage that the crew had got to hear of this story, and the chief mate said it had been brought aboard by the carpenter, who had picked it up from some of the dockyard labourers.

'I well recollect two uncomfortable circumstances: we sailed on a Friday, and the able and ordinary seamen were thirteen in number, the idlers and ourselves aft bringing up the ship's company to nineteen souls! when, I suppose, in her prime the *Ocean King* never left port short of seventy or eighty seamen, not to mention stewards, cooks, cooks' mates, butcher, butcher's mate, baker, and the rest of them. But double topsailyards were now in; besides, I understood that the vessel's masts had been reduced and her yards shortened, and we carried stump fore and mizzen topgallantmasts.

'All being ready, a tug got hold of our tow-rope, and away we went down the river and out to sea.

'I don't believe myself that any stories which had been told the men about this ship impressed them much. Sailors are very superstitious, but they are not to be scared till something has happened to frighten them. Your merely telling them that there's a ghost aboard the ship they're in won't alarm them till they've caught sight of the ghost. But once let a man say to the others, "There's a bloomin' sperrit in this ship. Lay your head agin the forehatch, and you'll hear him gnashing his teeth and rattlin' his chains," and then let another man go and listen, and swear, and perhaps very honestly, that he "heerd the noises plain," and you'll have all hands in a funk, talking in whispers, and going aloft in the dark nervously.

'In our ship nothing happened for some days. We were deep and slow, and rolled along solemnly, the sea falling away from the vessel's powerful round bows as from a rock. Pile what we could upon her, with tacks aboard, staysails drawing, and the wind hitting her best sailing point, we could seldom manage to get more than seven knots out of her. One night I had the first watch. It was about two bells. There was a nice wind, the sea smooth, and a red moon crawling up over our starboard beam. We were under all plain sail, leaning away from the wind a trifle, and the water washed along under the bends in lines through which the starlight ran glimmering. I was thinking over the five or six months' voyages which old waggons after the pattern of this ship took in getting to India, when, seeing a squall coming along, I sung out for hands to stand by the main royal and mizzen topgallant halliards. It drove down dark, and not knowing what was behind I ordered the main royal to be clewed up and furled. Two youngsters went aloft. By the time they were on the yard the squall thinned, but I fancied there was another bearing down, and thought it best to let the ordinary seamen roll the sail up. On a sudden down they both trotted hand over hand, leaving the sail flapping in the clutch of the clewlines.

'I roared out, "What d'ye mean by coming down before you've furled that sail?"

'They stood together in the main rigging, and one of them answered, "Please, sir, there's a ghost somewhere up aloft on the foretopsail-yard."

'"A ghost, you fool!" I cried.

'"Yes, sir," he answered. "He says, 'Jim, your mother wants

yer.' I says, 'What?' and he says, 'Your mother wants yer,' in the hollowest o' voices. Dick here heard it. There's no one aloft forrards, sir."

'I sung out to them to jump aloft again, and finding that they didn't move I made a spring, on which they dropped like lightning on deck, and began to beg and pray of me in the eagerest manner not to send them aloft, as they were too frightened to hold on. Indeed, the fellow named Jim actually began to shiver and cry when I threatened him; so as the royal had to be furled I sent an able seaman aloft, who, after rolling up the sail, came down and said that no voice had called to him, and that he rather reckoned it was a bit of skylarking on the part of the boys to get out of stowing the sail. However, I noticed that the man was wonderfully quick over the job, and that afterwards the watch on deck stood talking in low voices in the waist.

'Jim was a fool of a youth, but Dick was a smart lad, aged about nineteen, and good-looking, with a lively tongue, and I heard afterwards that he could spin a yarn to perfection all out of his imagination. I called him to me, and asked him if he had really heard a voice, and he swore he had.

'"Did it say," said I, "'Jim, your mother wants you'?"

'"Ay, sir," he answered, with a bit of a shudder, "as plain as you yourself say it. It seemed to come off the foretopgallant-yard, where I fancied I see something dark a-moving; but I was too frightened to take particular notice."

'Well, it was not long after this, about eleven o'clock in the morning, that, the captain being on deck, the cook steps out of the galley, comes walking along the poop, and going up to the skipper, touches his cap, and stands looking at him.

'"What d'ye want?" said the captain, eyeing him as if he took him to be mad.

'"Didn't you call, sir?" says the cook.

'"Call!" cries the skipper. "Certainly not."

'The man looked stupid with surprise, and, muttering something to himself, went forward. Ten minutes after he came up again to the skipper, and says, "Yes, sir!" as a man might who answers to a call. The skipper began to swear at him, and called him a lunatic, and so on; but the man, finding he was wrong again, grew white, and swore that if he was on his deathbed he'd maintain that the captain had called him twice.

'The skipper, who was a rather nervous man, turned to me, and said, "What do you make of this, Mr Green? I can't doubt the cook's word. Who's calling him in my voice?"

'"Oh, it's some illusion, sir," said I, feeling puzzled for all that.

'But the cook, with the tears actually standing in his eyes, declared it was no illusion; he'd know the captain's voice if it was nine miles off. And he then walked in a dazed way towards the forecastle, singing out that whether the voice he had heard belonged to a ghost or a Christian man, it might go on calling "Cook!" for the next twenty years without his taking further notice of it. This thing coming so soon after the call to Jim that had so greatly alarmed the two ordinary seamen, made a great impression on the crew; and I never regret anything more than that my position should have prevented me from getting into their confidence, and learning their thoughts, for there is no doubt I should have stowed away memories enough to serve me for many a hearty laugh in after years.

'A few days rolled by without anything particular happening. One night it came to my turn to have the first watch. It was a quiet night, with wind enough to keep the sails still whilst the old ship went drowsily rolling along her course to the African port. Suddenly I heard a commotion forward, and, fearing that some accident had happened, I called out to know what the matter was. A voice answered, "Ghost or no ghost, there's somebody a-talking in the forehold; come and listen, sir." The silence that followed suggested a good deal of alarm. I sang out as I approached the men, "Perhaps there's a stowaway below."

'"It's no living voice," was the reply; "it sounds as if it comes from a skelington."

'I found a crowd of men standing in awed postures near the hatch, and the most frightened of all looked to me to be the ordinary seaman Dick, who had backed away on the other side of the hatch, and stood looking on, leaning with his hands on his knees, and staring as if he was fascinated. I waited a couple or three minutes, which, in a business of this kind, seems a long time, and hearing nothing, I was going to ridicule the men for their nervousness, when a hollow voice under the hatch said distinctly, "It's a terrible thing to be a ghost and not be able to get out." I was greatly startled, and ran aft to tell the captain, who agreed with me that there must be a stowaway in the hold, and that he had gone mad. We both went forward and the hatch was lifted, and we looked on top of the coal; and I was then about to ask some of the men to join me in a search in the forepeak, for upon my word I had no taste single-handed for a job of that kind at such a moment, when the voice said, "There's no use looking, you'll never find me. I'm not to be seen."

"'Confound me!" cried the skipper, polishing his forehead with a pocket-handkerchief, "if ever I heard of such a thing. I'll tell you what it is," he shouted, looking into the hatch, "dead men can't talk, and so, as you're bound to be alive, you'd better come up out of that, and smartly too – d'ye hear? – or you'll find this the worst attempt at skylarking that was ever made."

'There was a short silence, and you'd see all hands straining their ears, for there was light enough for that, given out by a lantern one of the men held.

"'You couldn't catch me because you couldn't see me," said the voice in a die-away tone, and this time it came from the direction of the main hatch, as though it had flitted aft.

"'Well," says the captain, "may I be jiggered!" and without another word he walked away on to the poop.

'I told the men to clap the hatches on again, and they did this in double-quick time, evidently afraid that the ghost might pop up out of the hold if they didn't mind their eye.

'All this made us very superstitious, from the captain down to the boys. We talked it over in the cabin, and the mate was incredulous, and disposed to ridicule me.

"'Any way," said he, "it's strange that his voice is only heard in your watch. It's never favoured *me* with any remarks. The creaking and groaning of an old wooden ship is often like spoken words, and what you've been hearing may be nothing but a deception of the ear."

"'A deception in your eye!" cried the skipper. "The timbers of an old wooden ship may strain and creak in the Dutch language, but hang me if they ever talked good sensible English. However, I'm not going to worry. For my part," said he, with a nervous glance around him, "I don't believe in ghosts; whatever it is that's talking in the hold may go on jawing, so long as he sticks to that, and don't frighten the men with an ugly mug, nor come upon us for a man's allowance."

"'If it's anybody's ghost," said I, "it must be the Italian's, the chap that was starved in the forepeak."

"'I doubt that,' said the skipper. "I didn't detect anything foreign in what he said. To my ear it sounded more like Whitechapel than Italiano."

'Well, for another week we heard little more of the ghost. It's true that one middle watch a chap I had sent aloft to loose the mainroyal had hardly stepped out of the lower rigging, after lingering in the crosstrees to overhaul his clewlines, when he comes rushing up to me and cries out, "I've been hailed from aloft, sir! a voice has just sung out, 'Tommy, jump aloft again that I may have a good look at you!'"

"'Who's up, there?" I asked him, staring into the gloom where the mast and yards went towering.

"'There's no one up there, sir: I'll swear it. I was bound to see him had any one been there,' he answered, evidently very much frightened.

'It occurred to me that some one of the crew might be lying hid in the top, and that if I could catch him I might find out who the ghost was. So I jumped into the rigging and trotted aloft, keeping my eye on the lee rigging, to make sure that no one descended by it. I gained the top, but nobody was there. I mounted to the crosstrees, but the deuce a sign of any one could I see. I came down, feeling both foolish and scared; for you see I had heard the voice myself in the hold, there was no question that there *was* a voice, belonging to nobody knew what, knocking about the ship, and consequently it was now impossible to help believing a man when he said he heard it.

'However, it was necessary to keep the men in heart, and this was not to be done by captain and mates appearing scared; so I reasoned a bit with the man, told him that there were no such things as ghosts, that a voice was bound to come from a live person, because a spectre couldn't possibly have lungs, those organs being of a perishable nature, and then sent him forward, but no easier in his mind, I suspect, than I was. Anyhow I was glad when eight bells were struck and it was my turn to go below. But, as I have said, nothing much came of this – at least, nothing that reached my ears. But not many nights following the ship lay becalmed – there wasn't a breath of air, and the sea lay smooth as polished jet. This time I had the middle watch again. I was walking quietly up and down the poop, on the look-out for a deeper shadow upon the sea to indicate the approach of wind, when a man came up the ladder and said, "There's someone a-talking to the ship under the bows."

"'Are you awake?" said I.

"'Heaven help me, as I stand here, sir," exclaimed the fellow, solemnly, "if that there voice which talked in the hold t'other day ain't now over the side."

'I ran forward, and found most of the watch huddled together near the starboard cathead. I peered over, and there was a dead silence.

"'What are you looking over that side for? I'm here!" said a thin, faint voice, that seemed more in the air than in the sea.

"'There!" exclaimed one of the seamen, in a hoarse whisper, "That's the third time. Whichever side we look, he's on the other."

"'But there must be some one in the water," said another man. "Anybody see his outline? cuss me if I couldn't swear I see a chap swimmin' just now."

"'No, no," answered some one gruffly, "nothing but phosphorus, Joe, and the right sort o' stuff too, for if this ain't Old Nick – "

"'You're a liar, Sam!" came the voice clear and as one could swear, plain from over the side.

'There was a general recoil, and a sort of groan ran among the men.

'At the same moment I collared a figure standing near me, and slewed him round to bring his face fair to the starlight, clear of the staysail. "Come you along with me, Master Dick," said I; and I marched him off the forecastle, along the main deck, and up on to the poop. "So *you're* the ghost, eh?" said I. "Why, to have kept your secret you should have given my elbow a wider berth. No wonder the Voice only makes observations in my watch. You're too lazy, I suppose, to leave your hammock to try your wonderful power on the mate, eh? Now see here," said I, finding him silent, and noticing how white his face glimmered to the stars, "I know you're the man, so you'd better confess. Own the truth and I'll keep your secret, providing you belay all further tricks of this same kind; deny that you're the ghost and I'll speak to the captain and set the men upon you."

'This fairly frightened him. "Well, sir, it's true; I'm the Voice, sir; but for God's sake keep the secret, sir. The men 'ud have my life if they found out that it was me as scared them."

'This confession was what I needed, for though when standing pretty close to him on the forecastle I could have sworn that it was he who uttered the words which perplexed and awed the sailors, yet so perfect was the deception, so fine, in short, was his skill as a ventriloquist that, had he stoutly denied and gone on denying that he was the "voice," I should have believed him and continued sharing in the wonder and superstition of the crew. I kept his secret as I promised; but, somehow or other, it leaked out in time that he could deceive the ear by apparently pitching his voice among the rigging, or under the deck, or over the side, though the discovery was not made until the "ghost" had for a long time ceased to trouble the ship's company, and until the men's superstitious awe had faded somewhat, and they had recovered their old cheerfulness. We then sent for Dick to the cabin, where he gave a real entertainment as a ventriloquist, imitating all sorts of animals and producing sounds as of women in distress and men singing out for help in the berths; indeed, such was the skill that I'd often see the skipper and mate turning startled to look in the direction whence the voices proceeded. He made his peace with the men by amusing them in the same way; so that, instead of getting the rope's-ending aft and the pummelling forward which he deserved, he ended as a real and general favourite, and one of the most amusing fellows that a man ever was shipmate with. I used to tell him that if he chose to perform ashore he was sure to make plenty of money, since such ventriloquial powers as his were the rarest thing in the world; and I'd sometimes fancy he meant to take my advice. But whether he died or kept on going to sea I don't know, for after he left the ship I never saw nor heard of him again."

J. HABAKUK
JEPHSON'S STATEMENT

Sir Arthur Conan Doyle

The mystery of W. Clark Russell's 'A Bewitched Ship' was explained simply enough, but the sea has a great many famous true mysteries which have defied all attempts to explain them. The legend of the phantom ship The Flying Dutchman, which I have already mentioned, is one; while the curious case of the abandoned vessel the Marie Celeste is another which has intrigued a lot of people for many years. In the next two stories a pair of distinguished writers attempt to offer solutions to these puzzling cases.

In 'J. Habakuk Jephson's Statement', Sir Arthur Conan Doyle (1859–1930) uses the kind of clever analytical powers that his famous detective Sherlock Holmes possessed to try to unravel the mystery of the brigantine Marie Celeste, found drifting and deserted at sea in 1873. Conan Doyle poses an intriguing and unexpected solution, which I will not discuss here to avoid spoiling your enjoyment. However, I must just say that when the story was first published anonymously in the Cornhill Magazine in 1884 it was taken as a serious account by certain officials in the British government.

I think all keen students of the Sherlock Holmes' stories will know why I have placed this tale immediately after that by W. Clark Russell. Russell's stories were, of course, the favourite reading material of the good Doctor Watson!

IN THE MONTH of December in the year 1873, the British Ship *Dei Gratia* steered into Gibraltar, having in tow the derelict brigantine *Marie Celeste* which had been picked up in latitude 38° 40', longitude 17° 14' W. There were several circumstances in connection with the condition and appearance of this abandoned vessel which excited considerable comment at the time, and aroused a curiosity which has never been satisfied. What these circumstances were was summed up in an able article which appeared in the *Gibraltar Gazette*. The curious can find it in the issue for January 4, 1874, unless my memory deceives me. For the benefit of those, however, who may be unable to refer to the paper in question, I shall subjoin a few extracts which touch upon the leading features of the case.

'We have ourselves,' says the anonymous writer in the *Gazette*, 'been over the derelict *Marie Celeste*, and have closely questioned the officers of the *Dei Gratia* on every point which might throw light on the affair. They are of opinion that she had been abandoned several days, or perhaps weeks, before being picked up. The official log, which was found in the cabin, states that the vessel sailed from Boston to Lisbon, starting upon October 16. It is, however, most imperfectly kept, and affords little information. There is no reference to rough weather, and, indeed, the state of the vessel's paint and rigging excludes the idea that she was abandoned for any such reason. She is perfectly watertight. No signs of a struggle or of violence are to be detected, and there is absolutely nothing to account for the disappearance of the crew. There are several indications that a lady was present on board, a sewing-machine being found in the cabin and some articles of female attire. These probably belonged to the captain's wife, who is mentioned in the log as having accompanied her husband. As an instance of the mildness of the weather, it may be remarked that a bobbin of silk was found standing upon the sewing-machine, though the least roll of the vessel would have precipitated it to the floor. The boats were intact and slung upon the davits; and the cargo, consisting of tallow and American clocks, was untouched. An old-fashioned sword of curious workmanship was discovered among some lumber in the forecastle, and this weapon is said to exhibit a longitudinal striation on the steel, as if it had been recently wiped. It has been placed in the hands of the police, and submitted to Dr Monaghan, the analyst, for inspection. The result of his examination has not yet been published. We may remark, in conclusion, that Captain Dalton, of the *Dei Gratia*, an able and intelligent seaman, is of opinion that the *Marie Celeste* may have been abandoned a considerable distance from the spot at which she was picked up, since a powerful current runs up in that latitude from the African coast. He confesses his inability, however, to advance any hypothesis which can reconcile all the facts of the case. In the utter absence of a clue or grain of evidence, it is to be feared that the fate of the crew of the *Marie Celeste* will be added to those numerous mysteries of the deep which will never be solved until the great day when the sea shall give up its dead. If crime has been committed, as is much to be suspected, there is little hope of bringing the perpetrators to justice.'

I shall supplement this extract from the *Gibraltar Gazette* by quoting a telegram from Boston, which went the round of the English papers, and represented the total amount of information which had been collected about the *Marie Celeste*. 'She was,' it said, 'a brigantine of 170 tons burden, and belonged to White, Russell & White, wine importers, of this city. Captain J. W. Tibbs was an old servant of the firm, and was a man of known ability and tried probity. He was accompanied by his wife, aged thirty-one, and their youngest child, five years old. The crew consisted of seven hands, including two coloured seamen, and a boy. There were three passengers, one of whom was the well-known Brooklyn specialist on consumption, Dr Habakuk Jephson, who was a distinguished advocate for Abolition in the early days of the movement, and whose pamphlet, entitled "Where is thy Brother?" exercised a strong influence on public opinion before the war. The other passengers were Mr J. Harton, a writer in the employ of the firm, and Mr Septimius Goring, a half-caste gentleman, from New Orleans. All investigations have failed to throw any light upon the fate of these fourteen human beings. The loss of Dr Jephson will be felt both in political and scientific circles.'

I have here epitomised, for the benefit of the public, all that has been hitherto known concerning the *Marie Celeste* and her crew, for the past ten years have not in any way helped to elucidate the mystery. I have now taken up my pen with the intention of telling all that I know of the ill-fated voyage. I consider that it is a duty which I owe to society, for symptoms which I am familiar with in others lead me to believe that before many months my tongue and hand may be alike incapable of conveying information. Let me remark, as a preface to my narrative, that I am Joseph Habakuk Jephson, Doctor of Medicine of the University of Harvard, and ex-Consulting Physician of the Samaritan Hospital of Brooklyn.

Many will doubtless wonder why I have not proclaimed myself before, and why I have suffered so many conjectures and surmises to pass unchallenged. Could the ends of justice have been served in any way by my revealing the facts in my possession I should unhesitatingly have done so. It seemed to me, however, that there was no possibility of such a result; and when I attempted after the occurrence, to state my case to an English official, I was met with such offensive incredulity that I determined never again to expose myself to the chance of such an indignity. I can excuse the discourtesy of the Liverpool magistrate, however, when I reflect upon the treatment which I received at the hands of my own relatives, who, though they knew my unimpeachable character, listened to my statement with an indulgent smile as if humouring the delusion of a monomaniac. This slur upon my veracity led to a quarrel between myself and John Vanburger, the brother of my wife, and confirmed me in my resolution to let the matter sink into oblivion – a determination which I have only altered through my son's solicitations. In order to make my narrative intelligible, I must run lightly over one or two incidents in my former life which throw light upon subsequent events.

My father, William K. Jephson, was a preacher of the sect called Plymouth Brethren, and was one of the most respected citizens of Lowell. Like most of the other Puritans of New England, he was a determined opponent of slavery, and it was from his lips that I received those lessons which tinged every action of my life. While I was studying medicine at Harvard University, I had already made a mark as an advanced Abolitionist; and when, after taking my degree, I bought a third share of the practice of Dr Willis, of Brooklyn, I managed, in spite of my professional duties to devote a considerable time to the cause which I had at heart, my pamphlet, 'Where is thy Brother?' (Swarburgh, Lister & Co., 1859) attracting considerable attention.

When the war broke out I left Brooklyn and accompanied the 113th New York Regiment through the campaign. I was present at the second battle of Bull's Run and at the battle of Gettysburg. Finally, I was severely wounded at Antietam, and would probably have perished on the field had it not been for the kindness of a gentleman named Murray, who had me carried to his house and provided me with every comfort. Thanks to his charity, and to the nursing which I received from his black domestics, I was soon able to get about the plantation with the help of a stick. It was during this period of convalescence that an incident occurred which is closely connected with my story.

Among the most assiduous of the negresses who had watched my couch during my illness there was one old crone who appeared to exert considerable authority over the others. She was exceedingly attentive to me, and I gathered from the few words that passed between us that she had heard of me, and that she was grateful to me for championing her oppressed race.

One day as I was sitting alone in the verandah, basking in the sun, and debating whether I should rejoin Grant's army, I was surprised to see this old creature hobbling towards me. After looking cautiously around to see that we were alone, she fumbled in the front of her dress, and produced a small chamois leather bag which was hung round her neck by a white cord.

'Massa,' she said, bending down and croaking the words into my ear, 'me die soon. Me very old woman. Not stay long on Massa Murray's plantation.'

'You may live a long time yet, Martha,' I answered. 'You know I am a doctor. If you feel ill let me know about it, and I will try to cure you.'

'No wish to live – wish to die. I'm gwine to join the heavenly host.' Here she relapsed into one of those half-heathenish rhapsodies in which negroes indulge.

'But, massa, me have one thing must leave behind me when I go. No able to take it with me across the Jordan. That one thing very precious, more precious and more holy than all thing else in the world. Me, a poor old black woman, have this because my people, very great people, 'spose they was back in the old country. But you cannot understand this same as black folk could. My fader give it me, and his fader give it him, but now who shall I give it to? Poor Martha hab no child, no relation, nobody. All round I see black man very bad man. Black woman very stupid woman. Nobody worthy of the stone. And so I say, Here is Massa Jephson who write books and fight for coloured folk – he must be a good man, and he shall have it though he is white man, and nebber can know what it mean or where it came from.' Here the old woman fumbled in the chamois leather bag and pulled out a flattish black stone with a hole through the middle of it. 'Here, take it,' she said, pressing it into my hand; 'take it. No harm nebber come from anything good. Keep it safe – nebber lose it!' and with a warning gesture the old crone hobbled away in the same cautious way as she had come, looking from side to side to see if we had been observed.

I was more amused than impressed by the old woman's earnestness, and was only prevented from laughing during her oration by the fear of hurting her feelings. When she was gone I took a good look at the stone which she had given me. It was intensely black, of extreme hardness, and oval in shape – just such a flat stone as one would pick up on the seashore if one wished to throw a long way. It was about three inches long, and an inch and a half broad at the middle, but rounded off at the extremities. The most curious part about it was several well-marked ridges which ran in semicircles over its surface, and gave it exactly the appearance of a human ear. Although I was rather interested in my new possession and determined to submit it, as a geological specimen to my friend Professor Shroeder of the New York Institute upon the earliest opportunity. In the meantime I thrust it into my pocket, and rising from my chair started off for a short stroll in the shrubbery, dismissing the incident from my mind.

As my wound had nearly healed by this time, I took my leave of Mr Murray shortly afterwards. The Union armies were everywhere victorious and converging on Richmond, so that my assistance seemed unnecessary, and I returned to Brooklyn. There I resumed my practice, and married the second daughter of Josiah Vanburger, the well-known wood engraver. In the course of a few years I built up a good connection and acquired considerable reputation in the treatment of pulmonary complaints. I still kept the old black stone in my pocket, and frequently told the story of the dramatic way in which I had become possessed of it. I also kept my resolution of showing it to Professor Shroeder, who was much interested both by the anecdote and the specimen. He pronounced it to be a piece of meteoric stone, and drew my attention to the fact that its resemblance to an ear was not accidental, but that it was most carefully worked into that shape. A dozen little anatomical points showed that the worker had been as accurate as he was skilful. 'I should not wonder,' said the Professor, 'if it were broken off from some larger statue, though how such hard material could be so perfectly worked is more than I can understand. If there is a statue to correspond I should like to see it!' So I thought at the time, but I have changed my opinion since.

The next seven or eight years of my life were quiet and uneventful. Summer followed spring, and spring followed winter, without any variation in my duties. As the practice increased I admitted J. S. Jackson as partner, he to have one-fourth of the profits. The continued strain had told upon my constitution, however, and I became at last so unwell that my wife insisted upon my consulting Dr Kavanagh Smith, who was my colleague at the Samaritan Hospital. That gentleman examined me, and pronounced the apex of my left lung to be in a state of consolidation, recommending me at the same time to go through a course of medical treatment and to take a long sea-voyage.

My own disposition, which is naturally restless, predisposed me strongly in favour of the latter piece of advice, and the matter was clinched by my meeting young Russell, of the firm of White, Russell & White, who offered me a passage in one of his father's ships, the *Marie Celeste*, which was just starting from Boston. 'She is a snug little ship,' he said, 'and Tibbs, the captain, is an excellent fellow. There is nothing like a sailing ship for an invalid.' I was very much of the same opinion myself, so I closed with the offer on the spot.

My original plan was that my wife should accompany me on my travels. She has always been a very poor sailor, however, and there were strong family reasons against her exposing herself to any risk at the time, so we determined that she should remain at home. I am not a religious or an effusive man; but oh, thank God for that! As to leaving my practice, I was easily reconciled to it, as Jackson, my partner, was a reliable and hard-working man.

I arrived in Boston on October 12, 1873, and proceeded immediately to the office of the firm in order to thank them for their courtesy. As I was sitting in the counting-house waiting until they should be at liberty to see me, the words *Marie Celeste* suddenly attracted my attention. I looked round and saw a very tall, gaunt man, who was leaning across the polished mahogany counter asking some questions of the clerk at the other side. His face was turned half towards me, and I could see that he had a strong dash of negro blood in him, being probably a quadroon or even nearer akin to the black. His curved aquiline nose and straight lank hair showed the white strain; but the dark, restless eye, sensuous mouth, and gleaming teeth all told of his African origin. His complexion was of a sickly, unhealthy yellow, and as his face was deeply pitted with small-pox, the general impression was so unfavourable as to be almost revolting. When he spoke, however, it was in a soft, melodious voice, and in well-chosen words, and he was evidently a man of some education.

'I wished to ask a few questions about the *Marie Celeste*,' he repeated, leaning across to the clerk. 'She sails the day after to-morrow, does she not?'

'Yes, sir,' said the young clerk, awed into unusual politeness by the glimmer of a large diamond in the stranger's shirt front.

'Where is she bound for?'

'Lisbon.'

'How many of a crew?'

'Seven, sir.'

'Passengers?'

'Yes, two. One of our young gentlemen, and a doctor from New York.'

'No gentleman from the South?' asked the stranger eagerly.

'No, none, sir.'

'Is there room for another passenger?'

'Accommodation, for three more,' answered the clerk.

'I'll go,' said the quadroon decisively; 'I'll go, I'll engage my passage at once. Put it down, will you – Mr Septimius Goring, of New Orleans.'

The clerk filled up a form and handed it over to the stranger, pointing to a black space at the bottom. As Mr Goring stooped over to sign it I was horrified to observe that the fingers of his right hand had been lopped off, and that he was holding the pen between his thumb and the palm. I have seen thousands slain in battle, and assisted at every conceivable operation, but I cannot recall any sight which gave me such a thrill of disgust as that great brown sponge-like hand with the single member protruding from it. He used it skilfully enough, however, for, dashing off his signature, he nodded to the clerk and strolled out of the office just as Mr White sent out word that he was ready to receive me.

I went down to the *Marie Celeste* that evening, and looked over my berth, which was extremely comfortable considering the small size of the vessel. Mr Goring, whom I had seen in the

morning, was to have the one next mine. Opposite was the
captain's cabin and a small berth for Mr John Harton, a
gentleman who was going out in the interests of the firm. These
little rooms were arranged on each side of the passage which led
from the main-deck to the saloon. The latter was a comfortable
room, the panelling tastefully done in oak and mahogany, with a
rich Brussels carpet and luxurious settees. I was very much
pleased with the accommodation, and also with Tibbs the
captain, a bluff, sailor-like fellow, with a loud voice and hearty
manner, who welcomed me to the ship with effusion, and
insisted upon our splitting a bottle of wine in his cabin. He told
me that he intended to take his wife and youngest child with him
on the voyage, and that he hoped with good luck to make Lisbon
in three weeks. We had a pleasant chat and parted the best of
friends, he warning me to make the last of my preparations next
morning, as he intended to make a start by the mid-day tide,
having now shipped all his cargo. I went back to my hotel where
I found a letter from my wife awaiting me, and, after a refreshing
night's sleep, returned to the boat in the morning. From this
point I am able to quote from the journal which I kept in order to
vary the monotony of the long sea-voyage. If it is somewhat bald
in places I can at least rely upon its accuracy in details, as it was
written conscientiously from day to day.

October 16th—Cast off our warps at half-past two and were
towed out into the bay, where the tug left us, and with all sail set
we bowled along at about nine knots. I stood upon the poop
watching the low land of America sinking gradually upon the
horizon until the evening haze hid it from my sight. A single red
light, however, continued to blaze balefully behind us, throwing
a long track like a trail of blood upon the water, and it is still
visible as I write, though reduced to a mere speck. The captain is
in a bad humour, for two of his hands disappointed him at the
last moment, and he was compelled to ship a couple of negroes
who happened to be on the quay. The missing men were steady,
reliable fellows, who had been with him several voyages, and
their non-appearance puzzled as well as irritated him. Where a
crew of seven men have to work a fair-sized ship the loss of two
experienced seamen is a serious one, for though the negroes may

take a spell at the wheel or swab the decks, they are of little or no use in rough weather. Our cook is also a black man, and Mr Septimius Goring has a little darkie servant, so that we are rather a piebald community. The accountant, John Harton, promises to be an acquisition, for he is a cheery, amusing young fellow. Strange how little wealth has to do with happiness! He has all the world before him and is seeking his fortune in a far land, yet he is as transparently happy as a man can be. Goring is rich, if I am not mistaken, and so am I; but I know that I have a lung, and Goring has some deeper trouble still, to judge by his features. How poorly do we both contrast with the careless, penniless clerk!

October 17th—Mrs Tibbs appeared upon the deck for the first time this morning – a cheerful, energetic woman, with a dear little child just able to walk and prattle. Young Harton pounced on it at once, and carried it away to his cabin, where no doubt he will lay the seeds of future dyspepsia in the child's stomach. Thus medicine doth make cynics of us all! The weather is still all that could be desired, with a fine fresh breeze from the west-sou'-west. The vessel goes so steadily that you would hardly know that she was moving were it not for the creaking of the cordage, the bellying of the sails, and the long white furrow in our wake. Walked the quarter-deck all morning with the captain, and I think the keen fresh air has already done my breathing good, for the exercise did not fatigue me in any way. Tibbs is a remarkably intelligent man, and we had an interesting argument about Murray's observations on ocean currents, which we terminated by going down into his cabin to consult the work. There we found Goring, rather to the captain's surprise, as it is not usual for passengers to enter that sanctum unless specially invited. He apologised for his intrusion, however, pleading his ignorance of the usages of ship life; and the good-natured sailor simply laughed at the incident, begging him to remain and favour us with his company. Goring pointed to the chronometers, the case of which he had opened, and remarked that he had been admiring them. He has evidently some practical knowledge of mathematical instruments, as he told at a glance which was the most trustworthy of the three, and also named their price within a few dollars. He had a discussion with the captain too upon the variation of the compass, and when we came back to the ocean currents he showed a thorough grasp of the subject. Altogether he rather improves upon acquaintance, and is a man of decided culture and refinement. His voice harmonises with his conversation, and both are the very antithesis of his face and figure.

The noonday observation shows that we have run two hundred and twenty miles. Towards evening the breeze freshened up, and the first mate ordered reefs to be taken in the topsails and top-gallant sails in expectation of a windy night. I observe that the barometer has fallen to twenty-nine. I trust our voyage will not be a rough one, as I am a poor sailor, and my health would probably derive more harm than good from a stormy trip, though I have the greatest confidence in the captain's seamanship and in the soundness of the vessel. Played cribbage with Mrs Tibbs after supper, and Harton gave us a couple of tunes on the violin.

October 18th—The gloomy prognostications of last night were not fulfilled, as the wind died away again and we are lying now in a long greasy swell, ruffled here, and there by a fleeting catspaw which is insufficient to fill the sails. The air is colder than it was yesterday, and I have put on one of the thick woollen jerseys which my wife knitted for me. Harton came into my cabin in the morning and we had a cigar together. He says that he remembers having seen Goring in Cleveland, Ohio, in '69. He was, it appears, a mystery then as now, wandering about without any visible employment, and extremely reticent on his own affairs. The man interests me as a psychological study. At breakfast this morning I suddenly had that vague feeling of uneasiness which comes over some people when closely stared at, and, looking quickly up, I met his eyes bent upon me with an intensity which amounted to ferocity, though their expression instantly softened as he made some conventional remark upon the weather. Curiously enough, Harton says that he had a very similar experience yesterday upon deck. I observe that Goring frequently talks to the coloured seamen as he strolls about – a trait which I rather admire, as it is common to find half-breeds ignore their dark strain and treat their black kinsfolk with greater intolerance than a white man would do. His little page is devoted to him, apparently, which speaks well for his treatment of him. Altogether, the man is a curious mixture of incongruous qualities, and unless I am deceived in him will give me food for observation during the voyage.

The captain is grumbling about his chronometers, which do not register exactly the same time. He says it is the first time that they have ever disagreed. We were unable to get a noonday observation on account of the haze. By dead reckoning, we have done about a hundred and seventy miles in the twenty-four hours. The dark seamen have proved, as the skipper prophesied, to be very inferior hands, but as they can both manage the wheel well they are kept steering, and so leave the more experienced men to work the ship. These details are trivial enough, but a small thing serves as food for gossip aboard ship. The appearance of a whale in the evening caused quite a flutter among us. From its sharp back and forked tail, I should pronounce it to have been a rorqual, or 'finner', as they are called by the fishermen.

October 19th—Wind was cold, so I prudently remained in my cabin all day, only creeping out for dinner. Lying in my bunk I can, without moving, reach my books, pipes, or anything else I may want, which is one advantage of a small apartment. My old wound began to ache a little to-day, probably from the cold. Read *Montaigne's Essays* and nursed myself. Harton came in in the afternoon with Doddy, the captain's child, and the skipper himself followed, so that I held quite a reception.

October 20th and 21st—Still cold, with a continual drizzle or rain, and I have not been able to leave the cabin. This confinement makes me feel weak and depressed. Goring came in to see me, but his company did not tend to cheer me up much, as he hardly uttered a word, but contented himself with staring at me in a peculiar and rather irritating manner. He then got up and stole out of the cabin without saying anything. I am beginning to suspect that the man is a lunatic. I think I mentioned that his cabin is next to mine. The two are simply divided by a thin wooden partition which is cracked in many places, some of the cracks being so large that I can hardly avoid, as I lie in my bunk, observing his motions in the adjoining room. Without any wish to play the spy, I see him continually stooping over what appears to be a chart and working with a pencil and compasses. I have remarked the interest he displays in matters connected with navigation, but I am surprised that he should take the trouble to work out the course of the ship. However, it is a harmless amusement enough, and no doubt he verifies his results by those of the captain.

I wish the man did not run in my thoughts so much. I had a nightmare on the night of the 20th, in which I thought my bunk was a coffin, that I was laid out in it, and that Goring was endeavouring to nail up the lid, which I was frantically pushing away. Even when I woke up, I could hardly persuade myself that I was not in a coffin. As a medical man, I know that a nightmare is simply a vascular derangement of the cerebral hemispheres, and yet in my weak state I cannot shake off the morbid impression which it produces.

October 22nd—A fine day, with hardly a cloud in the sky, and a fresh breeze from the sou'-west which wafts us gaily on our way. There has evidently been some heavy weather near us, as there is a tremendous swell on, and the ship lurches until the end of the fore-yard nearly touches the water. Had a refreshing walk up and down the quarter-deck, though I have hardly found my sealegs yet. Several small birds – chaffinches, I think – perched in the rigging.

4.40 p.m.—While I was on deck this morning I heard a sudden explosion from the direction of my cabin, and, hurrying down, found that I had very nearly met with a serious accident. Goring was cleaning a revolver, it seems, in his cabin, when one of the barrels which he thought was unloaded went off. The ball passed through the side partition and imbedded itself in the bulwarks in the exact place where my head usually rests. I have been under fire too often to magnify trifles, but there is no doubt that if I had been in the bunk it must have killed me. Goring, poor fellow, did not know that I had gone on deck that day, and must therefore have felt terribly frightened. I never saw such emotion in a man's face as when, on rushing out of his cabin with the smoking pistol in his hand, he met me face to face as I came down from the deck. Of course, he was profuse in his apologies, though I simply laughed at the incident.

11 p.m.—A misfortune has occurred so unexpected and so horrible that my little escape of the morning dwindles into insignificance. Mrs Tibbs and her child have disappeared – utterly and entirely disappeared. I can hardly compose myself to write the sad details. About half-past eight Tibbs rushed into my cabin with a very white face and asked me if I had seen his wife. I answered that I had not. He then ran wildly into the saloon and began groping about for any trace of her, while I followed him, endeavouring vainly to persuade him that his fears were ridiculous. We hunted over the ship for an hour and a half without coming on any sight of the missing woman or child. Poor Tibbs lost his voice completely from calling her name. Even the sailors, who are generally stolid enough, were deeply affected by the sight of him as he roamed bareheaded and dishevelled about the deck, searching with feverish anxiety the most impossible places, and returning to them again and again with a piteous pertinacity. The last time she was seen was about seven o'clock, when she took Doddy on to the poop to give him a breath of fresh air before putting him to bed. There was no one there at the time except the black seaman at the wheel, who denies having seen her at all. The whole affair is wrapped in mystery. My own theory is that while Mrs Tibbs was holding the child and standing near the bulwarks it gave a spring and fell overboard, and that in her convulsive attempt to catch or save it, she followed it. I cannot account for the double disappearance in any other way. It is quite feasible that such a tragedy should be enacted without the knowledge of the man at the wheel, since it was dark at the time, and the peaked skylights of the saloon screen the greater part of the quarter-deck. Whatever the truth may be it is a terrible catastrophe, and has cast the darkest gloom upon our voyage. The mate has put the ship about, but of course there is not the slightest hope of picking them up. The captain is lying in a state of stupor in his cabin. I gave him a powerful dose of opium in his coffee that for a few hours at least his anguish may be deadened.

October 23rd—Woke with a vague feeling of heaviness and misfortune, but it was not until a few moments' reflection that I was able to recall our loss of the night before. When I came on deck I saw the poor skipper standing gazing back at the waste of waters behind us which contains everything dear to him upon earth. I attempted to speak to him, but he turned brusquely away, and began pacing the deck with his head sunk upon his breast. Even now, when the truth is so clear, he cannot pass a boat or an unbent sail without peering under it. He looks ten years older than he did yesterday morning. Harton is terribly cut up, for he was fond of little Doddy, and Goring seems sorry too. At least he has shut himself up in his cabin all day, and when I got a casual glance at him his head was resting on his two hands as if in a melancholy reverie. I fear we are about as dismal a crew as ever sailed. How shocked my wife will be to hear of our disaster! The swell has gone down now, and we are doing about eight knots with all sail set and a nice little breeze. Hyson is practically in command of the ship, as Tibbs, though he does his best to bear up and keep a brave front, is incapable of applying himself to serious work.

October 24th—Is the ship accursed? Was there ever a voyage which began so fairly and which changed so disastrously? Tibbs shot himself through the head during the night. I was awakened about three o'clock in the morning by an explosion, and immediately sprang out of bed and rushed into the captain's cabin to find out the cause, though with a terrible presentiment in my heart. Quickly as I went, Goring went more quickly still, for he was already in the cabin stooping over the dead body of the captain. It was a hideous sight, for the whole front of his face was blown in, and the little room was swimming in blood. The pistol was lying beside him on the floor, just as it had dropped from his hand. He had evidently put it to his mouth before pulling the trigger. Goring and I picked him reverently up and laid him on his bed. The crew had all clustered into his cabin, and the six white men were deeply grieved, for they were old hands who had sailed with him many years. There were dark looks and murmurs among them too, and one of them openly declared that the ship was haunted. Harton helped to lay the poor skipper out, and we did him up in canvas between us. At twelve o'clock the fore-yard was hauled aback, and we committed his body to the deep, Goring reading the Church of England burial service. The breeze has freshened up, and we have done ten knots all day and sometimes twelve. The sooner we reach Lisbon and get away from this accursed ship the better pleased shall I be. I feel as though we were in a floating coffin. Little wonder that the poor sailors are superstitious when I, an educated man, feel it so strongly.

October 25th—Made a good run all day. Feel listless and depressed.

October 26th—Goring, Harton, and I had a chat together on deck in the morning. Harton tried to draw Goring out as to his profession, and his object in going to Europe, but the quadroon parried all his questions and gave us no information. Indeed, he seemed to be slightly offended by Harton's pertinacity, and went down into his cabin. I wonder why we should both take such an interest in this man! I suppose it is his striking appearance, coupled with his apparent wealth, which piques our curiosity. Harton has a theory that he is really a detective, that he is after some criminal who has got away to Portugal, and that he chooses this peculiar way of travelling that he may arrive unnoticed and pounce upon his quarry unawares. I think the supposition is rather a far-fetched one, but Harton bases it upon a book which Goring left on deck, and which he picked up and glanced over. It was a sort of scrap-book, it seems, and contained a large number of newspaper cuttings. All these cuttings related to murders which had been committed at various times in the States during the last twenty years or so. The curious thing which Harton observed about them, however, was that they were invariably murders the authors of which had never been brought to justice. They varied in every detail, he says, as to the manner of execution and the social status of the victim, but they uniformly wound up with the same formula that the murderer was still at large, though, of course, the police had every reason to expect his speedy capture. Certainly the incident seems to support Harton's theory, though it may be a mere whim of Goring's, or, as I suggested to Horton, he may be collecting materials for a book which shall outvie De Quincy. In any case it is no business of ours.

October 27th, 28th—Wind still fair, and we are making good progress. Strange how easily a human unit may drop out of its place and be forgotten! Tibbs is hardly ever mentioned now; Hyson has taken possession of his cabin, and all goes on as before. Were it not for Mrs Tibbs's sewing-machine upon a side-table we might forget that the unfortunate family had ever existed. Another accident occurred on board to-day, though fortunately not a very serious one. One of our white hands had gone down the afterhold to fetch up a spare coil of rope, when one of the hatches which he had removed came crashing down on top of him. He saved his life by springing out of the way, but one of his feet was terribly crushed, and he will be of little use for the remainder of the voyage. He attributes the accident to the carelessness of his negro companion, who had helped him to shift the hatches. The latter, however, puts it down to the roll of the ship. Whatever be the cause, it reduces our short-handed crew still further. This run of ill-luck seems to be depressing Harton, for he has lost his usual good spirits and joviality. Goring is the only one who preserves his cheerfulness. I see him still working at his chart in his own cabin. His nautical knowledge would be useful should anything happen to Hyson – which God forbid!

October 29th, 30th—Still bowling along with a fresh breeze. All quiet and nothing of note to chronicle.

October 31st—My weak lungs, combined with the exciting episodes of the voyage, have shaken my nervous system so much that the most trivial incident affects me. I can hardly believe that I am the same man who tied the external iliac artery, an operation requiring the nicest precision, under a heavy rifle fire at Antietam. I am as nervous as a child. I was lying half dozing last night about four bells in the middle watch trying in vain to drop into a refreshing sleep. There was no light inside my cabin, but a single ray of moonlight streamed in through the port-hole, throwing a silvery flickering circle upon the door. As I lay I kept my drowsy eyes upon this circle, and was conscious that it was gradually becoming less well-defined as my senses left me, when I was suddenly recalled to full wakefulness by the appearance of a small dark object in the very centre of the luminous disc. I lay quietly and breathlessly watching it. Gradually it grew larger and plainer, and then I perceived that it was a human hand which had been cautiously inserted through the chink of the half-closed door – a hand which, as I observed with a thrill of horror, was not provided with fingers. The door swung cautiously backwards, and Goring's head followed his hand. It appeared in the centre of the moonlight, and was framed as it were in a ghastly uncertain halo, against which his features showed out plainly. It seemed to me that I had never seen such an utterly fiendish and merciless expression upon a human face. His eyes were dilated and glaring, his lips drawn back so as to show his white fangs, and his straight black hair appeared to bristle over his low forehead like the hood of a cobra. The sudden and noiseless apparition had such an effect upon me that I sprang up in bed trembling in every limb, and held out my hand towards my revolver. I was heartily ashamed of my hastiness when he explained the object of his intrusion, as he immediately did in the most courteous language. He had been suffering from toothache, poor fellow! and had come in to beg some laudanum, knowing that I possessed a medicine chest. As to a sinister expression he is never a beauty, and what with my state of nervous tension and the effect of the shifting moonlight it was easy to conjure up something horrible. I gave him twenty drops, and he went off again, with many expressions of gratitude. I can hardly say how much this trivial incident affected me. I have felt unstrung all day.

A week's record of our voyage is here omitted, as nothing eventful occurred during the time, and my log consists merely of a few pages of unimportant gossip.

November 7th—Harton and I sat on the poop all the morning, for the weather is becoming very warm as we come into southern latitudes. We reckon that we have done two-thirds of our voyage. How glad we shall be to see the green banks of the Tagus, and leave this unlucky ship for ever! I was endeavouring to amuse Harton to-day and to while away the time by telling him some of the experiences of my past life. Among others I related to him how I came into the possession of my black stone, and as a finale I rummaged in the side pocket of my old shooting coat and produced the identical object in question. He and I were bending over it together, I pointing out to him the curious ridges upon its surface, when we were conscious of a shadow falling between us and the sun, and looking round saw Goring standing behind us glaring over our shoulders at the stone. For some reason or other he appeared to be powerfully excited, though he was evidently trying to control himself and to conceal his emotion. He pointed once or twice at my relic with his stubby thumb before he could recover himself sufficiently to ask what it was and how I obtained it – a question put in such a brusque manner that I should have been offended had I not known the man to be an eccentric. I told him the story very much as I had told it to Harton. He listened with the deepest interest and then asked me if I had any idea what the stone was. I said I had not, beyond that it was meteoric. He asked me if I had ever tried its effect upon a negro. I said I had not. 'Come,' said he, 'we'll see what our black friend at the wheel thinks of it.' He took the stone in his hand and went across to the sailor, and the two examined it carefully. I could see the man gesticulating and nodding his head excitedly as if making some assertion, while his face betrayed the utmost astonishment, mixed, I think, with some reverence. Goring came across the deck to us presently, still holding the stone in his hand. 'He says it is a worthless, useless thing,' he said, 'and fit only to be chucked overboard,' with which he raised his hand and would most certainly have made an end of my relic, had the black sailor behind him not rushed forward and seized him by the wrist. Finding himself secured Goring dropped the stone and turned away with a very bad grace to avoid my angry remonstrances at his breach of faith. The black picked up the stone and handed it to me with a low bow and every sign of profound respect. The whole affair is inexplicable. I am rapidly coming to the conclusion that Goring is a maniac or something very near one. When I compare the effect produced by the stone upon the sailor, however, with the respect shown to Martha on the plantation, and the surprise of Goring on its first production, I cannot but come to the conclusion that I have really got hold of some powerful talisman which appeals to the whole dark race. I must not trust it in Goring's hands again.

November 8th, 9th—What splendid weather we are having! Beyond the little blow, we have had nothing but fresh breezes the whole voyage. These two days we have made better runs than any hitherto. It is a pretty thing to watch the spray fly up from our prow as it cuts through the waves. The sun shines through it and breaks it up into a number of miniature rainbows – 'sundogs' the sailors call them. I stood on the fo'c'sle-head for several hours to-day watching the effect, and surrounded by a halo of prismatic colours. The steersman has evidently told the other blacks about my wonderful stone, for I am treated by them all with the greatest respect. Talking about optical phenomena, we had a curious one yesterday evening which was pointed out to me by Hyson. This was the appearance of a triangular well-defined object high up in the heavens to the north of us. He explained that it was exactly like the Peak of Teneriffe as seen from a great distance – the peak was, however, at that moment at least five hundred miles to the south. It may have been a cloud, or it may have been one of those strange reflections of which one reads. The weather is very warm. The mate says that he never knew it so warm in these latitudes. Played chess with Harton in the evening.

November 10th—It is getting warmer and warmer. Some land birds came and perched in the rigging to-day, though we are still a considerable way from our destination. The heat is so great that we are too lazy to do anything but lounge about the decks and smoke. Goring came over to me to-day and asked me some more questions about my stone; but I answered him rather shortly, for I have not quite forgiven him yet for the cool way in which he attempted to deprive me of it.

November 11th, 12th—Still making good progress. I had no idea Portugal was ever as hot as this, but no doubt it is cooler on land. Hyson himself seemed surprised at it, and so do the men.

November 13th—A most extraordinary event has happened, so extraordinary as to be almost inexplicable. Either Hyson has blundered wonderfully, or some magnetic influence has disturbed our instruments. Just about daybreak the watch on the fo'c'sle-head shouted out that he heard the sound of surf ahead, and Hyson that he saw the loom of land. The ship was put about, and, though no lights were seen, none of us doubted that we had struck the Portuguese coast a little sooner than we had expected. What was our surprise to see the scene which was revealed to us at break of day! As far as we could look on either side was one long line of surf, great, green billows rolling in and breaking into a cloud of foam. But behind the surf what was there! Not the green banks nor the high cliffs of the shores of Portugal, but a great sandy waste which stretched away and away until it blended with the skyline. To right and left, look where you would, there was nothing but yellow sand, heaped in some places into fantastic mounds, some of them several hundred feet high, while in other parts were long stretches as level apparently as a billiard board. Harton and I, who had come on deck together, looked at each other in astonishment, and Harton burst out laughing. Hyson is exceedingly mortified at the occurrence, and protests that the instruments have been tampered with. There is no doubt that this is the mainland of Africa, and that it was really the Peak of Teneriffe which we saw some days ago upon the northern horizon. At the time when we saw the land birds we must have been passing some of the Canary Islands. If we continued on the same course, we are now to the north of Cape Blanco, near the unexplored country which skirts the great Sahara. All we can do is to rectify our instruments as far as possible and start afresh for our destination.

8.30 p.m.—Have been lying in a calm all day. The coast is now about a mile and a half from us. Hyson has examined the instruments, but cannot find any reason for their extraordinary deviation.

This is the end of my private journal, and I must make the remainder of my statement from memory. There is little chance of my being mistaken about facts, which have seared themselves into my recollection. That very night the storm which had been brewing so long burst over us, and I came to learn whither all those little incidents were tending which I had recorded so aimlessly. Blind fool that I was not to have seen it sooner! I shall tell what occurred as precisely as I can.

I had gone into my cabin about half-past eleven, and was preparing to go to bed, when a tap came at my door. On opening it I saw Goring's little black page, who told me that his master would like to have a word with me on deck. I was rather surprised that he should want me at such a late hour, but I went up without hesitation. I had hardly put my foot on the quarter-deck before I was seized from behind, dragged down upon my back, and a handkerchief slipped round my mouth. I struggled as hard as I could, but a coil of rope was rapidly and firmly wound round me, and I found myself lashed to the davit of one of the boats, utterly powerless to do or say anything, while the point of a knife pressed to my throat warned me to cease my struggles. The night was so dark that I had been unable hitherto to recognize my assailants, but as my eyes became accustomed to the gloom, and the moon broke out through the clouds that obscured it, I made out that I was surrounded by the two negro sailors, the black cook, and my fellow-passenger, Goring. Another man was crouching on the deck at my feet, but he was in the shadow and I could not recognize him.

All this occurred so rapidly that a minute could hardly have elapsed from the time I mounted the companion until I found myself gagged and powerless. It was so sudden that I could scarce bring myself to realize it, or to comprehend what it all meant. I heard the gang round me speaking in short, fierce whispers to each other, and some instinct told me that my life was the question at issue. Goring spoke authoritatively and angrily – the others doggedly and all together, as if disputing his commands. Then they moved away in a body to the opposite side of the deck, where I could still hear them whispering, though they were concealed from my view by the saloon skylights.

All this time the voices of the watch on deck chatting and laughing at the other end of the ship were distinctly audible, and I could see them gathered in a group, little dreaming of the dark doings which were going on within thirty yards of them. Oh! That I could have given them one word of warning, even though I had lost my life in doing it! but it was impossible. The moon was shining fitfully through the scattered clouds, and I could see the silvery gleam of the surge, and beyond it the vast weird desert with its fantastic sand-hills. Glancing down, I saw that the man who had been crouching on the deck was still lying there, and as I gazed at him a flickering ray of moonlight fell full upon his upturned face. Great heaven! even now, when more than twelve years have elapsed, my hand trembles as I write that, in spite of distorted features and projecting eyes, I recognized the face of Harton, the cheery young clerk who had been my companion during the voyage. It needed no medical eye to see that he was quite dead, while the twisted handkerchief round the neck, and the gag in his mouth, showed the silent way in which the hell-hounds had done their work. The clue which explained every event of our voyage came upon me like a flash of light as I gazed on poor Harton's corpse. Much was dark and unexplained, but I felt a great dim perception of the truth.

I heard the striking of a match at the other side of the skylights, and then I saw the tall, gaunt figure of Goring standing up on the bulwarks and holding in his hands what appeared to be a dark lantern. He lowered this for a moment over the side of the ship, and, to my inexpressible astonishment, I saw it answered instantaneously by a flash among the sand-hills on shore, which came and went so rapidly, that unless I had been following the direction of Goring's gaze, I should never have detected it. Again he lowered the lantern, and again it was answered from the shore. He then stepped down from the bulwarks, and in doing so slipped, making such a noise, that for a moment my heart bounded with the thought that the attention of the watch would be directed to his proceedings. It was a vain hope. The night was calm and the ship motionless, so that no idea of duty kept them vigilant. Hyson, who after the death of Tibbs was in command of both watches, had gone below to snatch a few hours' sleep, and the boatswain, who was left in charge, was standing with the other two men at the foot of the foremast. Powerless, speechless, with the cords cutting into my flesh and the murdered man at my feet, I awaited the next act in the tragedy.

The four ruffians were standing up now at the other side of the deck. The cook was armed with some sort of a cleaver, the others had knives, and Goring had a revolver. They were all leaning over the rail and looking out over the water as if watching for something. I saw one of them grasp another's arm and point as if at some object, and following the direction I made out the loom of a large moving mass making towards the ship. As it emerged from the gloom I saw that it was a great canoe crammed with men and propelled by at least a score of paddles. As it shot under our stern the watch caught sight of it also, and raising a cry hurried aft. They were too late, however. A swarm of gigantic negroes clambered over the quarter, and led by Goring swept down the deck in an irresistible torrent. All opposition was overpowered in a moment, the unarmed watch were knocked over and bound, and the sleepers dragged out of their bunks and secured in the same manner. Hyson made an attempt to defend the narrow passage leading to his cabin, and I heard a scuffle, and his voice shouting for assistance. There was none to assist, however, and he was brought on to the poop with the blood streaming from a deep cut in his forehead. He was gagged like the others, and a council was held upon our fate by the negroes. I saw our black seamen pointing towards me and making some statement, which was received with murmurs of astonishment and incredulity by the savages. One of them then came over to me, and plunging his hand into my pocket took out my black stone and held it up. He then handed it to a man who appeared to be a chief, who examined it as minutely as the light would permit, and muttering a few words passed it on to the warrior beside him, who also scrutinized it and passed it on until it had gone from hand to hand round the whole circle. The chief then said a few words to Goring in the native tongue, on which the quadroon addressed me in English. At this moment I seem to see the scene. The tall masts of the ship with the moonlight streaming down, silvering the yards and bringing the network of cordage into hard relief; the group of dusky warriors leaning on their spears; the dead man at my feet; the line of white-faced prisoners, and in front of me the loathsome half-breed, looking in his white linen and elegant clothes a strange contrast to his associates.

'You will bear me witness,' he said in his softest accents, 'that I am no party to sparing your life. If it rested with me you would die as these other men are about to do. I have no personal grudge against either you or them, but I have devoted my life to the destruction of the white race, and you are the first that has ever been in my power and has escaped me. You may thank that stone of yours for your life. These poor fellows reverence it, and indeed if it really be what they think it is they have cause. Should it prove when we get ashore that they are mistaken, and that its shape and material is a mere chance, nothing can save your life. In the meantime we wish to treat you well, so if there are any of your possessions which you would like to take with you, you are at liberty to get them.' As he finished he gave a sign, and a couple of the negroes unbound me, though without removing the gag. I was led down into the cabin, where I put a few valuables into my pockets, together with a pocket-compass and my journal of the voyage. They then pushed me over the side into a small canoe, which was lying beside the large one, and my guards followed me, and shoving off began paddling for the shore. We had got about a hundred yards or so from the ship when our steersman held up his hand, and the paddlers paused for a moment and listened. Then on the silence of the night I heard a sort of dull, moaning sound, followed by a succession of splashes in the water. That is all I know of the fate of my poor shipmates. Almost immediately afterwards the large canoe followed us, and the deserted ship was left drifting about – a dreary spectre-like hulk. Nothing was taken from her by the savages. The whole fiendish transaction was carried through as decorously and temperately as though it were a religious rite.

The first grey of daylight was visible in the east as we passed through the surge and reached the shore. Leaving half a dozen men with the canoes, the rest of the negroes set off through the sand-hills, leading me with them, but treating me very gently and respectfully. It was difficult walking, as we sank over our ankles into the loose, shifting sand at every step, and I was nearly dead beat by the time we reached the native village, or town rather, for it was a place of considerable dimensions. The houses were conical structures not unlike bee-hives, and were made of compressed seaweed cemented over with a rude form of mortar, there being neither stick nor stone upon the coast nor anywhere within many hundreds of miles. As we entered the town an enormous crowd of both sexes came swarming out to meet us, beating tom-toms and howling and screaming. On seeing me they redoubled their yells and assumed a threatening attitude, which was instantly quelled by a few words shouted by my escort. A buzz of wonder succeeded the war-cries and yells of the moment before, and the whole dense mass proceeded down the broad central street of the town, having my escort and myself in the centre.

My statement hitherto may seem so strange as to excite doubt in the minds of those who do not know me, but it was the fact which I am now about to relate which caused my own brother-in-law to insult me by disbelief. I can but relate the occurrence in the simplest words, and trust to chance and time to prove their truth. In the centre of this main street there was a large building, formed in the same primitive way as the others, but towering high above them; a stockade of beautifully polished ebony rails was planted all round it, the framework of the door was formed by two magnificent elephant's tusks sunk in the ground on each side and meeting at the top, and the aperture was closed by a screen of native cloth richly embroidered with gold. We made our way to this imposing-looking structure, but on reaching the opening in the stockade, the multitude stopped and squatted down upon their hams, while I was led through into the enclosure by a few of the chiefs and elders of the tribe, Goring accompanying us, and in fact directing the proceedings. On reaching the screen which closed the temple – for such it evidently was – my hat and my shoes were removed, and I was then led in, a venerable old negro leading the way carrying in his hand my stone, which had been taken from my pocket. The building was only lit up by a few long slits in the roof, through which the tropical sun poured, throwing broad golden bars upon the clay floor, alternating with intervals of darkness.

The interior was even larger than one would have imagined from the outside appearance. The walls were hung with native mats, shells, and other ornaments, but the remainder of the great space was quite empty, with the exception of a single object in the centre. This was the figure of a colossal negro, which I at first thought to be some real king or high priest of titanic size, but as I approached it I saw by the way in which the light was reflected from it that it was a statue admirably cut in jet-black stone. I was led up to this idol, for such it seemed to be, and looking at it closer I saw that though it was perfect in every other respect, one of its ears had been broken short off. The grey-

haired negro who held my relic mounted upon a small stool, and
stretching up his arm fitted Martha's black stone on to the jagged
surface on the side of the statue's head. There could not be a
doubt that the one had been broken off from the other. The parts
dovetailed together so accurately that when the old man
removed his hand the ear stuck in its place for a few seconds
before dropping into his open palm. The group around me
prostrated themselves on the ground at the sight with a cry of
reverence, while the crowd outside, to whom the result was
communicated, set up a wild whooping and cheering.

In a moment I found myself converted from a prisoner into a
demi-god. I was escorted back through the town in triumph, the
people pressing forward to touch my clothing and to gather up
the dust on which my foot had trod. One of the largest huts was
put at my disposal, and a banquet of every native delicacy was
served me. I still felt, however, that I was not a free man, as
several spearmen were placed as a guard at the entrance of my
hut. All day my mind was occupied with plans of escape, but
none seemed in any way feasible. On the one side was the great
arid desert stretching away to Timbuctoo, on the other was a sea
untraversed by vessels. The more I pondered over the problem
the more hopeless did it seem. I little dreamed how near I was to
its solution.

Night had fallen, and the clamour of the negroes had died
gradually away. I was stretched on the couch of skins which had
been provided for me, and was still meditating over my future,
when Goring walked stealthily into the hut. My first idea was
that he had come to complete his murderous holocaust by
making away with me, the last survivor, and I sprang up upon
my feet, determined to defend myself to the last. He smiled
when he saw the action, and motioned me down again while he
seated himself upon the other end of the couch.

'What do you think of me?' was the astonishing question with
which he commenced our conversation.

'Think of you!' I almost yelled. 'I think you the vilest, most
unnatural renegade that ever polluted the earth. If we were away
from these black devils of yours I would strangle you with my
hands!'

'Don't speak so loud,' he said, without the slightest appearance of irritation. 'I don't want our chat to be cut short. So you would strangle me, would you!' he went on, with an amused smile. 'I suppose I am returning good for evil, for I have come to help you to escape.'

'You!' I gasped incredulously.

'Yes, I,' he continued. 'Oh, there is no credit to me in the matter. I am quite consistent. There is no reason why I should not be perfectly candid with you. I wish to be king over these fellows – not a very high ambition, certainly, but you know what Cæser said about being first in a village in Gaul. Well, this unlucky stone of yours has not only saved your life, but has turned all their heads so that they think you are come down from heaven, and my influence will be gone until you are out of the way. That is why I am going to help you to escape, since I cannot kill you' – this in the most natural and dulcet voice, as if the desire to do so were a matter of course.

'You would give the world to ask me a few questions,' he went on, after a pause; 'but you are too proud to do it. Never mind, I'll tell you one or two things, because I want your fellow white men to know them when you go back – if you are lucky enough to get back. About that cursed stone of yours, for instance. These negroes, or at least so the legend goes, were Mahometans originally. While Mahomet himself was still alive, there was a schism among his followers, and the smaller party moved away from Arabia, and eventually crossed Africa. They took away with them, in their exile, a valuable relic of their old faith in the shape of a large piece of the black stone of Mecca. The stone was a meteoric one, as you may have heard, and in its fall upon the earth it broke into two pieces. One of these pieces is still at Mecca. The larger piece was carried away to Barbary, where a skilful worker modelled it into the fashion which you saw to-day. These man are the descendants of the original seceders from Mahomet, and they have brought their relic safely through all their wanderings until they settled in this strange place, where the desert protects them from their enemies.'

'And the ear?' I asked, almost involuntarily.

'Oh, that was the same story over again. Some of the tribe

wandered away to the south a few hundred years ago, and one of them, wishing to have good luck for the enterprise, got into the temple at night and carried off one of the ears. There has been a tradition among the negroes ever since that the ear would come back some day. The fellow who carried it was caught by some slaver, no doubt, and that was how it got into America, and so into your hands – and you have had the honour of fulfilling the prophecy.'

He paused for a few minutes, resting his head upon his hands, waiting apparently for me to speak. When he looked up again, the whole expression of his face had changed. His features were firm and set, and he changed the air of half-levity with which he had spoken before for one of sternness and almost ferocity.

'I wish you to carry a message back,' he said, 'to the white race, the great dominating race whom I hate and defy. Tell them that I have battened on their blood for twenty years, that I have slain them until even I became tired of what had once been a joy, that I did this unnoticed and unsuspected in the face of every precaution which their civilization could suggest. There is no satisfaction in revenge when your enemy does not know who has struck him. I am not sorry, therefore, to have you as a messenger. There is no need why I should tell you how this great hate became born in me. See this,' and he held up his mutilated hand; 'that was done by a white man's knife. My father was white, my mother was a slave. When he died she was sold again, and I, a child then, saw her lashed to death to break her of some of the little airs and graces which her late master had encouraged in her. My young wife, too, oh, my young wife!' a shudder ran through his whole frame. 'No matter! I swore my oath, and I kept it. From Maine to Florida, and from Boston to San Francisco, you could track my steps by sudden deaths which baffled the police. I warred against the whole white race as they for centuries had warred against the black one. At last, as I tell you, I sickened of blood. Still, the sight of a white face was abhorrent to me, and I determined to find some bold free black people and to throw in my lot with them, to cultivate their latent powers and to form a nucleus for a great coloured nation. This idea possessed me, and I travelled over the world for two years seeking for what I desired. At last I almost despaired of finding it. There was no hope of regeneration in the slave-dealing Soudanese, the debased Fantee, or the Americanized negroes of Liberia. I was returning from my quest when chance brought me in contact with this magnificent tribe of dwellers in the desert, and I threw in my lot with them. Before doing so, however, my old instinct of revenge prompted me to make one last visit to the United States, and I returned from it in the *Marie Celeste*.

'As to the voyage itself, your intelligence will have told you by this time that, thanks to my manipulation, both compasses and chronometers were entirely untrustworthy. I alone worked out the course with correct instruments of my own, while the steering was done by my black friends under my guidance. I pushed Tibbs's wife overboard. What! You look surprised and shrink away. Surely you had guessed that by this time. I would have shot you that day through the partition, but unfortunately you were not there. I tried again afterwards, but you were awake. I shot Tibbs. I think the idea of suicide was carried out rather neatly. Of course when once we got on the coast the rest was simple. I had bargained that all on board should die; but that stone of yours upset my plans. I also bargained that there should be no plunder. No one can say we are pirates. We have acted from principle, not from any sordid motive.'

I listened in amazement to the summary of his crimes which this strange man gave me, all in the quietest and most composed of voices, as though detailing incidents of every-day occurrence. I still seem to see him sitting like a hideous nightmare at the end of my couch, with the single rude lamp flickering over his cadaverous features.

'And now,' he continued, 'there is no difficulty about your escape. These stupid adopted children of mine will say that you have gone back to heaven from whence you came. The wind blows off the land. I have a boat all ready for you, well stored with provisions and water. I am anxious to be rid of you, so you may rely that nothing is neglected. Rise up and follow me.'

I did what he commanded, and he led me through the door of the hut. The guards had either been withdrawn, or Goring had arranged matters with them. We passed unchallenged through the town and across the sandy plain. Once more I heard the roar of the sea, and saw the long white line of the surge. Two figures were standing upon the shore arranging the gear of a small boat. They were the two sailors who had been with us on the voyage.

'See him safely through the surf,' said Goring. The two men sprang in and pushed off, pulling me in after them. With mainsail and jib we ran out from the land and passed safely over the bar. Then my two companions without a word of farewell sprang overboard, and I saw their heads like black dots on the white foam as they made their way back to the shore, while I scudded away into the blackness of the night. Looking back I caught my last glimpse of Goring. He was standing upon the summit of a sand-hill, and the rising moon behind him threw his gaunt angular figure into hard relief. He was waving his arms frantically to and fro; it may have been to encourage me on my way, but the gestures seemed to me at the time to be threatening ones, and I have often thought that it was more likely that his old savage instinct had returned when he realized that I was out of his power. Be that as it may, it was the last that I ever saw or ever shall see of Septimius Goring.

There is no need for me to dwell upon my solitary voyage. I steered as well as I could for the Canaries, but was picked up upon the fifth day by the British and African Steam Navigation Company's boat *Monrovia*. Let me take this opportunity of tendering my sincerest thanks to Captain Stornoway and his officers for the great kindness which they showed me from that time till they landed me in Liverpool, where I was enabled to take one of the Guion boats to New York.

From the day on which I found myself once more in the bosom of my family I have said little of what I have undergone. The subject is still an intensely painful one to me, and the little which I have dropped has been discredited. I now put the facts before the public as they occurred, careless how far they may be believed, and simply writing them down because my lung is growing weaker, and I feel the responsibility of holding my peace longer. I make no vague statement. Turn to your map of Africa. There above Cape Blanco, where the land trends away north and south from the westernmost point of the continent, there it is that Septimius Goring still reigns over his dark subjects unless retribution has overtaken him; and there, where the long green ridges run swiftly in to roar and hiss upon the hot yellow sand, it is there that Harton lies with Hyson and the other poor fellows who were done to death in the *Marie Celeste*.

THE BENEVOLENT
GHOST AND CAPTAIN
LOWRIE

Richard Sale

The Flying Dutchman, *a ghostly ship which is doomed to sail the oceans of the world as punishment for its captain's blasphemy, has been a subject of interest for generations. It provided the great composer Richard Wagner with the idea for one of his most famous operas,* Die Fliegende Hollander, *written in 1843. The captain of the ship, generally called Vanderdecken, was said to have been a Dutchman who defied God and the elements while trying to sail through a storm around the Cape of Good Hope, and was thereafter condemned to roam the oceans until he could find another vessel willing to take letters begging forgiveness back to his home in Holland. According to legend any other ship which came into contact with the Dutchman similarly became doomed, and so sailors everywhere steered clear of the ancient sailing craft.*

Although there have, of course, been lots of stories of ghostly vessels seen on the world's oceans, none has so captured the imagination of writers and readers as The Flying Dutchman. *As I mentioned earlier, both Captain Marryatt and Clark Russell took up the idea, as did the German poet Heinrich Heine, who created a very successful fictitious account in 1834. None, though, has come as near to solving the mystery as the well-known American writer and film director, Richard Sale (1911-) in* 'The Benevolent Ghost and Captain Lowrie' *(published in 1940).*

Richard Sale's love affair with the sea has produced fine books such as Not Too Narrow, Not Too Deep *(1936) which was filmed four years later under the title* Strange Cargo *starring Clark Gable, Joan Crawford and Peter Lorre. Sale also wrote the powerful screenplay for the movie* Abandon Ship *made in 1957. In the following tale he offers what I think may well be the best key to the riddle of the phantom ship – that is, until it finally comes in to harbour*
. . .

I

NORTH OF THEM, across the miles of black wet, howling night, Cape Town reposed upon the sturdy rocks of Africa, feeling the storm, too, but not the shock of the ocean.

The *S.S. Mary Watson*, Baltimore, Maryland, was an old ship. That did not mean she was senile. She had been with the sea a long time and she knew its foibles and handled herself with uncanny dexterity. But she had not been built originally to stand such buffeting, and her age made her joints creak when the heavy seas pounded her.

It was Bruno's watch and he listened to the high crying of the wind as it searched with harsh fingers through every crack and cranny of his clothing. Its pressure lay against his chest and cheeks alike, binding both arms against his chest and making a relentless skirt about his legs. Pushing into the weight of the gale, he fought its thrust as he balanced like a tight-rope walker above the rise and pitch of the restless deck. His heart boomed roughly as the ship smashed forward, expert but weary and old.

It was Bruno's watch, and he did not like it. Only once before, east in the Caribbean Sea, after a sore and foggy dawn, had he seen a wind with such velocity. They would soon be in trouble, and he knew it, and so called up the old man and put the responsibility where it belonged.

The night was black, yet they could see some of it because the bridge was even blacker. Where the combers burst upon the forepiece and swept the *Mary Watson*'s deck to the beam, there to be spit back into the sea through the scuppers, the water exploded alternately white and green against the tapestry of darkness.

Outside, as Captain John Lowrie soon found, the night was filled with the wind and the ocean, the rain had slackened perceptibly, but the wind hauled southwest the port side, and it nearly blew his teeth into his throat.

He gripped the rail and went up the stairs toward the bridge, catching a glimpse of the *Mary Watson*'s lonely funnels staggering overhead in the dark. Forward, he was barely able to discern the bridge wingtips with their glass weatherbreaks. The high howls of the wind on the boat deck smothered the deep thunder of the raging seas alongside as they swept by, white, mad, hungry.

He stepped off the bridge and slammed the door shut behind him, shaking his shoulders, soaking with rain. He stared across the darkness of the bridge at Bruno, and said, 'It's a fine night to call a man out.'

Bruno said nothing. There was nothing to say. The weather conditions spoke for themselves, and even a seasick landlubber could tell by the way the *Mary Watson* pitched and rolled that all was not well.

Captain Lowrie walked over to the helmsman, who clung to the wheel nervously, his eyes wide as he peered through the rain-studded window. The helmsman's name was Murphy, and he was young. He was nervous because he was having his first taste of a whole gale.

'How does she go, Mister?' asked Captain Lowrie.

'She goes hard and heavy, sir,' replied Murphy, his voice flat.

Bruno said, 'I've been in communication with Mr McNulty, sir, in the engine room, and he reports excessive vibration in the shaft. I changed speed to dead slow, but that seemed to make little difference. To my way of thinking we should heave to for the night, until this blows out.'

'To *my* way of thinking, there's little sense in that,' said Captain Lowrie. 'Change your course, mister. Due southwest, nothing off. Look alive now.'

There was thunder in the seas as the helmsman brought her over. Her blunt prow dug in hard and firm, the blows running through her body. The starboard bow vanished under the weighted seas, but in another moment it was clear and she was dead in the wind, pitching and tossing, the sickening rolls now gone.

They could all feel the difference at once. The strain went out of her rusty plates. Her fore and aft motion was short and sharp, as a good pitch should be. Mr Murphy at the helm relaxed.

'Well, now,' said Captain Lowrie, 'that was a small thing to get a man out in this kind of night for. How did you expect her to go easy with the waves on her beam?'

Bruno did not mind the jibe. Indeed, Captain Lowrie did not mean for it to be taken seriously. They both knew that the course could be changed only with the captain's permission. And for all the heartiness in Captain Lowrie's voice, there was still a troubled look around his eyes. Bruno noticed it and knew what it meant. For dead in the wind, her blunt bow rebuffing the staggering blows of the giant waves, the *Mary Watson* was safe enough. But there were many things that could happen: a broken screw, a burned-out bearing, or another ship out there in the darkness, unseen. Power was the thing. Without it, they were lost.

Captain Lowrie said, 'What does Sparks report?'

'Sparks was in touch with Cape Town half an hour ago, and he reports there ain't a ship within seventy miles of us. The nearest one is the *Nichyo Maru*. She's due west of us, so we've nothing to worry about in the way of a collision.'

'It's nice to know,' said Captain Lowrie. 'A lookout couldn't sight the devil's own seven masters on a night like this.'

Bruno shivered. 'Aye, sir,' he said, 'I've seen a night like this only once in fourteen years at sea. And I never want to see another. It's the sort of black dark night when seamen's yarns come true. Mr Franklin was telling me a while back that he saw St Elmo's fire on the mast.'

Franklin was second officer of the *Mary Watson*.

'St Elmo's fire!' Captain Lowrie exclaimed. 'And what's so

mythical about St Elmo's fire? I've seen it many a time at sea, and not a stormy night needed for it, either. When I was mate of the schooner *Chaff*, fishing the Grand Banks out of Gloucester, a long time ago, I seen St Elmo's fire time and again. Little crackling flames, sharp and clear, dancing across the yardarms. St Elmo's fire is no myth.'

Murphy at the helm stirred uneasily and opened his mouth. But he shut it again without saying anything.

Captain Lowrie stared at him. 'Was you goin' to say something, mister?'

Murphy wet his lips, swallowed hard. 'You were talking of seamen's yarns, Captain, and it was just that I was remembering some others I've heard. Tales of the Sargasso, the mystery of the *Marie Celeste*, and of the Flying Dutchman.'

'Ah,' said Captain Lowrie. 'The Dutchman!' He rubbed his hand through his shaggy mustache, and the bristly sound of it filled the bridge. 'The Dutchman indeed.'

He said it with such fervour that Bruno turned and stared at him. 'Surely, sir,' he said, 'you don't believe them old wives' tales?'

Captain Lowrie did not reply at once. He stared out through the storm window above the faint miserly glow which illumined the compass card, and he locked his hands behind his back and swayed easily with the motion of the freighter.

'Old wives' tales, eh?' He shook his head slowly. 'You're young, Mr Bruno, and maybe that's the reason; but me – I've been a seaman nigh on twenty-five years, and there's strange things happen in the seas. Strange indeed.'

Mr Murphy swallowed again, so hard this time that he made a clucking sound. There wasn't much light on the bridge, but the little there was showed his face pale and white. The sound of his gulp drew the old man's eyes.

'Feeling seasick, mister?' the captain said.

'No, sir,' replied Mr Murphy. 'I was just rememberin'.'

'Rememberin' what?'

'I was rememberin', Captain, that we're off the Cape of Good Hope in a blow. And that's just about what happened to the Flying Dutchman, isn't it?'

'Mind the helm!' Mr Bruno said sharply. He glanced at the quartermaster with some contempt. 'You're nervous enough, mister, without getting scared about a ghost.'

'Yes, sir,' Mr Murphy said.

II

'Aye,' Captain Lowrie ruminated soberly. 'There's strange things in the sea. You, Mr Bruno, you don't believe in sea serpents, I take it. There's more things in heaven and earth and ocean than a man could ever dream about.

'*I* believe in sea serpents. I believe there is things in the ocean no man has ever seen. Why, bless St Christopher, it was near this very spot that a trawler hauled a fish out of the sea that was supposed to have been dead for fifty million years. Them scientific fellows have been reconstructing it from fossils they found some place in Europe.

'And right here, near Cape Town, a smelly trawler hauls it topside. Extinct for fifty million years, and yet not dead at all! I tell you, Mr Bruno, no man knows what's under the sea. And for that matter, no man knows what's above the sea, either. So who's to say the legend of the Flying Dutchman ain't true?'

Bruno sniffed. 'Personally, sir, I don't believe in ghosts,' he said.

Captain Lowrie snorted gruffly. 'And I suppose you don't think it's bad luck to kill an albatross or a gull? I suppose you don't think a ship is a "she". I suppose you don't think a shark following in the wake is bad luck. Silly superstitions for old fools like me, eh?'

'I didn't say that, sir.'

'What's the difference, man, if you think it?'

Bruno shrugged. Captain Lowrie continued:

'When I was mate aboard the *S.S. Gulf City* – she was a Standard Oil tanker in the coastwise trade – we had two seamen die of ptomaine poisoning. We buried them at sea, somewhere off Hatteras. I'd always heard that yarn about a dead man following the ship he loved, just as easily as a rat deserted a ship that was doomed.

'Next day, the watch spied one of the corpses floating in our wake, right after us. He thought maybe his eyes were tricking him, so he ran to get a camera to take a picture. But when he came back, the corpse was gone. We all joshed him about it.

'Two days later, off the Virginia Cape – now mind you, we buried them off Hatteras – the watch spied both them men floating in our wake! This time he had a camera with him, and he took a picture. He wanted to make sure that he would have something to prove his word, this time.

'But he needn't have been in such a hurry, because this time they didn't disappear. They hung on our wake all day long, and every member of the ship got an eyeful of them. They were there as plain as day; you could even see their faces. From Hatteras to the Virginia Cape, mind you, and no explanation for that, eh, Mr Bruno?

'Finally, off Cape May, they disappeared and we didn't see them again. Every word of that story is true, Mr Bruno, and there are the pictures to back it up. So clear and good were they, that a big New York magazine published them, and lots of people tried to explain it away. But you couldn't explain away two dead men following a ship over six hundred miles, lying there in the wake as plain as day.'

Bruno's brow was furrowed. 'Wasn't there some explanation offered, to the effect that the suction of the ship's wake might have held the corpses behind her?'

Captain Lowrie chuckled sardonically. 'There may have been some such explanation, Mr Bruno. But you yourself at this very moment take little stock in it.'

'Oh, well,' Bruno muttered. 'I'll admit that strange things happen on land or sea and that sometimes there isn't much explanation for them. But the legend of the Flying Dutchman is something else again, unless I've got it all wrong.'

Captain Lowrie seated himself in a chair and tipped it back against the wall, balancing there precariously as the freighter pitched in the ponderous sea. He seemed quite at ease. He rubbed at his mustache with his left hand, and then proceeded to address himself to Mr Bruno.

'The Flying Dutchman is the Wandering Jew of the ocean. Nobody knows what his name is now; it's forgotten over the years. But a long time ago, and on such a night as this, the Dutchman was rounding the Cape of Good Hope in a three-masted schooner. She was called the *Fliegende Hollander*.

'He was a turbulent and headstrong sailor, this Dutchman. The storm was against him. The winds were against him. The men on his decks begged him to turn back, but he refused. "I'll round the Cape of Good Hope tonight," he said, "in spite of wind or storm or Heaven or Hell."

'For thus defying the elements and the Devil, he was cursed, condemned to roam the oceans of the world until the crack of Doomsday. And there was only one thing could save him; the love of a woman who would be faithful to him after death.'

Captain Lowrie chuckled. 'You can see where the poor man never had a chance. Ain't a woman alive could redeem him. It would take a lot of faith in these streamlined days.'

Bruno grunted. 'And do you actually believe, sir, that the Flying Dutchman exists today?'

'I don't say I do,' replied Captain Lowrie, 'and I don't say I don't.'

A sliver of lightning cut across the night sky, followed by a reverberating crash of thunder. Murphy, at the helm, jerked, startled by its sound, and nearly loosed his grip upon the spoke. 'He could be here,' the helmsman faltered. 'He could be right here, where he made his oath that stormy night some hundred years ago.'

Bruno sprang to the wheel and grasped it. 'Mind the course, you fool! You've dropped five points.'

He turned and stared accusingly at Captain Lowrie who still perched on the chair, little bothered by the fact that the *Mary Watson*'s bow had swung off the wind.

'There you see, sir, what good these tales of phantom ships can do. If it were only that they lent some colour or adventure or glamour to the sea, I wouldn't mind them. But they make for terror and incompetency. They make men afraid and inefficient. That's why I don't believe in ghosts, Captain. And I'm a better seaman for it.'

Captain Lowrie's bushy white eyebrows came far down over his eyes. He glowered at Bruno. 'If it were only that such tales made men afraid,' he said, 'I would agree with you, Mr Bruno. But why in the name of Davy Jones this lubber is afraid of the Dutchman is more than I can see. He's shaking like a leaf. I'll wager he cannot tell you why.'

Murphy, his mouth grim and taut, clung to the helm and said nothing.

'Look here, man,' said Captain Lowrie, 'you expect the Dutchman will be out on a night like this looking for you to take you along to Hell with himself. Were he here, the Dutchman, poor soul, would only be trying to make the same passage we are, around the Cape against the storm.

'By the beard of St Christopher, if he has one, I'd just as leave give him a tow if we met up with him. It would be the common courtesy of one seaman to another. And like as not he'd do the same for me. But the Dutchman, God save him, is busy on another sea in this world tonight, I'll wager.'

He stirred in the chair and rose unsteadily to his feet as the freighter wallowed in the trough. 'It's that late that I'm sleepy. So I'll catch forty winks. The wind is holding steadily now, and should be dropping soon, and we'll be on our way. Tell Mr McNulty to stand by in case we need him. Keep a weather eye peeled for a shift in the wind. And if things don't get better, call me up again.'

'Aye, sir,' said Bruno.

III

Near three o'clock in the morning, some time after the ship's chronometer had rung out five bells, the wind began to slacken. The heavy dangerous sea did not abate in force, but the rain vanished and the wind dropped off so sharply that the spume on the breaking crest was no longer visible.

Down in the black hole of Calcutta, where the gleaming polished propeller-shaft faithfully ground out its r.p.m.'s,

McNulty, the chief engineer, felt the *Mary Watson* gaining headway. The wind which had held them back now dissipated, allowing her, even at dead slow, to forge ahead.

Where before the freighter had expended only enough energy to equalize her position in the wind, now she was under way once more. And McNulty, a Scotchman who liked scones, Scotch and Beethoven, was glad of it. A few minutes later, and the engine room, telegraphed from the bridge, clanged its way to half speed.

NcNulty marked the telegraph gyrations, and then turned up the turbine engine. It was a pleasure to feel the *Mary Watson* bite steadily and head due east once more.

On the bridge, where the remnants of the wind still howled past the corners, Bruno noted his course on the chart. He felt very good. But he was enough of a realist to know that they were not out of the woods yet. He no longer doubted they would make the passage safely; but he was afraid that in making it the *Mary Watson* would reach Zanzibar with a stove-in hatch.

Still there was no choice. The gale had blown them far west of their course, and they had lost both precious time and fuel. Bruno telephoned the captain, and the old man agreed with him that the steady old tub should be pushed with as much speed as she could safely handle in the seaway.

At three-fifteen, the ragged clouds vanished, and the darkness of the bridge was suddenly illumined with pale moonlight. It was very faint, for streaky will-o'-the-wisps still scurried across its slender face. But there was, at least, some visibility and Bruno was heartened.

The wave crest ran high, but no longer broke. The glassy hollows, where salt bubbles split rapidly, were long and deep. One moment, as the *Mary Watson* topped a grayback, Mr Bruno could see miles of ridged, pocked-marked sea. Then would follow the awesome drop into the trough, where the horizon would merely be at the top of the next wave away.

Eastbound, the sea was on their corners, and the *Mary Watson* rolled alarmingly in the swell. But her speed steadied her somewhat, even though the going was very wet forward. And

Bruno knew that by dawn the Cape of Good Hope would be astern.

Franklin, the second officer, presently joined Bruno on the bridge. It was not his stint, but it had been a rotten night to sleep, and Franklin was just as glad to be out of his bunk.

At three-thirty a.m., a strange intensity pervaded the entire ship. Overhead, the moon suddenly hid itself behind a bulky cloud. There was only the faintest indication of moonlight left upon the turbulent crest.

In his cabin Captain John Lowrie, who had been snoring lustily, suddenly awoke out of a sound sleep for no reason at all and sat up in his bunk, disturbed and apprehensive.

In the engine rooms, McNulty, who had all but surrendered his duties to his assistant, McAdoo, content that the ship was well out of trouble, returned suddenly to his post, vaguely worried and not knowing why.

In the galley, where the ship's cook had bedded himself down for the night, Toby, the ship's cat, who had been sleeping serenely upon the breadbox, suddenly awoke, backed to a corner and began to growl, the long hairs down his back standing straight up on end.

On the bridge they felt it, too. Bruno looked up from his place at the chart table and shivered. He was not cold, and he did not know why he had done it. Franklin, who had been sitting in the chair that Captain Lowrie had vacated, suddenly stirred uneasily and rubbed the backs of his hands briskly.

'That's funny,' he said. 'I've just had the strangest feeling—'
Bruno met his eyes. They stared at each other.

The starboard door of the bridge opened, and Captain Lowrie walked in. He did not say anything, just walked to the chart table and sat down beside Bruno. There was a frown on his face and he looked worried.

'It was as if,' Captain Lowrie would tell his wife some months later, in Boston, 'we had all gone to a concert. It was that moment of great sense of silence, as the baton goes up just before the music begins.'

It was like that, that charged moment before the baton drops, when you can almost imagine you hear the music even before it has begun. The sea, there, pounding on her starboard quarter, might have been a kettle-drum. The dying wind, still whining high, might have been the first violin.

And under their feet, the freighter dropped into a deep and darkened valley. The boat wallowed there a moment, panting, and then with sovereign dignity forced her blunt bow up the wall of water which came rushing on. And when she reached the peak of that watery mountain she paused, as if to survey the studded voyage before her.

Young Murphy at the helm suddenly gaped into the faintly luminescent night before his eyes.

'In the name of Heaven!' Murphy said hollowly.

The other three – Captain Lowrie, Bruno, and Franklin – moved as one man. They sprang to their feet, instantly aware of Murphy's contorted face.

It was fear, Captain Lowrie knew. He had seen it often enough. The eyes, all white and glazed, the blanched skin, the dropped jaw which hung on Murphy's chest, the quivering mouth. They, too, faced the sea and watched expectantly beyond the waves.

Out of the night, like a great white ghost, they saw the ship. She was about a hundred feet long, her sails all set and filled. Captain Lowrie had never seen such a colour in sails before. Blood red they were, like a dying sunset; the strangest colour his eyes had ever seen: for the moonlight was faint, and in the back of his mind he wondered how sails of any colour could be that bright.

She was on the starboard tack, heeled well over, and she had a white bone in her teeth. There were moving shadows of men on her decks. The *Mary Watson* was bound east, but this strange schooner with her blood-red sails was bound due north and she seemed to come right at them.

Her speed was amazing. She seemed to plunge ahead much faster than the wind which filled her sails.

Through binoculars, Captain Lowrie could see a name upon her bow; but it was hazy and indistinct through the glass, and he could not make it out.

But he could make out her figurehead. At the base of the bowsprit, wet and glistening as the heavy bow plunged into the waves, he made out the grinning death's head.

Three masts, sticking up into the sky nakedly like inverted streaks of lightning, a death's head at the bow, blood-red sails; a schooner in a storm at the Cape of Good Hope, and an oath with the Devil.

'The Dutchman!' Captain Lowrie roared. 'The Flying Dutchman!'

IV

Bruno wrenched the binoculars away from the captain's grasp and peered out into the night himself. The glasses trembled in his hand. They were seven-power glasses and hard to hold upon the scene, but he managed it a moment and then dropped them from his eyes; and he was white and shaking.

'It's not The Dutchman,' he said savagely. 'It's a ship, a sailing ship, and she's running without lights. Sheer off, helmsman, sheer off to port. She'll strike us!'

But Franklin had already wrested the wheel from the quartermaster and he was bringing it hard over. The freighter's bow swung northward from east, and in the cross-sea the *Mary Watson* rolled dangerously.

'She's a phantom,' Captain Lowrie said hoarsely. 'She's the Dutchman out of Holland, trying to round the Cape.'

'You're mad!' Bruno snapped. 'She's just a ship, an old sea trader, perhaps.'

Captain Lowrie had the binoculars again. He held them on her bow as she came closer to them. '*Fliegende Hollander*,' he said, his voice trembling. 'It's there on the bow, under the bowsprit, as plain as day. Look for yourself, man! Her name is there, right there – the *Fliegende Hollander*, and her hailing port is Amsterdam.'

'It's your imagination; you are all filled up with the Dutchman's lore,' Bruno replied.

And then he said nothing more. There was no time to say

anything more. Silently and tensely, they watched her come. She was a savage ship, and she laid the water white around her bow, her bowsprit stabbing the sea like a guard sword.

She was very close now; so close that they could see the sailors on her deck. They seemed to be Norwegian. And back on the poop deck, by the great helm, there stood a tall, broad man with a great black cape around his shoulders.

His nose was large, and he had a heavy beard; and as the schooner bore upon them, Captain Lowrie could see this man wave a burly hand.

For a moment, it looked as if she would strike them near the stern, as if to slash the combing and the screw clean off, and leave the rest of the Mary Watson floating in the ocean, a powerless hulk. In that breathless moment, Captain Lowrie saw her flag, curling out to leeward above the blood-red sails. It was the flag of Holland.

Bruno saw it too. 'It could be a Dutch ship, and nothing more,' he whispered. 'A Dutch ship, an ordinary ship, and nothing more.' He was talking to reassure himself, but they all heard him.

'She's the Dutchman,' Captain Lowrie said, quietly now. 'Stand by for a crash.'

But there was no crash. The black ship, when she had forced the Mary Watson to turn due north, suddenly sheered off. They could see her captain, that big bearded man at the helm, swinging the wheel hard, and her bow, with a death's head for a figurehead, swung off the freighter's stern and turned northwest.

Swiftly she was abaft. They saw her dip into the deep trough between two towering crests. Only her curling flag and the tops of the three masts were left visible. And suddenly they sank down, too, and seemed to vanish.

When the next wave away reached that spot to lift her to its top, she did not rise. Indeed, she was no longer there.

'She's gone!' Franklin gasped.

'Gone, indeed,' Captain Lowrie said.

Bruno, his brow lined with multiple wrinkles, peered intently at the spot where he had last seen her. 'Has she sunk?' he said.

'Did she go down?'

Nobody answered his questions. Captain Lowrie murmured, 'He sheered off. Did you see him sheer off? He didn't mean to strike us in the first place. He was satisfied to push us off our course. That was all he wanted. It was as plain as day; and having done that he's gone and vanished like any good ghost should.'

The blood was flowing back into Bruno's cheeks. He straightened, and felt more assured.

'Ghost, my eye!' he snapped. 'He would have cut us in half if he hadn't seen us at the last moment. The captain of that ship is a fool. I wish we could have got her name, and reported her. He picked a fine stormy night to be running without lights.'

He scanned the turbulent seas for some sign of her. But there was none. 'But where did she go?'

Captain Lowrie did not attempt to answer him. He addressed himself to Franklin.

'Bring her back, mister,' he said. 'Bring her back on the eastbound route. I don't know the meaning of it, but it's over and done. So let's be on our way again, with the sea on the quarter. This old lady is panting – she never did like a following sea.'

Franklin brought back the helm, and the *Mary Watson* soon turned slowly eastward, where a faint leaden glow was beginning to touch the sky, off in eternity where the sea met the heavens.

The telephone rang. Captain Lowrie answered it. It was McNulty, calling from the black hole of Calcutta, annoyed and bothered. 'Captain, sir,' he said, 'must we be staying in a following sea? When my screws are near the surface, they all but shake my shaft out of its bearings.'

'I've other things to worry about beside your shaft,' Captain Lowrie replied. 'The course is my concern, and the shaft is yours, Mr McNulty. So mind your P's and Q's. There'll be no more following seas if we can help it. But then again, I ain't in a position to make any promises.'

He hung up abruptly.

About ten minutes had passed since they had last seen the three-masted will-o'-the-wisp bury itself in that trough.

The wind had all but died. The rain had definitely vanished.

The seas were beginning to drop. But only slightly. The cloud which hid the moon passed on, and the night was once again filled with a silver glow.

The four men stood up at the weatherbreak now, watching the night sharply. Only Captain Lowrie's face seemed relaxed. Murphy's was afraid. Bruno's was taut. Franklin's was harried.

And while they stood there, they felt it again, that strange fluttering feeling upon their heartstrings. Like violins in tremolo. Bruno shivered; his hands felt icy cold.

'Mind the helm,' Captain Lowrie said sharply.

Franklin had raised his left hand. He pointed it out past the weatherbreak. In awed, sepulchral tone he said, 'Look!'

They looked. But Captain Lowrie had already seen it. 'Aye,' he said coolly. 'She's back again.'

Mr Murphy, the quartermaster, tried to keep his teeth from chattering. But he could not manage it. The cracking sound of them filled the bridge.

It was true enough. She was back again. But this time she came from the north. All of her sails were set, and her lee scuppers were awash. She was running close-hauled, and her bow was under a wall of water most of the time.

Bruno stared at the flag upon his own mast. It curled to the south. That meant the wind had shifted.

'But how,' Bruno asked in a choked voice, 'can she run close-hauled against the wind which is directly astern of her?'

'She ain't no ordinary ship,' Captain Lowrie replied. 'And not a ship to be afraid of, either, mister,' he remarked to the trembling quartermaster. 'Only three hours back, I offered the Dutchman a tow around Good Hope, if need be. It ain't like one good seaman to return ill to another good seaman, when only good has been offered. He means well, no doubt. But what he means, I can't yet fathom.'

Bruno said, 'But the wind has all but died. How can a ship point down with such speed when there isn't any wind to push her?'

'I told you, mister,' answered Captain Lowrie, 'she ain't no ordinary ship.'

* * *

No more was said. They all stood stock still, tense, and watched her come. She had seemed far ahead of them to port when they first sighted her again. But already she was much closer. There was white water all around her. She seemed to slash at the ocean. The *Mary Watson*'s own speed had carried her far ahead, so that now the schooner with the red sails was sharply off the port bow.

'A mirage,' Bruno said thickly. 'A mirage.' He spoke with hope, not with conviction. He, too, like the quartermaster, was trembling.

The schooner seemed so close now that they could have thrown a belaying pin upon her deck. And suddenly her intentions were plain. She held her way, adamantly, and every man on the fated bridge knew what she would do.

She was going to cut across their bow. Cut across them, sharp and close, impailing herself upon their forepiece if necessary. She would not give way this time, she would not sheer off. The bearded man at her helm, firm and resolute, had frozen there.

Captain Lowrie sprang to the engine-room telegraph and swung it to full speed astern. In the engine room, McNulty went crazy, wondering what was happening topside.

The *Mary Watson* groaned and paused in the seaway as her single engine went into reverse. The lone screw churned the water white behind her, imparting a terrific vibration through her hull, which threatened to split the rusty plates asunder.

The freighter almost made it, but not quite. Despite her revolving screw pulling her full speed astern, her impetus carried her forward. Under her bow, where her anchors clung to their niches, the schooner with the blood-red sails passed. She looked big and real now, although the men on her deck still seemed to be shadows.

Captain Lowrie and the others braced themselves for the crash. Surely it would be her beam, directly in their path. In a moment, there would be the splintering wood of her hull flying up, smacked by the steel bow of the *Mary Watson*. But she moved faster than even they had reckoned.

Her beam flashed by. Her foam-drenched combing went next, so close to the sharp prow of the freighter that the wash, compressed between the two, catapulted straight up high into the air and crashed upon the freighter's forepiece.

Captain Lowrie said, in a quiet low voice, 'We'll hit her stern, sure.' Automatically, he braced himself.

The other men seemed to be caught in a sort of paralysis.

V

It came. It was dull, not sharp. For all they knew, it might have been the blow of a chance sea. But they felt it distinctly.

A tremor ran through the *Mary Watson*'s spine. Captain Lowrie found himself on the exposed port wingtip of the bridge, shouting wildly. Bruno, inside, telegraphed the engine room to stand by.

There was no sound of broken wood. No sound, in fact, except the great roaring silence which swelled in their ears. The freighter paused, her screws stilled, and lolled there in the glassy interim which divided the crests.

Bruno stuck out his head from within the bridge. 'Where did she go?'

But Captain Lowrie could not answer that question, for he did not know himself. Where had she gone indeed? Captain Lowrie had seen her gaunt black stern go off the starboard, the windows high in the transom all soundlessly shattered. He had seen the gaping gash in her combing and bowline, where the *Mary Watson* had eaten into the planking.

But when the three-master was definitely a-starboard, she seemed to burn with a pale, mysterious moonlight; and in a few moments she was gone again, completely, gracefully, the seas slowly merging into every part of her, until there was nothing left but sea, all around where she had been.

From the wingtip where he stood, Captain Lowrie could fancy that he had seen that great Dutchman at the helm give one last lusty wave before the night swallowed him alive.

'We sank her!' Bruno cried.

'We sank nothing,' Captain Lowrie replied. 'Is Mr McNulty standing by?'

'Aye, sir.'

'Keep him standing by. Prepare to heave to for the night. I'll not let another inch of ocean fly past my barnacles until I can see by the light of day just where I'm going.'

'We've got to stand by anyway, sir,' Bruno said. 'She's gone down. There'll be survivors, perhaps.'

'There'll be no survivors.'

'If we could only have gotten her name,' Bruno faltered. 'We could have radioed Cape Town.'

'Radio no one, mind you. Radio no one, Mr Bruno. No word of this to get about until we see what's what.'

Dawn was long delayed; but it had a sun when it did come up. In that first cold light of dawn – and there is no colder light than the first sunless break of day upon a sea – Bruno went forward with some of the crew to inspect the damage to the bow. When he returned, his face was a picture of complete stupefaction.

'What was the damage?' Captain Lowrie asked.

Bruno's mouth worked. 'Not a sign of damage, sir. Not a scratch on her paint. Nothing, sir.'

Captain Lowrie stared. Ahead of him, the sun broke from the rim of the horizon, yellow and glaring. 'Aye;' he muttered, as if to himself. 'First he drove us to the north, off our eastern course. Then he cut across our bow to make us stop our way.

'He had a purpose, the Dutchman did. One good turn deserves another. Me, speaking offhand on a dark and stormy night, offering him a tow, wherever he might be. And him to reciprocate, out of a black dark sea, and maybe save my command.'

Bruno looked perplexed. 'I don't understand, sir,' he said.

'There are some things beyond understanding,' Captain Lowrie said. 'Send a look out aloft and tell him to keep a weather eye peeled, and signal Mr McNulty to proceed at dead slow until he gets further orders.'

The lookout went aloft, squatting in the crow's nest high above the bridge. Slowly and stubbornly, the *Mary Watson* ploughed along.

They did not have to wait long. By the time the sun had detached itself from the rim of the sea, painting their faces, the lookout reported. From the crow's nest, in the windless quiet of the morning, his excited cry dropped down on Bruno, who stood beneath him on the boatdeck.

'Whale, ho!' the lookout bellowed.

'Where away?' Mr Bruno replied.

'Dead ahead,' said the lookout. 'Just rolling there. I can hardly see him. It's the rim of his spine above water, and nothing more!'

Bruno instantly relayed this news to the bridge. The *Mary Watson* paused in her stride and then stopped. Captain Lowrie, peering through his binoculars, found the hump in the ocean. He stared at it for a long time. 'Whale, my eye!' he grunted. 'Have a look, Mr Bruno.'

Bruno accepted the glasses eagerly. He peered through them for a long time, too. Finally he said, in a hollow voice. 'You're right, sir. That's no whale. It's a hulk, a floating derelict, and from what I see of her upturned keel she's a big one.'

Captain Lowrie nodded. 'Two hundred feet of her, at least,' he said reflectively. 'And all her wood probably water-logged. Nice to have struck upon her. You might just as well have put dynamite in our bow, for the hole she would have torn there.'

'An old clipper ship, sir,' Franklin hazarded.

'Maybe so, mister,' Captain Lowrie said. 'I ain't seen a keel like that in a long, long time.'

Bruno's face held an odd expression. He ruminated slowly, 'The storm must have driven her northward. That would have put her more to the south a few hours back. If we had continued in our eastbound track, we might have struck her.

'Then we turned north. But the wind and waves were blowing her north, too. Good Lord, sir, it gives me the creeps to think of what might have happened if we had not hove to until daybreak.'

'Thanks to the Dutchman, and a ready tow for him,' said Captain Lowrie soberly. 'Whether he be in the seas of Heaven, or in the oceans of Hell.'

'It's a strange thing,' Bruno said, his eyes smoky with thought. 'A very strange thing. And not the sort of thing a man can tell his wife in Boston when he sees home again.'

Captain Lowrie nodded. 'Right, mister. And you only to be ridiculed and laughed at for the telling of such a tale. And if your hair were a mite gray, the younger blades might be calling *you* an old fool, too.'

'It could have been a mirage,' Bruno said, as if he didn't believe it himself.

'It could have been,' Captain Lowrie agreed. 'But mirage or no, it did its work, and all of us should be grateful for it. Helmsman, point her head off that wreck. Mr Bruno, you may telegraph Mr McNulty to proceed at half speed.

'Mr Franklin, will you kindly stop by at the radio shack and tell Sparks to wireless Cape Town, a warning to all shipping in the vicinity of Good Hope. Give the location of the wreck and our present position. That will do. As for myself, I'm going below. If I'm needed, you've only to call me up again.'

Bruno stared through the weatherbreak as the freighter gained way again. 'Look,' he said, 'look off there! Porpoises. A whole island of them!'

At the door, Captain Lowrie paused. There was a faint smile on his face. 'And what does that mean, mister?'

'It means, sir,' replied Bruno quietly, 'that we shall have a good passage from here to Zanzibar.'

'Aye,' Captain Lowrie nodded, and he went out. But as he went, you could see by the expression on his face that he was very well pleased with his first officer.

MAKE
WESTING

Jack London

Cape Horn is one of the most famous stretches of water in the world, and features in the following story by a writer regarded by many as one of the best maritime novelists, Jack London (1876–1916). This romantic, revolutionary figure whose wild, drunken, adventurous life has helped preserve his fame as well as giving added appeal to his books, loved the sea with a passionate intensity which is mirrored in much that he wrote.

During his life, London sailed almost from one end of the globe to the other. At one period of time he was an 'oyster pirate' in Oakland Bay, at another a seal hunter out of San Francisco. He even tried to circumnavigate the world in a ketch long before such round-the-globe voyages were even thought of, let alone popular pursuits; and for a year and more was a tramp sailor in the South Seas. It made little difference to him where he was as long as he had a deck beneath his feet and cracking canvas above his head.

Jack London's nautical books are classics of their kind: The Cruise of the Dazzler *(1902),* The Sea Wolf *(1904),* Tales of the Fish Patrol *(1905), and* The Mutiny of the 'Elsinore' *(1914) all draw on his incredible adventures. This next short story was written by him in 1911 and is full of the elemental power of the sea and the strange effects it can have on those who challenge it.*

'Whatever you do, make westing! make westing!'
—Sailing directions for Cape Horn

FOR SEVEN WEEKS the *Mary Rogers* had been 50° south in the Atlantic and 50° south in the Pacific, which meant that for seven weeks she had been struggling to round Cape Horn. For seven weeks she had been either in dirt, or close to dirt, save once, and then, following upon six days of excessive dirt, which she had ridden out under the shelter of the redoubtable Terra del Fuego coast, she had almost gone ashore during a heavy swell in the dead calm that had suddenly fallen. For seven weeks she had wrestled with the Cape Horn greybeards, and in return had been buffeted and smashed by them. She was a wooden ship, and her ceaseless straining had opened her seams, so that twice a day the watch took its turn at the pumps.

The *Mary Rogers* was strained, the crew was strained, and big Dan Cullen, master, was likewise strained. Perhaps he was strained most of all, for upon him rested the responsibility of that titanic struggle. He slept most of the time in his clothes, though he rarely slept. He haunted the deck at night, a great, burly, robust ghost, black with the sunburn of thirty years of sea and hairy as an orang-outang. He, in turn, was haunted by one thought of action, a sailing direction for the Horn: *Whatever you do, make westing! make westing!* It was an obsession. He thought of nothing else, except, at times, to blaspheme God for sending such bitter weather.

115

Make Westing! He hugged the Horn, and a dozen times lay hove to with the iron Cape bearing east-by-north, or north-north-east, a score of miles away. And each time the eternal west wind smote him back and he made easting. He fought gale after gale, south to 64°, inside the antarctic drift-ice, and pledged his immortal soul to the Powers of darkness, for a bit of westing, for a slant to take him around. And he made easting. In despair, he had tried to make the passage through the Straits of Le Maire. Halfway through, the wind hauled to the north'ard of north-west, the glass dropped to 28·88, and he turned and ran before a gale of cyclonic fury, missing, by a hair's breadth, piling up the *Mary Rogers* on the black-toothed rocks. Twice he had made west to the Diego Ramirez Rocks, one of the times saved between two snow-squalls by sighting the gravestones of ships a quarter of a mile dead ahead.

Blow! Captain Dan Cullen instanced all his thirty years at sea to prove that never had it blown so before. The *Mary Rogers* was hove to at the time he gave the evidence, and, to clinch it, inside half an hour the *Mary Rogers* was hove down to the hatches. Her new maintopsail and brand new spencer were blown away like tissue paper; and five sails, furled and fast under double gaskets, were blown loose and stripped from the yards. And before morning the *Mary Rogers* was hove down twice again, and holes were knocked in her bulwarks to ease her decks from the weight of ocean that pressed her down.

On an average of once a week Captain Dan Cullen caught glimpses of the sun. Once, for ten minutes, the sun shone at midday, and ten minutes afterwards a new gale was piping up, both watches were shortening sail, and all was buried in the obscurity of a driving snow-squall. For a fortnight, once, Captain Dan Cullen was without a meridian or a chronometer sight. Rarely did he know his position within half of a degree, except when in sight of land; for sun and stars remained hidden behind the sky, and it was so gloomy that even at the best the horizons were poor for accurate observations. A grey gloom shrouded the world. The clouds were grey; the great driving seas were leaden grey; the smoking crests were a grey churning; even the occasional albatrosses were grey, while the snow-flurries were not white, but grey, under the sombre pall of the heavens.

Life on board the *Mary Rogers* was grey – grey and gloomy. The faces of the sailors were blue grey; they were afflicted with sea-cuts and sea-boils, and suffered exquisitely. They were shadows of men. For seven weeks, in the forecastle or on deck, they had not known what it was to be dry. They had forgotten what it was to sleep out a watch, and all watches it was, 'All hands on deck!' They caught the snatches of agonized sleep, and they slept in their oil-skins ready for the everlasting call. So weak and worn were they that it took both watches to do the work of one. That was why both watches were on deck so much of the time. And no shadow of a man could shirk duty. Nothing less than a broken leg could enable a man to knock off work; and there were two such, who had been mauled and pulped by the seas that broke overboard.

One other man who was the shadow of a man was George Dorety. He was the only passenger on board, a friend of the firm, and he had elected to make the voyage for his health. But seven weeks off Cape Horn had not bettered his health. He gasped and panted in his bunk through the long, heaving nights; and when on deck he was so bundled up for warmth that he resembled a peripatetic old-clothes shop. At midday, eating at the cabin table in a gloom so deep that the swinging sea-lamps burned always, he looked as blue-grey as the sickest, saddest man for'ard. Nor did gazing across the table at Captain Dan Cullen have any cheering effect upon him. Captain Cullen chewed and scowled and kept silent. The scowls were for God, and with every chew he reiterated the sole thought of his existence, which was *make westing*. He was a big, hairy brute, and the sight of him was not stimulating to the other's appetite. He looked upon George Dorety as a Jonah, and told him so once each meal savagely transferring the scowl from God to the passenger and back again.

Nor did the mate prove a first aid to a languid appetite. Joshua Higgins by name, a seaman by profession and pull, but a pot-walloper by capacity, he was a loose-jointed, sniffling creature, heartless and selfish and cowardly, without a soul, in fear of his life of Dan Cullen, and a bully over the sailors, who knew that behind the mate was Captain Cullen, the law-giver and compeller, the driver and the destroyer, the incarnation of a dozen bucko mates. In that wild weather at the southern end of the earth, Joshua Higgins ceased washing. His grimy face usually robbed George Dorety of what little appetite he managed to accumulate. Ordinarily this lavatorial dereliction would have caught Captain Cullen's eye and vocabulary, but in the present his mind was filled with making westing, to the exclusion of all other things not contributory thereto. Whether the mate's face was clean or dirty had no bearing upon westing. Later on, when 50° south in the Pacific had been reached, Joshua Higgins would wash his face very abruptly. In the meantime, at the cabin table, where grey twilight alternated with lamplight while the lamps were being filled, George Dorety sat between the two men, one a tiger and the other a hyena, and wondered why God had made them. The second mate, Matthew Turner, was a true sailor and a man, but George Dorety did not have the solace of his company, for he ate by himself, solitary, when they had finished.

On Saturday morning, July 24, George Dorety awoke to a feeling of life and headlong movement. On deck he found the *Mary Rogers* running off before a howling south-easter. Nothing was set but the lower topsails and the foresail. It was all she could stand, yet she was making fourteen knots, as Mr Turner shouted in Dorety's ear when he came on deck. And it was all westing. She was going round the Horn at last . . . if the wind held. Mr Turner looked happy. The end of the struggle was in sight. But Captain Cullen did not look happy. He scowled at Dorety in passing. Captain Cullen did not want God to know that he was pleased with that wind. He had a conception of a malicious God, and believed in his secret soul that if God knew it was a desirable wind, God would promptly efface it and send a snorter from the west. So he walked softly before God, smothering his joy down under scowls and muttered curses, and, so, fooling God, for God was the only thing in the universe of which Dan Cullen was afraid.

All Saturday and Saturday night the *Mary Rogers* raced her westing. Persistently she logged her fourteen knots, so that by Sunday morning she had covered three hundred and fifty miles. If the wind held, she would make around. If it failed, and the snorter came from anywhere between southwest and north, back the *Mary Rogers* would be hurled and be no better off than she had been seven weeks before. And on Sunday morning the wind *was* failing. The big sea was going down and running smoother. Both watches were on deck setting sail after sail as fast as the ship could stand it. And now Captain Cullen went around brazenly before God, smoking a big cigar, smiling jubilantly, as if the failing wind delighted him, while down underneath he was raging against God for taking the life out of the blessed wind. *Make westing!* So he would, if God would only leave him alone. Secretly, he pledged himself to the Powers of Darkness, if they would let him make westing. He pledged himself so easily because he did not believe in the Powers of Darkness. He really believed only in God, though he did not know it. And in his inverted theology God was really the Prince of Darkness. Captain Cullen was a devil-worshipper, but he called the devil by another name, that was all.

At midday, after calling eight bells, Captain Cullen ordered the royals on. The men went aloft faster than they had gone in weeks. Not alone were they nimble because of the westing, but a benignant sun was shining down and limbering their stiff bodies. George Dorety stood aft, near Captain Cullen, less bundled in clothes than usual, soaking in the grateful warmth as he watched the scene. Swiftly and abruptly the incident occurred. There was a cry from the foreroyal-yard of 'Man overboard!' Somebody threw a life-buoy over the side, and at the same instant the second mate's voice came aft, ringing and peremptory –

'Hard down your helm!'

The man at the wheel never moved a spoke. He knew better, for Captain Dan Cullen was standing alongside of him. He wanted to move a spoke, to move all the spokes, to grind the wheel down, hard down, for his comrade drowning in the sea. He glanced at Captain Dan Cullen, and Captain Dan Cullen gave no sign.

'Down! Hard down!' the second mate roared, as he sprang aft.

But he ceased springing and commanding, and stood still, when he saw Dan Cullen by the wheel. And big Dan Cullen puffed at his cigar and said nothing. Astern, and going astern fast, could be seen the sailor. He had caught the life-buoy and was clinging to it. Nobody spoke. Nobody moved. The men aloft clung to the royal yards and watched with terror-stricken faces. And the *Mary Rogers* raced on, making her westing. A long, silent minute passed.

'Who was it?' Captain Cullen demanded.

'Mops, sir,' eagerly answered the sailor at the wheel.

Mops topped a wave astern and disappeared temporarily in the trough. It was a large wave, but it was no greybeard. A small boat could live easily in such a sea, and in such a sea the *Mary Rogers* could easily come to. But she could not come to and make westing at the same time.

For the first time in all his years, George Dorety was seeing a real drama of life and death – a sordid little drama in which the scales balanced an unknown sailor named Mops against a few miles of longitude. At first he had watched the man astern, but now he watched big Dan Cullen, hairy and black, vested with power of life and death, smoking a cigar.

Captain Dan Cullen smoked another long, silent minute. Then he removed the cigar from his mouth. He glanced aloft at the spars of the *Mary Rogers*, and overside at the sea.

'Sheet home the royals!' he cried.

Fifteen minutes later they sat at table, in the cabin, with food served before them. On one side of George Dorety sat Dan Cullen, the tiger, on the other side, Joshua Higgins, the hyena. Nobody spoke. On deck the men were sheeting home the skysails. George Dorety could hear their cries, while a persistent vision haunted him of a man called Mops, alive and well, clinging to a life-buoy miles astern in that lonely ocean. He glanced at Captain Cullen, and experienced a feeling of nausea, for the man was eating his food with relish, almost bolting it.

'Captain Cullen,' Dorety said, 'you are in command of this ship, and it is not proper for me to comment now upon what you do. But I wish to say one thing. There is a hereafter, and yours will be a hot one.'

Captain Cullen did not even scowl. In his voice was regret as he said –

'It was blowing a living gale. It was impossible to save the man.'

'He fell from the royal-yard,' Dorety cried hotly. 'You were setting the royals at the time. Fifteen minutes afterwards you were setting the skysails.'

'It was a living gale, wasn't it, Mr Higgins?' Captain Cullen said, turning to the mate.

'If you'd brought her to, it'd have taken the sticks out of her' was the mate's answer. 'You did the proper thing, Captain Cullen. The man hadn't a ghost of a show.'

George Dorety made no answer, and to the meal's end no one spoke. After that, Dorety had his meals served in his state-room. Captain Cullen scowled at him no longer, though no speech was exchanged between them, while the *Mary Rogers* sped north toward warmer latitudes. At the end of the week, Dan Cullen cornered Dorety on deck.

'What are you going to do when we get to 'Frisco?' he demanded bluntly.

'I am going to swear out a warrant for your arrest,' Dorety answered quietly. 'I am going to charge you with murder, and I am going to see you hanged for it.'

'You're almighty sure of yourself,' Captain Cullen sneered, turning on his heel.

A second week passed, and one morning found George Dorety standing in the coach-house companionway at the for'ard end of the long poop, taking his first gaze around the deck. The *Mary Rogers* was reaching full-and-by, in a stiff breeze. Every sail was set and drawing, including the staysails. Captain Cullen strolled for'ard along the poop. He strolled carelessly, glancing at the passenger out of the corner of his eye. Dorety was looking the other way, standing with head and shoulders outside the companionway, and only the back of his head was to be seen. Captain Cullen, with swift eye, embraced the mainstaysail-block and the head and estimated the distance. He glanced about him. Nobody was looking. Aft, Joshua Higgins, pacing up and down, had just turned his back and was going the other way. Captain Cullen bent over suddenly and cast the staysail-sheet off from its pin. The heavy block hurtled through the air, smashing

Dorety's head like an egg-shell and hurtling on and back and forth as the staysail whipped and slatted in the wind. Joshua Higgins turned around to see what had carried away, and met the full blast of the vilest portion of Captain Cullen's profanity.

'I made the sheet fast myself,' whimpered the mate in the first lull, 'with an extra turn to make sure. I remember it distinctly.'

'Made fast?' the Captain snarled back, for the benefit of the watch as it struggled to capture the flying sail before it tore to ribbons. 'You couldn't make your grandmother fast, you useless hell's scullion. If you made that sheet fast with an extra turn, why in hell didn't it stay fast? That's what I want to know. Why in hell didn't it stay fast?'

The mate whined inarticulately.

'Oh, shut up!' was the final word of Captain Cullen.

Half an hour later he was as surprised as any when the body of George Dorety was found inside the companionway on the floor. In the afternoon, alone in his room, he doctored up the log.

'Ordinary seaman, Karl Brun,' he wrote, 'lost overboard from foreroyal-yard in a gale of wind. Was running at the time, and for the safety of the ship did not dare to come up the wind. Nor could a boat have lived in the sea that was running.'

On another page he wrote:

'Had often warned Mr Dorety about the danger he ran because of his carelessness on deck. I told him, once, that some day he would get his head knocked off by a block. A carelessly fastened mainstaysail sheet was the cause of the accident, which was deeply to be regretted because Mr Dorety was a favourite with all of us.'

Captain Dan Cullen read over his literary effort with admiration, blotted the page, and closed the log. He lighted a cigar and stared before him. He felt the *Mary Rogers* lift, and heel, and surge along, and knew that she was making nine knots. A smile of satisfaction slowly dawned on his black and hairy face. Well, anyway, he had made his westing and fooled God.

THE BLACK
MATE

Joseph Conrad

Another outstanding writer of sea stories is Joseph Conrad (1857–1924). Like so many of the other contributors to this book he became fascinated by the sea when he was young, and never lost his interest in all the mystery and strangeness of life on the ocean. He too based his work on years of experience at sea; some of it spent in the most dangerous circumstances.

Conrad was actually born in Poland, but went to sea in an English merchant ship and in 1884 became a naturalised British subject. After gaining his master's certificate, he spent a number of years in the Far East where the boats he sailed in plied between Singapore and Borneo. This gave him an unrivalled knowledge of the mysterious creeks and jungles of the area which were later featured in some of his best work.

Just before the turn of the century, he abandoned the sea and settled in England where he began to produce the various books which made his reputation; including such outstanding maritime tales as The Nigger of the Narcissus *(1897),* Lord Jim *(1900),* Twixt Land and Sea *(1912) and superb short stories like 'Typhoon', 'The Shadow Line' and 'The Black Mate' (published in 1912). This last tale is perhaps my favourite Conrad short story, and its weird atmosphere and surprise ending make it an ideal selection for this collection.*

A GOOD MANY years ago there were several ships loading at the Jetty, London Dock. I am speaking here of the 'eighties of the last century, of the time when London had plenty of fine ships in the docks, though not so many fine buildings in its streets.

The ships at the Jetty were fine enough; they lay one behind the other; and the *Sapphire*, third from the end, was as good as the rest of them, and nothing more. Each ship at the Jetty had, of course, her chief officer on board. So had every other ship in dock.

The policeman at the gates knew them all by sight, without being able to say at once, without thinking, to what ship any particular man belonged. As a matter of fact, the mates of the ships then lying in the London Dock were like the majority of officers in the Merchant Service – a steady, hard-working, staunch, unromantic-looking set of men, belonging to various classes of society, but with the professional stamp obliterating the personal characteristics, which were not very marked anyhow.

This last was true of them all, with the exception of the mate of the *Sapphire*. Of him the policemen could not be in doubt. This one had a presence.

He was noticeable to them in the street from a great distance; and when in the morning he strode down the Jetty to his ship, the lumpers and the dock labourers rolling the bales and trundling the cases of cargo on their hand-trucks would remark to each other:

'Here's the black mate coming along.'

That was the name they gave him, being a gross lot, who could have no appreciation of the man's dignified bearing. And to call him black was the superficial impressionism of the ignorant.

Of course, Mr Bunter, the mate of the *Sapphire*, was not black. He was no more black than you or I, and certainly as white as any chief mate of a ship in the whole of the Port of London. His complexion was of the sort that did not take the tan easily; and I happen to know that the poor fellow had had a month's illness just before he joined the *Sapphire*.

From this you will perceive that I knew Bunter. Of course I knew him. And, what's more, I knew his secret at the time, this secret which – never mind just now. Returning to Bunter's personal appearance, it was nothing but ignorant prejudice on the part of the foreman stevedore to say, as he did in my hearing: 'I bet he's a furriner of some sort.' A man may have black hair without being set down for a Dago. I have known a West-country sailor, boatswain of a fine ship, who looked more Spanish than any Spaniard afloat I've ever met. He looked like a Spaniard in a picture.

Competent authorities tell us that this earth is to be finally the inheritance of men with dark hair and brown eyes. It seems that already the great majority of mankind is dark-haired in various shades. But it is only when you meet one that you notice how men with really black hair, black as ebony, are rare. Bunter's hair was absolutely black, black as a raven's wing. He wore, too, all his beard (clipped, but a good length all the same), and his eyebrows were thick and bushy. Add to this steely blue eyes, which in a fair-haired man would have been nothing so extraordinary, but in that sombre framing made a startling contrast, and you will easily understand that Bunter was noticeable enough. If it had not been for the quietness of his movements, for the general soberness of his demeanour, one would have given him credit for a fiercely passionate nature.

Of course, he was not in his first youth; but if the expression 'in the force of his age' has any meaning, he realized it completely. He was a tall man, too, though rather spare. Seeing him from his poop indefatigably busy with his duties, Captain

Ashton, of the clipper ship *Elsinore*, lying just ahead of the *Sapphire*, remarked once to a friend that 'Johns has got somebody there to hustle his ship along for him.'

Captain Johns, master of the *Sapphire*, having commanded ships for many years, was well known without being much respected or liked. In the company of his fellows he was either neglected or chaffed. The chaffing was generally undertaken by Captain Ashton, a cynical and teasing sort of man. It was Captain Ashton who permitted himself the unpleasant joke of proclaiming once in company that 'Johns is of the opinion that every sailor above forty years of age ought to be poisoned – shipmasters in actual command excepted.'

It was in a City restaurant, where several well-known shipmasters were having lunch together. There was Captain Ashton, florid and jovial, in a large white waistcoat and with a yellow rose in his buttonhole; Captain Sellers in a sack-coat, thin and pale-faced, with his iron-gray hair tucked behind his ears, and, but for the absence of spectacles, looking like an ascetical mild man of books; Captain Hell, a bluff sea-dog with hairy fingers, in blue serge and a black felt hat pushed far back off the crimson forehead. There was also a very young shipmaster, with a little fair moustache and serious eyes, who said nothing, and only smiled faintly from time to time.

Captain Johns, very much startled, raised his perplexed and credulous glance, which, together with a low and horizontally wrinkled, brow, did not make a very intellectual *ensemble*. This impression was by no means mended by the slightly pointed form of his bald head.

Everybody laughed outright, and, thus guided, Captain Johns ended by smiling rather sourly, and attempted to defend himself. It was all very well to joke, but nowadays, when ships, to pay anything at all, had to be driven hard on the passage and in harbour, the sea was no place for elderly men. Only young men and men in their prime were equal to modern conditions of push and hurry. Look at the great firms: almost every single one of them was getting rid of men showing any signs of age. He, for one, didn't want any oldsters on board his ship.

And, indeed, in this opinion Captain Johns was not singular.

There was at that time a lot of seamen, with nothing against them but that they were grizzled, wearing out the soles of their last pair of boots on the pavements of the City in the heart-breaking search for a berth.

Captain Johns added with a sort of ill-humoured innocence that from holding that opinion to thinking of poisoning people was a very long step.

This seemed final but Captain Ashton would not let go his joke.

'Oh, yes. I am sure you would. You said distinctly "of no use". What's to be done with men who are "of no use?" You are a kind-hearted fellow, Johns. I am sure that if only you thought it over carefully you would consent to have them poisoned in some painless manner.'

Captain Sellers twitched his thin sinuous lips.

'Make ghosts of them,' he suggested, pointedly.

At the mention of ghosts Captain Johns became shy, in his perplexed, sly, and unlovely manner.

Captain Ashton winked.

'Yes. And then perhaps you would get a chance to have a communication with the world of spirits. Surely the ghosts of seamen should haunt ships. Some of them would be sure to call on an old shipmate.'

Captain Sellers remarked drily:

'Don't raise his hopes like this. It's cruel. He won't see anything. You know, Johns, that nobody has ever seen a ghost.'

At this intolerable provocation Captain Johns came out of his reserve. With no perplexity whatever, but with a positive passion of credulity giving momentary lustre to his dull little eyes, he brought up a lot of authenticated instances. There were books and books full of instances. It was merest ignorance to deny supernatural apparitions. Cases were published every month in a special newspaper. Professor Cranks saw ghosts daily. And Professor Cranks was no small potatoes either. One of the biggest scientific men living. And there was that newspaper fellow – what's his name? – who had a girl-ghost visitor. He printed in his paper things she said to him. And to say there were no ghosts after that!

'Why, they have been photographed! What more proof do you want?'

Captain Johns was indignant. Captain Bell's lips twitched, but Captain Ashton protested now.

'For goodness' sake, don't keep him going with that. And by the by, Johns, who's that hairy pirate you've got for your new mate? Nobody in the Dock seems to have seen him before.'

Captain Johns, pacified by the change of subjects, answered simply that Willy, the tobacconist at the corner of Fenchurch Street, had sent him along.

Willy, his shop, and the very house in Fenchurch Street, I believe, are gone now. In his time, wearing a careworn, absent-minded look on his pasty face, Willy served with tobacco many southern-going ships out of the Port of London. At certain times of the day the shop would be full of shipmasters. They sat on casks, they lounged against the counter.

Many a youngster found his first lift in life there; many a man got a sorely needed berth by simply dropping in for four pennyworth of birds'-eye at an auspicious moment. Even Willy's assistant, a red-headed, uninterested, delicate-looking young fellow, would hand you across the counter sometimes a bit of valuable intelligence with your box of cigarettes, in a whisper, lips hardly moving, thus: 'The *Bellona*, South Dock. Second officer wanted. You may be in time for it if you hurry up.'

And didn't one just fly!

'Oh, Willy sent him,' said Captain Ashton. 'He's a very striking man. If you were to put a red sash round his waist and a red handkerchief round his head he would look exactly like one of them buccaneering chaps that made men walk the plank and carried women off into captivity. Look out, Johns, he don't cut your throat for you and run off with the *Sapphire*. What ship has he come out of last?'

Captain Johns, after looking up credulously as usual, wrinkled his brow, and said placidly that the man had seen better days. His name was Bunter.

'He's had command of a Liverpool ship, the *Samaria*, some years ago. He lost her in the Indian Ocean, and had his certificate suspended for a year. Ever since then he has not been able to get another command. He's been knocking about in the Western Ocean trade lately.'

'That accounts for him being a stranger to everybody about the Docks,' Captain Ashton concluded as they rose from table.

Captain Johns walked down to the Dock after lunch. He was short of stature and slightly bandy. His appearance did not inspire the generality of mankind with esteem; but it must have been otherwise with his employers. He had the reputation of being an uncomfortable commander, meticulous in trifles, always nursing a grievance of some sort and incessantly nagging. He was not a man to kick up a row with you and be done with it, but to say nasty things in a whining voice; a man capable of making one's life a perfect misery if he took a dislike to an officer.

That very evening I went to see Bunter on board, and sympathized with him on his prospects for the voyage. He was subdued. I suppose a man with a secret locked up in his breast loses his buoyancy. And there was another reason why I could not expect Bunter to show a great elasticity of spirits. For one thing he had been very seedy lately, and besides – but of that later.

Captain Johns had been on board that afternoon and had loitered and dodged about his chief mate in a manner which had annoyed Bunter exceedingly.

'What could he mean?' he asked with calm exasperation. 'One would think he suspected I had stolen something and tried to see in what pocket I had stowed it away; or that somebody told him I had a tail and he wanted to find out how I managed to conceal it. I don't like to be approached from behind several times in one afternoon in that creepy way and then to be looked up at suddenly in front from under my elbow. Is it a new sort of peep-bo game? It doesn't amuse me. I am no longer a baby.'

I assured him that if anyone were to tell Captain Johns that he – Bunter – had a tail, Johns would manage to get himself to believe the story in some mysterious manner. He would. He was suspicious and credulous to an inconceivable degree. He would believe any silly tale, suspect any man of anything, and crawl about with it and ruminate the stuff, and turn it over and over in his mind in the most miserable, inwardly whining perplexity. He would taken the meanest possible view in the end, and discover the meanest possible course of action by a sort of natural genius for that sort of thing.

Bunter also told me that the mean creature had crept all over the ship on his little, bandy legs, taking him along to grumble and whine to about a lot of trifles. Crept about the decks like a wretched insect – like a cockroach, only not so lively.

Thus did the self-possessed Bunter express himself with great disgust. Then, going on with his usual stately deliberation, made sinister by the frown of his jet-black eyebrows:

'And the fellow is mad, too. He tried to be sociable for a bit, and could find nothing else but to make big eyes at me, and ask me if I believed "in communication beyond the grave." Communication beyond – I didn't know what he meant at first. I didn't know what to say. "A very solemn subject, Mr Bunter," says he. "I've given a great deal of study to it."'

Had Johns lived on shore he would have been the predestined prey of fraudulent mediums; or even if he had had any decent opportunities between the voyages. Luckily for him, when in England, he lived somewhere far away in Leytonstone, with a maiden sister ten years older than himself, a fearsome virago twice his size, before whom he trembled. It was said she bullied him terribly in general; and in the particular instance of his spiritualistic leanings she had her own views.

These leanings were to her simply satanic. She was reported as having declared that, 'With God's help, she would prevent that fool from giving himself up to the Devils.' It was beyond doubt that Johns' secret ambition was to get into personal communication with the spirits of the dead – if only his sister would let him. But she was adamant. I was told that while in London he had to account to her for every penny of the money he took with him in the morning, and for every hour of his time. And she kept the bankbook, too.

Bunter (he had been a wild youngster, but he was well connected; had ancestors; there was a family tomb somewhere in the home counties) – Bunter was indignant, perhaps on account of his own dead. Those steely-blue eyes of his flashed with positive ferocity out of that black-bearded face. He impressed me – there was so much dark passion in his leisurely contempt.

'The cheek of the fellow! Enter into relations with . . . A mean little cad like this! It would be an impudent intrusion. He wants to enter! . . . What is it? A new sort of snobbishness or what?'

I laughed outright at this original view of spiritism – or whatever the ghost craze is called. Even Bunter himself condescended to smile. But it was an austere, quickly vanished smile. A man in his almost, I may say, tragic position couldn't be expected – you understand. He was really worried. He was ready eventually to put up with any dirty trick in the course of the voyage. A man could not expect much consideration should he find himself at the mercy of a fellow like Johns. A misfortune is a misfortune, and there's an end of it. But to be bored by mean, low-spirited, inane ghost stories in the Johns style, all the way out to Calcutta and back again, was an intolerable apprehension to be under. Spiritism was indeed a solemn subject to think about in that light. Dreadful, even!

Poor fellow! Little we both thought that before very long he himself . . . However, I could give him no comfort. I was rather appalled myself.

Bunter had also another annoyance that day. A confounded berthing master came on board on some pretence or other, but in reality, Bunter thought, simply impelled by an inconvenient curiosity – inconvenient to Bunter, that is. After some beating about the bush, that man suddenly said:

'I can't help thinking. I've seen you before somewhere, Mr Mate. If I heard your name, perhaps – '

Bunter – that's the worst of a life with a mystery in it – was much alarmed. It was very likely that the man had seen him before – worse luck to his excellent memory. Bunter himself could not be expected to remember every casual dock walloper he might have had to do with. Bunter brazened it out by turning upon the man, making use of that impressive, black-as-night sternness of expression his unusual hair furnished him with:

'My name's Bunter, sir. Does that enlighten your inquisitive intellect? And I don't ask what your name may be. I don't want to know. I've no use for it, sir. An individual who calmly tells me to my face that he is *not sure* if he has seen me before, either means to be impudent or is no better than a worm, sir. Yes, I said a worm – a blind worm!'

Brave Bunter. That was the line to take. He fairly drove the beggar out of the ship, as if every word had been a blow. But the pertinacity of that brass-bound Paul Pry was astonishing. He cleared out of the ship, of course, before Bunter's ire, not saying anything, and only trying to cover up his retreat by a sickly smile. But once on the jetty he turned deliberately round, and set himself to stare in dead earnest at the ship. He remained planted there like a mooring-post, absolutely motionless, and with his stupid eyes winking no more than a pair of cabin portholes.

What could Bunter do? It was awkward for him, you know. He could not go and put his head into the bread-locker. What he did was to take up a position abaft the mizzen-rigging, and stare back as unwinking as the other. So they remained, and I don't know which of them grew giddy first; but the man on the jetty, not having the advantage of something to hold on to, got tired the soonest, flung his arm, giving the contest up, as it were, and went away at last.

Bunter told me he was glad the *Sapphire*, 'that gem amongst ships' as he alluded to her sarcastically, was going to sea next day. He had had enough of the Dock. I understood his impatience. He had steeled himself against any possible worry the voyage might bring, though it is clear enough now that he was not prepared for the extraordinary experience that was awaiting him already, and in no other part of the world than the Indian Ocean itself; the very part of the world where the poor fellow had lost his ship and had broken his luck, as it seemed for good and all, at the same time.

As to his remorse in regard to a certain secret action of his life, well, I understand that a man of Bunter's fine character would suffer not a little. Still, between ourselves, and without the slightest wish to be cynical, it cannot be denied that with the noblest of us the fear of being found out enters for some considerable part into the composition of remorse. I didn't say this in so many words to Bunter, but, as the poor fellow harped a bit on it, I told him that there were skeletons in a good many honest cupboards, and that, as to his own particular guilt, it wasn't writ large on his face for everybody to see – so he needn't worry as to that. And besides, he would be gone to sea in about twelve hours from now.

He said there was some comfort in that thought, and went off then to spend his last evening for many months with his wife. For all his wildness, Bunter had made no mistake in his marrying. He had married a lady. A perfect lady. She was a dear little woman, too. As to her pluck, I, who know what times they had to go through, I cannot admire her enough for it. Real, hard-wearing every day and day after day pluck that only a woman is capable of when she is of the right sort – the undismayed sort I would call it.

The black mate felt this parting with his wife more than any of the previous ones in all the years of bad luck. But she was of the undismayed kind, and showed less trouble in her gentle face than the black-haired, buccaneer-like, but dignified mate of the *Sapphire*. It may be that her conscience was less disturbed than her husband's. Of course, his life had no secret places for her; but a woman's conscience is somewhat more resourceful in finding good and valid excuses. It depends greatly on the person that needs them, too.

They had agreed that she should not come down to the Dock to see him off. 'I wonder you care to look at me at all,' said the sensitive man. And she did not laugh.

Bunter was very sensitive; he left her rather brusquely at the last. He got on board in good time, and produced the usual impression on the mud-pilot in the broken-down straw hat who took the *Sapphire* out of dock. The river-man was very polite to the dignified, striking-looking chief mate. 'The five-inch manilla for the check-rope, Mr – Bunter, thank you – Mr Bunter, please.' The sea-pilot who left the 'gem of ships' heading comfortably down Channel off Dover told some of his friends that, this voyage, the *Sapphire* had for a chief mate a man who seemed a jolly sight too good for old Johns. 'Bunter's his name. I wonder where he's sprung from? Never seen him before in any ship I piloted in or out all these years. He's the sort of man you don't forget. You couldn't. A thorough good sailor, too. And won't old Johns just worry his head off! Unless the old fool should take fright at him – for he does not seem the sort of man that would let himself be put upon without letting you know what he thinks of you. And that's exactly what old Johns would be more afraid of than anything else.'

As this is really meant to be the record of a spiritualistic experience which came, if not precisely to Captain Johns himself, at any rate to his ship, there is no use in recording the other events of the passage out. It was an ordinary passage, the crew was an ordinary crew, the weather was of the usual kind. The black mate's quiet, sedate method of going to work had given a sober tone to the life of the ship. Even in gales of wind everything went on quietly somehow.

There was only one severe blow which made things fairly lively for all hands for full four-and-twenty hours. That was off the coast of Africa, after passing the Cape of Good Hope. At the very height of it several heavy seas were shipped with no serious results, but there was a considerable smashing of breakable objects in the pantry and in the staterooms. Mr Bunter, who was so greatly respected on board, found himself treated scurvily by the Southern Ocean, which, bursting open the door of his room like a ruffianly burglar, carried off several useful things, and made all the others extremely wet.

Later, on the same day, the Southern Ocean caused the *Sapphire* to lurch over in such an unrestrained fashion that the two drawers fitted under Mr Bunter's sleeping-berth flew out altogether, spilling all their contents. They ought, of course, to have been locked, and Mr Bunter had only to thank himself for what had happened. He ought to have turned the key on each before going out on deck.

His consternation was very great. The steward, who was paddling about all the time with swabs, trying to dry out the flooded cuddy, heard him exclaim 'Hallo!' in a startled and dismayed tone. In the midst of his work the steward felt a sympathetic concern for the mate's distress.

Captain Johns was secretly glad when he heard of the damage. He was indeed afraid of his chief mate, as the sea-pilot had ventured to foretell, and afraid of him for the very reason the sea-pilot had put forward as likely.

Captain Johns, therefore, would have liked very much to hold that black mate of his at his mercy in some way or other. But the man was irreproachable, as near absolute perfection as could be. And Captain Johns was much annoyed, and at the same time congratulated himself on his chief officer's efficiency.

He made a great show of living sociably with him, on the principle that the more friendly you are with a man the more easily you may catch him tripping; and also for the reason that he wanted to have somebody who would listen to his stories of manifestations, apparitions, ghosts, and all the rest of the imbecile spook-lore. He had it all at his fingers' ends; and he spun those ghostly yarns in a persistent, colourless voice, giving them a futile turn peculiarly his own.

'I like to converse with my officers,' he used to say. 'There are masters that hardly ever open their mouths from beginning to end of a passage for fear of losing their dignity. What's that, after all – this bit of position a man holds!'

His sociability was most to be dreaded in the second dog-watch, because he was one of those men who grow lively towards the evening, and the officer on duty was unable then to find excuses for leaving the poop. Captain Johns would pop up the companion suddenly, and, sidling up in his creeping way to poor Bunter, as he walked up and down, would fire into him some spiritualistic proposition, such as:

'Spirits, male and female, show a good deal of refinement in a general way, don't they?'

To which Bunter, holding his black-whiskered head high, would mutter:

'I don't know.'

'Ah! that's because you don't want to. You are the most obstinate, prejudiced man I've ever met, Mr Bunter. I told you you may have any book out of my bookcase. You may just go into my stateroom and help yourself to any volume.'

And if Bunter protested that he was too tired in his watches below to spare any time for reading, Captain Johns would smile nastily behind his back, and remark that of course some people needed more sleep than others to keep themselves fit for work. If Mr Bunter was afraid of not keeping properly awake when on duty at night, that was another matter.

'But I think you borrowed a novel to read from the second mate the other day – a trashy pack of lies,' Captain Johns sighed. 'I am afraid you are not a spiritually minded man, Mr Bunter. That's what's the matter.'

Sometimes he would appear on deck in the middle of the night, looking very grotesque and bandy-legged in his sleeping suit. At that sight the persecuted Bunter would wring his hands stealthily, and break out into moisture all over his forehead. After standing sleepily by the binnacle, scratching himself in an unpleasant manner, Captain Johns was sure to start on some aspect or other of his only topic.

He would, for instance, discourse on the improvement of morality to be expected from the establishment of general and close intercourse with the spirits of the departed. The spirits, Captain Johns thought, would consent to associate familiarly with the living if it were not for the unbelief of the great mass of mankind. He would not care to have anything to do with a crowd that would not believe in his – Captain Johns' – existence. Then why should a spirit? This was asking too much.

He went on breathing hard by the binnacle and trying to reach round his shoulder-blades; then, with a thick, drowsy severity, declared:

'Incredulity, sir, is the evil of the age!'

It rejected the evidence of Professor Cranks and of the journalist chap. It resisted the production of photographs.

For Captain Johns believed firmly that certain spirits had been photographed. He had read something of it in the papers. And the idea of it having been done had got a tremendous hold on him, because his mind was not critical. Bunter said afterwards that nothing could be more weird than this little man, swathed in a sleeping suit three sizes too large for him, shuffling with excitement in the moonlight near the wheel, and shaking his fist at the serene sea.

'Photographs! Photographs!' he would repeat, in a voice as creaky as a rusty hinge.

The very helmsman just behind him got uneasy at that performance, not being capable of understanding exactly what the 'old man was kicking up a row with the mate about.'

Then Johns, after calming down a bit, would begin again.

'The sensitised plate can't lie. No, sir.'

Nothing could be more funny than this ridiculous little man's conviction – his dogmatic tone. Bunter would go on swinging up and down the poop like a deliberate, dignified pendulum. He said not a word. But the poor fellow had not a trifle on his conscience, as you know; and to have imbecile ghosts rammed down his throat like this on top of his own worry nearly drove him crazy. He knew that on many occasions he was on the verge of lunacy, because he could not help indulging in half-delirious visions of Captain Johns being picked up by the scruff of the neck and dropped over the taffrail into the ship's wake – the sort of thing no sane sailorman would think of doing to a cat or any other animal, anyhow. He imagined him bobbing up – a tiny black speck left far astern on the moonlit ocean.

I don't think that even at the worst moments Bunter really desired to drown Captain Johns. I fancy that all his disordered imagination longed for was merely to stop the ghostly inanity of the skipper's talk.

But, all the same, it was a dangerous form of self-indulgence. Just picture to yourself that ship in the Indian Ocean, on a clear, tropical night, with her sails full and still, the watch on deck stowed away out of sight; and on her poop, flooded with moonlight, the stately black mate walking up and down with measured, dignified steps, preserving an awful silence, and that grotesquely mean little figure in striped flannelette alternately creaking and droning of 'personal intercourse beyond the grave.'

It makes me creepy all over to think of. And sometimes the folly of Captain Johns would appear clothed in a sort of weird utilitarianism. How useful it would be if the spirits of the departed could be induced to take a practical interest in the affairs of the living! What a help, say, to the police, for instance, in the detection of crime! The number of murders, at any rate, would be considerably reduced, he guessed with an air of great sagacity. Then he would give way to grotesque discouragement.

Where was the use of trying to communicate with people that had no faith, and more likely than not would scorn the offered information? Spirits had their feelings. They were *all* feelings in a way. But he was surprised at the forbearance shown towards murderers by their victims. That was the sort of apparition that no guilty man would dare to pooh-pooh. And perhaps the undiscovered murderers – whether believing or not – were haunted. They wouldn't be likely to boast about it, would they?

'For myself,' he pursued, in a sort of vindictive, malevolent whine, 'if anybody murdered me I would not let him forget it. I would wither him up – I would terrify him to death.'

The idea of his skipper's ghost terrifying anyone was so ludicrous that the black mate, little disposed to mirth as he was, could not help giving vent to a weary laugh. And this laugh, the only acknowledgement of a long and earnest discourse, offended Captain Johns.

'What's there to laugh at in this conceited manner, Mr Bunter?' he snarled. 'Supernatural visitations have terrified better men than you. Don't you allow me enough soul to make a ghost of?'

I think it was the nasty tone that caused Bunter to stop short and turn about.

'I shouldn't wonder,' went on the angry fanatic of spiritism, 'if you weren't one of them people that take no more account of a man than if he were a beast. You would be capable, I don't doubt, to deny the possession of an immortal soul to your own father.'

And then Bunter, being bored beyond endurance, and also exasperated by the private worry, lost his self-possession.

He walked up suddenly to Captain Johns, and, stooping a little to look close into his face, said, in a low, even tone:

'You don't know what a man like me is capable of.'

Captain Johns threw his head back, but was too astonished to budge. Bunter resumed his walk; and for a long time his measured footsteps and the low wash of the water alongside were the only sounds which troubled the silence brooding over the great waters. Then Captain Johns cleared his throat uneasily, and, after sidling away towards the companionway for greater safety, plucked up enough courage to retreat under an act of authority:

'Raise the starboard clew of the mainsail, and lay the yards dead square, Mr Bunter. Don't you see the wind is nearly right aft?'

Bunter at once answered 'Ay, ay, sir,' though there was not the slightest necessity to touch the yards, and the wind was well out on the quarter. While he was executing the order Captain Johns hung on the companion-steps, growling to himself: 'Walk this poop like an admiral and don't even notice when the yards want trimming!' – loud enough for the helmsman to overhear. Then he sank slowly backwards out of the man's sight; and when he reached the bottom of the stairs he stood still and thought.

'He's an awful ruffian, with all his gentlemanly airs. No more gentleman mates for me.'

Two nights afterwards he was slumbering peacefully in his berth, when a heavy thumping just above his head (a well-understood signal that he was wanted on deck) made him leap out of bed, broad awake in a moment.

'What's up?' he muttered, running out barefooted. On passing through the cabin he glanced at the clock. It was the middle watch. 'What on earth can the mate want me for?' he thought.

Bolting out of the companion, he found a clear, dewy moonlit night and a strong, steady breeze. He looked around wildly. There was no one on the poop except the helmsman, who addressed him at once.

'It was me, sir. I let go the wheel for a second to stamp over your head. I am afraid there's something wrong with the mate.'

'Where's he got to?' asked the captain sharply.

The man, who was obviously nervous, said:

'The last I saw of him was as he fell down the port poop-ladder.'

'Fell down the poop-ladder! What did he do that for? What made him?'

'I don't know, sir. He was walking the port side. Then just as he turned towards me to come aft . . .'

'You saw him?' interrupted the captain.

'I did. I was looking at him. And I heard the crash, too – something awful. Like the mainmast going overboard. It was as if something had struck him.'

Captain Johns became very uneasy and alarmed.

'Come,' he said sharply. 'Did anybody strike him? What did you see?'

'Nothing, sir, so help me! There was nothing to see. He just gave a little sort of hallo! threw his hands before him, and over he went – crash. I couldn't hear anything more, so I just let go the wheel for a second to call you up.'

'You're scared!' said Captain Johns.

'I am, sir, straight!'

Captain Johns stared at him. The silence of his ship driving on her way seemed to contain a danger – a mystery. He was reluctant to go and look for his mate himself, in the shadows of the main-deck, so quiet, so still.

All he did was to advance to the break of the poop, and call for the watch. As the sleepy men came trooping aft, he shouted to them fiercely:

'Look at the foot of the port poop-ladder, some of you! See the mate lying there?'

Their startled exclamations told him immediately that they did see him. Somebody even screeched out emotionally:

'He's dead!'

Mr Bunter was laid in his bunk and when the lamp in his room was lit he looked indeed as if he were dead, but it was obvious also that he was breathing yet. The steward had been roused out, the second mate called and sent on deck to look after the ship, and for an hour or so Captain Johns devoted himself silently to the restoring of consciousness. Mr Bunter at last opened his eyes, but he could not speak. He was dazed and inert. The steward bandaged a nasty scalp-wound while Captain Johns held an additional light. They had to cut away a lot of Mr Bunter's jet-black hair to make a good dressing. This done, and after gazing for a while at their patient, the two left the cabin.

'A rum go, this, steward,' said Captain Johns in the passage.

'Yessir.'

'A sober man that's right in his head does not fall down a poop-ladder like a sack of potatoes. The ship's as steady as a church.'

'Yessir. Fit of some kind, I shouldn't wonder.'

'Well, I should. He doesn't look as if he were subject to fits and giddiness. Why, the man's in the prime of life. I wouldn't have another kind of mate – not if I knew it. You don't think he has a private store of liquor, do you, eh? He seemed to me a bit strange in his manner several times lately. Off his feed, too, a bit, I noticed.'

'Well, sir, if he ever had a bottle or two of grog in his cabin, that must have gone a long time ago. I saw him throw some broken glass overboard after the last gale we had; but that didn't amount to anything. Anyway, sir, you couldn't call Mr Bunter a drinking man.'

'No,' conceded the captain, reflectively. And the steward, locking the pantry door, tried to escape out of the passage, thinking he could manage to snatch another hour of sleep before it was time for him to turn out for the day.

Captain Johns shook his head.

'There's some mystery there.'

'There's special Providence that he didn't crack his head like an eggshell on the quarter-deck mooring-bits, sir. The men tell me he couldn't have missed them by more than an inch.'

And the steward vanished skilfully.

Captain Johns spent the rest of the night and the whole of the ensuing day between his own room and that of the mate.

In his own room he sat with his open hands reposing on his knees, his lips pursed up, and the horizontal furrows on his forehead marked very heavily. Now and then raising his arm by a slow, as if cautious movement, he scratched lightly the top of his bald head. In the mate's room he stood for long periods of time with his hands to his lips, gazing at the half-conscious man.

For three days Mr Bunter did not say a single word. He looked at people sensibly enough but did not seem to be able to hear any questions put to him. They cut off some more of his hair and swathed his head in wet cloths. He took some nourishment, and was made as comfortable as possible. At dinner on the third day the second mate remarked to the captain, in connection with the affair:

'These half-round brass plates on the steps of the poop-ladders are beastly dangerous things!'

'Are they?' retorted Captain Johns, sourly. 'It takes more than a brass plate to account for an able-bodied man crashing down in this fashion like a felled ox.'

The second mate was impressed by that view. There was something in that, he thought.

'And the weather fine, everything dry, and the ship going along as steady as a church!' pursued Captain Johns, gruffly.

As Captain Johns continued to look extremely sour, the second mate did not open his lips any more during the dinner. Captain Johns was annoyed and hurt by an innocent remark, because the fitting of the aforesaid brass plates had been done at his suggestion only the voyage before, in order to smarten up the appearance of the poop-ladders.

On the fourth day Mr Bunter looked decidedly better; very languid yet, of course, but he heard and understood what was said to him, and even could say a few words in a feeble voice.

Captain Johns, coming in, contemplated him attentively, without much visible sympathy.

'Well, can you give us your account of this accident, Mr Bunter?'

Bunter moved slightly his bandaged head, and fixed his cold blue stare on Captain Johns' face, as if taking stock and appraising the value of every feature; the perplexed forehead, the credulous eyes, the inane droop of the mouth. And he gazed so long that Captain Johns grew restive, and looked over his shoulder at the door.

'No accident,' breathed out Bunter, in a peculiar tone.

'You don't mean to say you've got the falling sickness,' said Captain Johns. 'How would you call it signing as chief mate of a clipper ship with a thing like that on you?'

Bunter answered him only by a sinister look. The skipper shuffled his feet a little.

'Well, what made you have that tumble, then?'

Bunter raised himself a little, and, looking straight into Captain Johns' eyes said, in a very distinct whisper:

'You – were – right!'

He fell back and closed his eyes. Not a word more could Captain Johns get out of him; and, the steward coming into the cabin, the skipper withdrew.

But that very night, unobserved, Captain Johns, opening the door cautiously, entered again the mate's cabin. He could wait no longer. The suppressed eagerness, the excitement expressed in all his mean, creeping little person, did not escape the chief mate, who was lying awake, looking frightfully pulled down and perfectly impassive.

'You are coming to gloat over me, I suppose,' said Bunter without moving, and yet making a palpable hit.

'Bless my soul!' exclaimed Captain Johns with a start, and assuming a sobered demeanour. 'There's a thing to say!'

'Well, gloat, then! You and your ghosts, you've managed to get over a live man.'

This was said by Bunter without stirring, in a low voice, and with not much expression.

'Do you mean to say,' inquired Captain Johns, in awe-struck whisper, 'that you had a supernatural experience that night? You saw an apparition, then, on board my ship?'

Reluctance, shame, disgust, would have been visible on poor Bunter's countenance if the great part of it had not been swathed up in cotton-wool and bandages. His ebony eyebrows, more sinister than ever amongst all that lot of white linen, came together in a frown as he made a mighty effort to say:

'Yes, I have seen.'

The wretchedness in his eyes would have awakened the compassion of any other man than Captain Johns. But Captain Johns was all agog with triumphant excitement. He was just a little bit frightened, too. He looked at that unbelieving scoffer laid low, and did not even dimly guess at his profound, humiliating distress. He was not generally capable of taking much part in the anguish of his fellow-creatures. This time, moreover, he was excessively anxious to know what had happened. Fixing his credulous eyes on the bandaged head, he asked, trembling slightly:

'And did it – did it knock you down?'

'Come! Am I the sort of man to be knocked down by a ghost?'

protested Bunter in a little stronger tone. 'Don't you remember
what you said yourself the other night? Better men than me—Ha!
You'll have to look a long time before you find a better man for a
mate of your ship.'

Captain Johns pointed a solemn finger at Bunter's bedplace.

'You've been terrified,' he said. 'That's what's the matter.
You've been terrified. Why, even the man at the wheel was
scared, though he couldn't see anything. He *felt* the
supernatural. You are punished for your incredulity, Mr
Bunter. You were terrified.'

'And suppose I was,' said Bunter. 'Do you know what I had
seen? Can you conceive the sort of ghost that would haunt a man
like me? Do you think it was a ladyish, afternoon call, another-
cup-of-tea-please apparition that visits your Professor Cranks
and that journalist chap you are always talking about? No; I can't
tell you what it was like. Every man has his own ghosts. You
couldn't conceive . . .'

Bunter stopped, out of breath; and Captain Johns remarked,
with the glow of inward satisfaction reflected in his tone:

'I've always thought you were the sort of man that was ready
for anything; from pitch-and-toss to wilful murder, as the saying
goes. Well, well! So you were terrified.'

'I stepped back,' said Bunter, curtly. 'I don't remember
anything else.'

'The man at the wheel told me you went backwards as if
something had hit you.'

'It was a sort of inward blow,' explained Bunter. 'Something
too deep for you, Captain Johns, to understand. Your life and
mine haven't been the same. Aren't you satisfied to see me
converted?'

'And you can't tell me any more?' asked Captain Johns,
anxiously.

'No, I can't. I wouldn't. It would be no use if I did. That sort of
experience must be gone through. Say I am being punished.
Well, I take my punishment, but talk of it I won't.'

'Very well,' said Captain Johns; 'you won't. But, mind, I can
draw my own conclusions from that.'

'Draw what you like; but be careful what you say, sir. You

don't terrify me. *You* aren't a ghost.'

'One word. Has it any connection with what you said to me on that last night, when we had a talk together on spiritualism?'

Bunter looked weary and puzzled.

'What did I say?'

'You told me that I couldn't know what a man like you was capable of.'

'Yes, yes. Enough!'

'Very good. I am fixed, then,' remarked Captain Johns. 'All I say is that I am jolly glad not to be you, though I would have given almost anything for the privilege of personal communication with the world of spirits. Yes, sir, but not in that way.'

Poor Bunter moaned pitifully.

'It has made me feel twenty years older.'

Captain Johns retired quietly. He was delighted to observe this overbearing ruffian humbled to the dust by the moralizing agency of the spirits. The whole occurrence was a source of pride and gratification; and he began to feel a sort of regard for his chief mate. It is true that in further interviews Bunter showed himself very mild and deferential. He seemed to cling to his captain for spiritual protection. He used to send for him, and say, 'I feel so nervous,' and Captain Johns would stay patiently for hours in the hot little cabin, and feel proud of the call.

For Mr Bunter was ill, and could not leave his berth for a good many days. He became a convinced spiritualist, not enthusiastically – that could hardly have been expected from him – but in a grim, unshakable way. He could not be called exactly friendly to the disembodied inhabitants of our globe, as Captain Johns was. But he was now a firm, if gloomy, recruit of spiritualism.

One afternoon, as the ship was already well to the north in the Gulf of Bengal, the steward knocked at the door of the captain's cabin, and said, without opening it:

'The mate asks if you could spare him a moment, sir. He seems to be in a state in there.'

Captain Johns jumped up from the couch at once.

'Yes. Tell him I am coming.'

He thought: Could it be possible there had been another

spiritual manifestation – in the daytime too!

He revelled in the hope. It was not exactly that, however. Still, Bunter, whom he saw sitting collapsed in a chair – he had been up for several days, but not on deck as yet – poor Bunter had something startling enough to communicate. His hands covered his face. His legs were stretched straight out, dismally.

'What's the news now?' croaked Captain Johns, not unkindly, because in truth it always pleased him to see Bunter – as he expressed it – tamed.

'News!' exclaimed the crushed sceptic through his hands. 'Ay, news enough, Captain Johns. Who will be able to deny the awfulness, the genuineness? Another man would have dropped dead. You want to know what I had seen. All I can tell you is that since I've seen it my hair is turning white.'

Bunter detached his hands from his face, and they hung on each side of his chair as if dead. He looked broken in the dusky cabin.

'You don't say!' stammered out Captain Johns. 'Turned white! Hold on a bit! I'll light the lamp!'

When the lamp was lit, the startling phenomenon could be seen plainly enough. As if the dread, the horror, the anguish of the supernatural were being exhaled through the pores of his skin, a sort of silvery mist seemed to cling to the cheeks and the head of the mate. His short beard, his cropped hair, were growing, not black, but gray – almost white.

When Mr Bunter, thin-faced and shaky, came on deck for duty, he was clean-shaven, and his head was white. The hands were awe-struck. 'Another man,' they whispered to each other. It was generally and mysteriously agreed that the mate had 'seen something,' with the exception of the man at the wheel at the time, who maintained that the mate was 'struck by something.'

This distinction hardly amounted to a difference. On the other hand, everybody admitted that, after he picked up his strength a bit, he seemed smarter in his movements than before.

One day in Calcutta, Captain Johns pointing out to a visitor his white-headed chief mate standing by the main-hatch, was heard to say oracularly:

'That man's in the prime of life.'

Of course, while Bunter was away, I called regularly on Mrs Bunter every Saturday, just to see whether she had any use for my services. It was understood I would do that. She had just his half-pay to live on – it amounted to about a pound a week. She had taken one room in a quiet little square in the East End.

And this was affluence to what I had heard that the couple were reduced to for a time after Bunter had to give up the Western Ocean trade – he used to go as mate of all sorts of hard packets after he lost his ship and his luck together – it was affluence to that time when Bunter would start at seven o'clock in the morning with but a glass of hot water and a crust of dry bread. It won't stand thinking about, especially for those who know Mrs Bunter. I had seen something of them, too, at that time; and it just makes me shudder to remember what that born lady had to put up with. Enough!

Dear Mrs Bunter used to worry a good deal after the *Sapphire* left for Calcutta. She would say to me: 'It must be so awful for poor Winston' – Winston is Bunter's name – and I tried to comfort her the best I could. Afterwards, she got some small children to teach in a family, and was half the day with them, and the occupation was good for her.

In the very first letter she had from Calcutta, Bunter told her he had had a fall down the poop-ladder, and cut his head, but no bones broken, thank God. That was all. Of course, she had other letters from him, but that vagabond Bunter never gave me a scratch of the pen the solid eleven months. I supposed, naturally, that everything was going on all right. Who could imagine what was happening?

Then one day dear Mrs Bunter got a letter from a legal firm in the City, advising her that her uncle was dead – her old curmudgeon of an uncle – a retired stockbroker, a heartless, petrified antiquity that had lasted on and on. He was nearly ninety, I believe; and if I were to meet his venerable ghost this minute, I would try to take him by the throat and strangle him.

The old beast would never forgive his niece for marrying Bunter; and years afterwards, when people made a point of letting him know that she was in London, pretty nearly starving at forty years of age, he only said: 'Serve the little fool right!' I believe he meant her to starve. And, lo and behold, the old cannibal died intestate, with no other relatives but that very identical little fool. The Bunters were wealthy people now.

Of course, Mrs Bunter wept as if her heart would break. In any other woman it would have been mere hypocrisy. Naturally, too, she wanted to cable the news to her Winston in Calcutta, but I showed her, *Gazette* in hand, that the ship was on the homeward-bound list for more than a week already. So we sat down to wait, and talked meantime of dear old Winston every day. There were just one hundred such days before the *Sapphire* got reported 'All well' in the chops of the Channel by an incoming mailboat.

'I am going to Dunkirk to meet him,' says she. The *Sapphire* had a cargo of jute for Dunkirk. Of course, I had to escort the dear lady in the quality of her 'ingenious friend'. She calls me 'our ingenious friend' to this day; and I've observed some people – strangers – looking hard at me, for the signs of the ingenuity, I suppose.

After settling Mrs Bunter in a good hotel in Dunkirk, I walked down to the docks – late afternoon it was – and what was my surprise to see the ship actually fast alongside. Either Johns or Bunter, or both, must have been driving her hard up Channel. Anyway, she had been in since the day before last, and her crew was already paid off. I met two of her apprenticed boys going off home on leave with their dunnage on a Frenchman's barrow, as happy as larks, and I asked them if the mate was on board.

'There he is, on the quay, looking at the moorings,' says one of the youngsters as he skipped past me.

You may imagine the shock to my feelings when I beheld his white head. I could only manage to tell him that his wife was at an hotel in town. He left me at once, to go and get his hat on board. I was mightily surprised by the smartness of his movements as he hurried up the gangway.

Whereas the black mate struck people as deliberate, and strangely stately in his gait for a man in the prime of life, this white-headed chap seemed the most wonderfully alert of old men. I don't suppose Bunter was any quicker on his pins than before. It was the colour of the hair that made all the difference in one's judgement.

The same with his eyes. Those eyes, that looked at you so steely, so fierce, and so fascinating out of a bush of a buccaneer's black hair, now had an innocent, almost boyish expression in their good-humoured brightness under those white eyebrows.

I led him without any delay into Mrs Bunter's private sitting-room. After she had dropped a tear over the late cannibal, given a hug to her Winston, and told him that he must grow his moustache again, the dear lady tucked her feet upon the sofa, and I got out of Bunter's way.

He started at once to pace the room, waving his long arms. He worked himself into a regular frenzy, and tore Johns limb from limb many times over that evening.

'Fell down? Of course I fell down, by slipping backwards on that fool's brass plates. 'Pon my word, I had been walking that poop in charge of the ship, and I didn't know whether I was in the Indian Ocean or in the moon. I was crazy. My head spun round and round with sheer worry. I had made my last application of your chemist's wonderful stuff.' (This to me.) 'All the store of bottles you gave me got smashed when those drawers fell out in the last gale. I had been getting some dry things to change, when I heard the cry: "All hands on deck!" and made one jump of it, without even pushing them in properly. Ass! When I came back and saw the broken glass and the mess, I felt ready to faint.

'No; look here – deception is bad; but not to be able to keep it up after one has been forced into it. You know that since I've been squeezed out of the Western Ocean packets by younger men, just on account of my grizzled muzzle – you know how much chance I had to ever get a ship. And not a soul to turn to. We have been a lonely couple, we two – she threw away everything for me – and to see her want a piece of dry bread –'

He banged with his fist fit to split the Frenchman's table in two.

'I would have turned a sanguinary pirate for her, let alone cheating my way into a berth by dyeing my hair. So when you came to me with your chemist's wonderful stuff –'

He checked himself.

'By the way, that fellow's got a fortune when he likes to pick it up. It is a wonderful stuff – you tell him salt water can do nothing to it. It stays on as long as your hair will.'

'All right,' I said, 'Go on.'

Thereupon he went for Johns again with a fury that frightened his wife, and made me laugh till I cried.

'Just you try to think what it would have meant to be at the mercy of the meanest creature that ever commanded a ship! Just fancy what a life that crawling Johns would have led me! And I knew that in a week or so the white hair would begin to show. And the crew. Did you ever think of that? To be shown up as a low fraud before all hands. What a life for me till we got to Calcutta! And once there – kicked out, of course. Half-pay stopped. Annie here alone without a penny – starving; and I on the other side of the earth, ditto. You see?

'I thought of shaving twice a day. But could I shave my head, too? No way – no way at all. Unless I dropped Johns overboard; and even then – Do you wonder now that with all these things boiling in my head I didn't know where I was putting down my foot that night? I just felt myself falling – then crash, and all dark.

'When I came to myself that bang on the head seemed to have steadied my wits somehow. I was so sick of everything that for two days I wouldn't speak to anyone. They thought it was a slight concussion of the brain. Then the idea dawned upon me as I was looking at that ghost-ridden, wretched fool. "Ah, you love ghosts," I thought. "Well, you shall have something from beyond the grave."

'I didn't even trouble to invent a story. I couldn't imagine a ghost if I wanted to. I wasn't fit to lie connectedly if I had tried. I just bulled him on to it. Do you know, he got, quite by himself, a notion that at some time or other I had done somebody to death in some way, and that –'

'Oh, the horrible man!' cried Mrs Bunter from the sofa. There was a silence.

'And didn't he bore my head off on the home passage!' began Bunter again in a weary voice. 'He loved me. He was proud of me. I was converted. I had had a manifestation. Do you know what he was after? He wanted me and him "to make a *seance*," in his own words, and to try to call up that ghost (the one that had turned my hair white – the ghost of my supposed victim), and, as he said, talk it over with him – the ghost – in a friendly way.

"'Or else, Bunter,' he said, "you may get another manifestation when you least expect it, and tumble overboard perhaps, or something. You ain't really safe till we pacify the spirit-world in some way."

'Can you conceive a lunatic like that? No – say?'

I said nothing. But Mrs Bunter did, in a very decided tone.

'Winston, I don't want you to go on board that ship again any more.'

'My dear,' says he, 'I have all my things on board yet.'

'You don't want the things. Don't go near that ship at all.'

He stood still; then, dropping his eyes with a faint smile, said slowly, in a dreamy voice:

'The haunted ship.'

'And your last,' I added.

We carried him off, as he stood, by the night train. He was very quiet; but crossing the Channel, as we two had a smoke on deck, he turned to me suddenly, and, grinding his teeth, whispered:

'He'll never know how near he was being dropped overboard!'

He meant Captain Johns. I said nothing.

But Captain Johns, I understand, made a great to-do about the disappearance of his chief mate. He set the French police scouring the country for the body. In the end, I fancy he got word from his owners' office to drop all this fuss – that it was all right. I don't suppose he ever understood anything of that mysterious occurrence.

To this day he tries at times (he's retired now, and his conversation is not very coherent) – he tries to tell the story of a black mate he once had, 'a murderous, gentlemanly ruffian,' with raven-black hair which turned white all at once in consequence of a manifestation from beyond the grave.' An avenging apparition. What with reference to black and white hair, to poop-ladders, and to his own feelings and views, it is difficult to make head or tail of it. If his sister (she's very vigorous still) should be present she cuts all this short — peremptorily:

'Don't you mind what he says. He's got devils on the brain.'

A MATTER
OF FACT

Rudyard Kipling

Sea monsters have been part of the lore of the sea for centuries, and though a great many sightings have subsequently been put down to figments of the imagination or just mistaken identification, there are others that have defied all explanation. For with so much that is mysterious about the sea, who could deny that creatures beyond the normal might not lurk beneath the grey-green waves? In the next story, 'A Matter of Fact', Rudyard Kipling (1865–1936) takes just such a premise as the basis for his curious tale.

Although Kipling will forever be associated with children's stories – the two Jungle Books *(1894–5),* Stalky and Co. *(1899), the* Just So Stories *(1902) and* Puck of Pook's Hill *(1906) – his mind often dwelt on the sea, and the discerning reader will find some of his very best work tucked away in collections such as* The Seven Seas *(1896) and individual stories like 'A Matter of Fact' which he wrote in 1893.*

Kipling was born in India, though he settled in England after travelling a great deal between the Far East, Britain and America. Much of this travel was by ship, and according to one Kipling expert it was on such a voyage that he had a bizarre experience very similar to the one described in this story. If that is so, it would seem to be a most aptly titled contribution.

And if ye doubt the tale I tell,
Steer through the South Pacific swell;
Go where the branching coral hives
Unending strife of endless lives,
Where, leagued about the 'wildered boat,
The rainbow jellies fill and float;
And, lilting where the laver lingers,
The starfish trips on all her fingers;
Where, 'neath his myriad spines ashock,
The sea-egg ripples down the rock;
An orange wonder dimly guessed,
From darkness where the cuttles rest,
Moored o'er the darker deeps that hide
The blind white Sea-snake and his bride
Who, drowsing, nose the long-lost ships
Let down through darkness to their lips.

—The Palms

ONCE A PRIEST, always a priest; once a mason, always a mason; but once a journalist, always and for ever a journalist.

There were three of us, all newspaper men, the only passengers on a little tramp steamer that ran where her owners told her to go. She had once been in the Bilbao iron ore business, had been lent to the Spanish Government for service at Manilla; and was ending her days in the Cape Town coolie-trade, with occasional trips to Madagascar and even as far as England. We found her going to Southampton in ballast, and shipped in her

155

because the fares were nominal. There was Keller, of an American paper, on his way back to the States from palace executions in Madagascar; there was a burly half-Dutchman, called Zuyland, who owned and edited a paper up country near Johannesberg; and there was myself, who had solemnly put away all journalism, vowing to forget that I had ever known the difference between an imprint and a stereo advertisement.

Ten minutes after Keller spoke to me, as the *Rathmines* cleared Cape Town, I had forgotten the aloofness I desired to feign, and was in heated discussion on the immorality of expanding telegrams beyond a certain fixed point. Then Zuyland came out of his cabin, and we were all at home instantly, because we were men of the same profession needing no introduction. We annexed the boat formally, broke open the passengers' bath-room door – on the Manilla lines the Dons do not wash – cleaned out the orange-peel and cigar-ends at the bottom of the bath, hired a Lascar to shave us throughout the voyage, and then asked each other's names.

Three ordinary men would have quarrelled through sheer boredom before they reached Southampton. We, by virtue of our craft, were anything but ordinary men. A large percentage of the tales of the world, the thirty-nine that cannot be told to ladies and the one that can, are common property coming of a common stock. We told them all, as a matter of form, with all their local and specific variants which are surprising. Then came, in the intervals of steady card-play, more personal histories of adventure and things seen and suffered: panics among white folk when the blind terror ran from man to man on the Brooklyn Bridge, and the people crushed each other to death they knew not why; fires, and faces that opened and shut their mouths horribly at red-hot window frames; wrecks in frost and snow, reported from the sleet-sheathed rescue-tug at the risk of frostbite; long rides after diamond thieves; skirmishes on the veldt and in municipal committees with the Boers; glimpses of lazy tangled Cape politics and the mule-rule in the Transvaal; card-tales, horse-tales, woman-tales, by the score and the half hundred; till the first mate, who had seen more than us all put together, but lacked words to clothe his tales with, sat open-mouthed far into the dawn.

When the tales were done we picked up cards till a curious hand or a chance remark made one or other of us say, 'That reminds me of a man who – or a business which – ' and the anecdotes would continue while the *Rathmines* kicked her way northward through the warm water.

In the morning of one specially warm night we three were sitting immediately in front of the wheel-house, where an old Swedish boatswain whom we called 'Frithiof the Dane' was at the wheel, pretending that he could not hear our stories. Once or twice Frithiof spun the spokes curiously, and Keller lifted his head from a long chair to ask, 'What is it? Can't you get any steerage-way on her?'

'There is a feel in the water,' said Frithiof, 'that I cannot understand. I think that we run downhills or somethings. She steers bad this morning.'

Nobody seems to know the laws that govern the pulses of the big waters. Sometimes even a landsman can tell that the solid ocean is atilt, and that the ship is working herself up a long unseen slope; and sometimes the captain says, when neither full steam nor fair wind justifies the length of a day's run, that the ship is sagging downhill; but how these ups and downs come about has not yet been settled authoritatively.

'No, it is a following sea,' said Frithiof; 'and with a following sea you shall not get good steerage-way.'

The sea was as smooth as a duck-pond, except for a regular oily swell. As I looked over the side to see where it might be following us from, the sun rose in a perfectly clear sky and struck the water with its light so sharply that it seemed as though the sea should clang like a burnished gong. The wake of the screw and the little white streak cut by the log-line hanging over the stern were the only marks on the water as far as eye could reach.

Keller rolled out of his chair and went aft to get a pine-apple from the ripening stock that was hung inside the after awning.

'Frithiof, the log-line has got tired of swimming. It's coming home,' he drawled.

'What?' said Frithiof, his voice jumping several octaves.

'Coming home,' Keller repeated leaning over the stern. I ran to his side and saw the log-line, which till then had been drawn tense over the stern railing, slacken, loop, and come up off the port quarter. Frithiof called up the speaking-tube to the bridge, and the bridge answered, 'Yes, nine knots.' Then Frithiof spoke again, and the answer was, 'What do you want of the skipper?' and Frithiof bellowed, 'Call him up.'

By this time Zuyland, Keller, and myself had caught something of Frithiof's excitement, for any emotion on shipboard is most contagious. The captain ran out of his cabin, spoke to Frithiof, looked at the log-line, jumped on the bridge, and in a minute we felt the steamer swing round as Frithiof turned her.

''Going back to Cape Town?' said Keller.

Frithiof did not answer, but tore away at the wheel. Then he beckoned us three to help, and we held the wheel down till the *Rathmines* answered it and we found ourselves looking into the white of our own wake, with the still oily sea tearing past our bows, though we were not going more than half steam ahead.

The captain stretched out his arm from the bridge and shouted. A minute later I would have given a great deal to have shouted too, for one-half of the sea seemed to shoulder itself above the other half, and came on in the shape of a hill. There was neither crest, comb, nor curl-over to it; nothing but black water with little waves chasing each other about the flanks. I saw it stream past and on a level with the *Rathmines*' bow-plates before the steamer hove up her bulk to rise, and I argued that this would be the last of all earthly voyages for me. Then we lifted for ever and ever and ever, till I heard Keller saying in my ear, 'The bowels of the deep, good Lord!' and the *Rathmines* stood poised, her screw racing and drumming on the slope of a hollow that stretched downwards for a good half-mile.

We went down that hollow, nose under for the most part, and the air smelt wet and muddy, like that of an emptied aquarium. There was a second hill to climb; I saw that much: but the water came aboard and carried me aft till it jammed me against the wheel-house door, and before I could catch breath or clear my eyes again we were rolling to and fro in the torn water, with the scuppers pouring like eaves in a thunderstorm.

'There were three waves,' said Keller; 'and the stokehold's flooded.'

The firemen were on deck waiting, apparently, to be drowned. The engineer came and dragged them below, and the crew, gasping, began to work the clumsy Board of Trade pump. That showed nothing serious, and when I understood that the *Rathmines* was really on the water, and not beneath it, I asked what had happened.

'The captain says it was a blow-up under the sea – a volcano,' said Keller.

'It hasn't warmed anything,' I said. I was feeling bitterly cold, and cold was almost unknown in those waters. I went below to change my clothes, and when I came up everything was wiped out in clinging white fog.

'Are there going to be any more surprises?' said Keller to the captain.

'I don't know. Be thankful you're alive, gentlemen. That's a tidal wave thrown up by a volcano. Probably the bottom of the sea has been lifted a few feet somewhere or other. I can't quite understand this cold spell. Our sea-thermometer says the surface water is 44°, and it should be 68° at least.'

'It's abominable,' said Keller, shivering. 'But hadn't you better attend to the fog-horn? It seems to me that I heard something.'

'Heard! Good heavens!' said the captain from the bridge, 'I should think you did.' He pulled the string of our fog-horn, which was a weak one. It sputtered and choked, because the stokehold was full of water and the fires were half-drowned, and at last gave out a moan. It was answered from the fog by one of the most appalling steam-sirens I have ever heard. Keller turned as white as I did, for the fog, the cold fog, was upon us, and any man may be forgiven for fearing a death he cannot see.

'Give her steam there!' said the captain to the engine-room. 'Steam for the whistle, if we have to go dead slow.'

We bellowed again, and the damp dripped off the awnings on to the deck as we listened for the reply. It seemed to be astern this time, but much nearer than before.

'The *Pembroke Castle* on us!' said Keller; and then, viciously,

'Well, thank God, we shall sink her too.'

'It's a side-wheel steamer,' I whispered. 'Can't you hear the paddles?'

This time we whistled and roared till the steam gave out, and the answer nearly deafened us. There was a sound of frantic threshing in the water, apparently about fifty yards away, and something shot past in the whiteness that looked as though it were gray and red.

'The *Pembroke Castle* bottom up,' said Keller, who, being a journalist, always sought for explanations. 'That's the colours of a Castle liner. We're in for a big thing.'

'The sea is bewitched,' said Frithiof from the wheel-house. 'There are *two* steamers!'

Another siren sounded on our bow, and the little steamer rolled in the wash of something that had passed unseen.

'We're evidently in the middle of a fleet,' said Keller quietly. 'If one doesn't run us down, the other will. Phew! What in creation is that?'

I sniffed, for there was a poisonous rank smell in the cold air – a smell that I had smelt before.

'If I was on land I should say that it was an alligator. It smells like musk,' I answered.

'Not ten thousand alligators could make that smell,' said Zuyland; 'I have smelt them.'

'Bewitched! Bewitched!' said Frithiof. 'The sea she is turned upside down, and we are walking along the bottom.'

Again the *Rathmines* rolled in the wash of some unseen ship, and a silver-gray wave broke over the bow, leaving on the deck a sheet of sediment – the gray broth that has its place in the fathomless deeps of the sea. A sprinkling of the wave fell on my face, and it was so cold that it stung as boiling water stings. The dead and most untouched deep water of the sea had been heaved to the top by the submarine volcano – the chill still water that kills all life and smells of desolation and emptiness. We did not need either the blinding fog or that indescribable smell of musk to make us unhappy – we were shivering with cold and wretchedness where we stood.

'The hot air on the cold water makes this fog,' said the captain;

'it ought to clear in a little time.'

'Whistle, oh! whistle, and let's get out of it,' said Keller.

The captain whistled again, and far and far astern the invisible twin steam-sirens answered us. Their blasting shriek grew louder, till at last it seemed to tear out of the fog just above our quarter, and I cowered while the *Rathmines* plunged bows under on a double swell that crossed.

'No more,' said Frithiof, 'it is not good any more. Let us get away, in the name of God.'

'Now if a torpedo-boat with a *City of Paris* siren went mad and broke her moorings and hired a friend to help her, it's just conceivable that we might be carried as we are now. Otherwise this thing is –'

The last words died on Keller's lips, his eyes began to start from his head, and his jaw fell. Some six or seven feet above the port bulwarks, framed in fog, and as utterly unsupported as the full moon, hung a Face. It was not human, and it certainly was not animal, for it did not belong to this earth as known to man. The mouth was open, revealing a ridiculously tiny tongue – as absurd as the tongue of an elephant; there were tense wrinkles of white skin at the angles of the drawn lips, white feelers like those of a barbel sprung from the lower jaw, and there was no sign of teeth within the mouth. But the horror of the face lay in the eyes, for those were sightless – white, in sockets as white as scraped bone, and blind. Yet for all this the face, wrinkled as the mask of a lion is drawn in Assyrian sculpture, was alive with rage and terror. One long white feeler touched our bulwarks. Then the face disappeared with the swiftness of a blindworm popping into its burrow, and the next thing that I remember is my own voice in my own ears, saying gravely to the mainmast. 'But the air-bladder ought to have been forced out of its mouth, you know.'

Keller came up to me, ashy white. He put his hand into his pocket, took a cigar, bit it, dropped it, thrust his shaking thumb into his mouth and mumbled, 'The giant gooseberry and the raining frogs! Gimme a light – gimme a light! Say, gimme a light.' A little bead of blood dropped from his thumb-joint.

I respected the motive, though the manifestation was absurd. 'Stop, you'll bite your thumb off,' I said, and Keller laughed brokenly as he picked up his cigar. Only Zuyland, leaning over the port bulwarks, seemed self-possessed. He declared later that he was very sick.

'We've seen it,' he said, turning round. 'That is it.'

'What?' said Keller, chewing the unlighted cigar.

As he spoke the fog was blown into shreds, and we saw the sea, gray with mud, rolling on every side of us and empty of all life. Then in one spot it bubbled and became like the pot of ointment that the Bible speaks of. From that wide-ringed trouble a Thing came up – a gray and red Thing with a neck – a Thing that bellowed and writhed in pain. Frithiof drew in his breath and held it till the red letters of the ship's name, woven across his jersey, straggled and opened out as though they had been type badly set. Then he said with a little cluck in his throat, 'Ah me! It is blind. *Hurilla!* That thing is blind,' and a murmur of pity went through us all, for we could see that the thing on the water was blind and in pain. Something had gashed and cut the great sides cruelly and the blood was spurting out. The gray ooze of the undermost sea lay in the monstrous wrinkles of the back, and poured away in sluices. The blind white head flung back and battered the wounds, and the body in its torment rose clear of the red and gray waves till we saw a pair of quivering shoulders streaked with weed and rough with shells, but as white in the clear spaces as the hairless, maneless, blind, toothless head. Afterwards, came a dot on the horizon and the sound of a shrill scream, and it was as though a shuttle shot all across the sea in one breath, and a second head and neck tore through the levels, driving a whispering wall of water to right and left. The two Things met – the one untouched and the other in its death-throe – male and female, we said, the female coming to the male. She circled round him bellowing, and laid her neck across the curve of his great turtle-back, and he disappeared under water for an instant, but flung up again, grunting in agony while the blood ran. Once the entire head and neck shot clear of the water and stiffened, and I heard Keller saying, as though he was watching a street accident, 'Give him air. For God's sake, give him air.' Then the death-struggle began, with crampings and twistings and jerkings of the white bulk to and fro, till our little steamer rolled again, and each gray wave coated her plates with gray slime. The sun was clear, there was no wind, and we watched, the whole crew, stokers and all, in wonder and pity, but chiefly pity. The Thing was so helpless, and, save for his mate, so alone. No human eye should have beheld him; it was monstrous and indecent to exhibit him there in trade waters between atlas degrees of latitude. He had been spewed up, mangled and dying, from his rest on the sea-floor, where he might have lived till the Judgment Day, and we saw the tides of his life go from him as an angry tide goes out across rocks in the teeth of a landward gale. His mate lay rocking on the water a little distance off, bellowing continually, and the smell of musk came down upon the ship making us cough.

At last the battle for life ended in a batter of coloured seas. We saw the writhing neck fall like a flail, the carcase turn sideways, showing the glint of a white belly and the inset of a gigantic hind leg or flipper. Then all sank, and sea boiled over it, while the mate swam round and round, darting her head in every direction. Though we might have feared that she would attack the steamer, no power on earth could have drawn any one of us from our places that hour. We watched, holding our breaths. The mate paused in her search; and we could hear the wash beating along her sides; reared her neck as high as she could reach, blind and lonely in all that loneliness of the sea, and sent one desperate bellow booming across the swells as an oyster-shell skips across a pond. Then she made off to the westward, the sun shining on the white head and the wake behind it, till nothing was left to see but a little pin point of silver on the horizon. We stood on our course again; and the *Rathmines*, coated with the sea-sediment from bow to stern, looked like a ship made gray with terror.

'We must pool our notes,' was the first coherent remark from Keller. 'We're three trained journalists – we hold absolutely the biggest scoop on record. Start fair.'

I objected to this. Nothing is gained by collaboration in journalism when all deal with the same facts, so we went to work each according to his own lights. Keller triple-headed his account, talked about our 'gallant captain,' and wound up with an allusion to American enterprise in that it was a citizen of Dayton, Ohio, that had seen the sea-serpent. This sort of thing would have discredited the Creation, much more a mere sea tale, but as a specimen of the picture-writing of a half-civilised people it was very interesting. Zuyland took a heavy column and a half, giving approximate lengths and breadths, and the whole list of the crew whom he had sworn on oath to testify to his facts. There was nothing fantastic or flamboyant in Zuyland. I wrote three-quarters of a leaded bourgeois column, roughly speaking, and refrained from putting any journalese into it for reasons that had begun to appear to me.

Keller was insolent with joy. He was going to cable from Southampton to the New York *World*, mail his account to America on the same day, paralyse London with his three columns of loosely knitted headlines, and generally efface the earth. 'You'll see how I work a big scoop when I get it,' he said.

'Is this your first visit to England?' I asked.

'Yes,' said he. 'You don't seem to appreciate the beauty of our scoop. It's pyramidal – the death of the sea-serpent! Good heavens alive, man, it's the biggest thing ever vouchsafed to a paper!'

'Curious to think that it will never appear in any paper, isn't it?' I said.

Zuyland was near me, and he nodded quickly.

'What do you mean?' said Keller. 'If you're enough of a Britisher to throw this thing away, I shan't. I thought you were a newspaperman.'

'I am. That's why I know. Don't be an ass, Keller. Remember, I'm seven hundred years your senior, and what your grandchildren may learn five hundred years hence, I learned from my grandfathers about five hundred years ago. You won't do it, because you can't.'

This conversation was held in the open sea, where everything seems possible, some hundred miles from Southampton. We passed the Needles Light at dawn, and the lifting day showed the stucco villas on the green and the awful orderlinesss of England – line upon line, wall upon wall, solid stone dock and monolithic pier. We waited an hour in the Customs shed, and there was ample time for the effect to soak in.

'Now, Keller, you face the music. The *Havel* goes out to-day. Mail by her, and I'll take you to the telegraph-office,' I said.

I heard Keller gasp as the influence of the land closed about him, cowing him as they say Newmarket Heath cows a young horse unused to open courses.

'I want to retouch my stuff. Suppose we wait till we get to London?' he said.

Zuyland, by the way, had torn up his account and thrown it overboard that morning early. His reasons were my reasons.

In the train Keller began to revise his copy, and every time that he looked at the trim little fields, the red villas, and the embankments of the line, the blue pencil plunged remorselessly through the slips. He appeared to have dredged the dictionary for adjectives. I could think of none that he had not used. Yet he was a perfectly sound poker-player and never showed more cards than were sufficient to take the pool.

Aren't you going to leave him a single bellow?' I asked sympathetically. 'Remember, everything goes in the States, from a trouser-button to a double-eagle.'

'That's just the curse of it,' said Keller below his breath. 'We've played 'em for suckers so often that when it comes to the golden truth – I'd like to try this on a London paper. You have first call there, though.'

'Not in the least. I'm not touching the thing in our papers. I shall be happy to leave 'em all to you; but surely you'll cable it home?'

'No. Not if I can make the scoop here and see the Britishers sit up.'

'You won't do it with three columns of slushy headline, believe me. They don't sit up as quickly as some people.'

'I'm beginning to think that too. Does *nothing* make any difference in this country?' he said, looking out of the window. 'How old is that farmhouse?'

'New. It can't be more than two hundred years at the most.'

'Um. Fields, too?'

'That hedge there must have been clipped for about eighty

years.'

'Labour cheap – eh?'

'Pretty much. Well, I suppose you'd like to try the *Times*, wouldn't you?'

'No,' said Keller, looking at Winchester Cathedral. 'Might as well try to electrify a haystack. And to think that the *World* would take three columns and ask for more – with illustrations too! It's sickening.'

'But the *Times* might,' I began.

Keller flung his paper across the carriage, and it opened in its austere majesty of solid type – opened with the crackle of an encyclopædia.

'Might! You *might* work your way through the bow-plates of a cruiser. Look at that first page!'

'It strikes you that way, does it?' I said. 'Then I'd recommend you to try a light and frivolous journal.'

'With a thing like this of mine – of ours? It's sacred history!'

I showed him a paper which I conceived would be after his own heart, in that it was modelled on American lines.

'That's homey, he said, 'but it's not the real thing. Now, I should like one of these fat old *Times* columns. Probably there'd be a bishop in the office, though.'

When we reached London Keller disappeared in the direction of the Strand. What his experiences may have been I cannot tell, but it seems that he invaded the office of an evening paper at 11.45 a.m. (I told him English editors were most idle at that hour), and mentioned my name as that of a witness to the truth of his story.

'I was nearly fired out,' he said furiously at lunch. 'As soon as I mentioned you, the old man said that I was to tell you that they didn't want any more of your practical jokes, and that you knew the hours to call if you had anything to sell, and that they'd see you condemned before they helped to puff one of your infernal yarns in advance. Say, what record do you hold for truth in the country, anyway?'

'A beauty. You ran up against it, that's all. Why don't you leave the English papers alone and cable New York? Everything goes over there.'

'Can't you see that's just why?' he repeated.

'I saw it a long time ago. You don't intend to cable then?'

'Yes, I do,' he answered, in the over-emphatic voice of one who does not know his own mind.

That afternoon I walked him abroad and about, over the streets that run between the pavements like channels of grooved and tongued lava, over the bridges that are made of enduring stone, through subways floored and sided with yard-thick concrete, between houses that are never rebuilt, and by river-steps hewn, to the eye, from the living rock. A black fog chased us into Westminster Abbey, and, standing there in the darkness, I could hear the wings of the dead centuries circling round the head of Litchfield A. Keller, journalist, of Dayton, Ohio, U.S.A., whose mission it was to make the Britishers sit up.

He stumbled gasping into the thick gloom, and the roar of the traffic came to his bewildered ears.

'Let's go to the telegraph-office and cable,' I said. 'Can't you hear the New York *World* crying for news of the great sea-serpent, blind, white, and smelling of musk, stricken to death by a submarine volcano, and assisted by his loving wife to die in mid-ocean, as visualised by an American citizen, the breezy, newsy, brainy newspaper man of Dayton, Ohio? 'Rah for the Buckeye State. Step lively! Both gates! Szz! Boom! Aah!' Keller was a Princeton man, and he seemed to need encouragement.

'You've got me on your own ground,' said he, tugging at his overcoat pocket. He pulled out his copy, with the cable forms – for he had written out his telegram – and put them all into my hand, groaning, 'I pass. If I hadn't come to your cursed country – If I'd sent it off at Southampton – If I ever get you west of the Alleghannies, if –'

'Never mind, Keller. It isn't your fault. It's the fault of your country. If you had been seven hundred years older you'd have done what I am going to do.'

'What are you going to do?'

'Tell it as a lie.'

'Fiction?' This with the full-blooded disgust of a journalist for the illegitimate branch of the profession.

'You can call it that if you like. I shall call it a lie.'

And a lie it has become; for Truth is a naked lady, and if by accident she is drawn up from the bottom of the sea, it behoves a gentleman either to give her a print petticoat or to turn his face to the wall and vow that he did not see.

THE FINDING
OF THE GRAIKEN

William Hope Hodgson

The Sargasso Sea is that legendary area of the Atlantic blighted by seaweed, in which for generations unwary ships and their crews were helplessly and fatally trapped. The rotting hulks which marked this dreadful place were also said to be filled with fearsome rats and the most terrible forms of sea life . . .

The man who immortalised the Sargasso Sea was William Hope Hodgson (1878–1918), for years a shamefully neglected writer, now at last gaining the international reputation he so richly deserves through new paperback editions of his best work. Born the second of twelve children of an Essex clergyman, he ran away to sea in his youth. Though his life afloat was extremely harsh and unhappy for years, it provided him with a cause – to better the lives of seamen – and the raw material for a whole succession of books and short stories about life at sea. He dwelt in particular on the wilder and lesser-known areas of ocean.

His first novel was the eerie Boats of the 'Glen Carrig' *(1907), followed by the even stranger* Ghost Pirates *(1909). He began to exploit his interest in the Sargasso Sea through a series of interrelated tales which, strangely, have never been collected in a single volume, although there have been several anthologies of his best sea stories including* The Luck of the Strong *(1916) and* Men of Deep Waters *(1917).*

William Hope Hodgson was killed while serving bravely with the Army in France in 1918, but it has taken well over half a century for his importance as a writer to be recognised. I am, therefore, pleased to be playing my own small part by returning to print one of his best Sargasso Sea stories, 'The Finding of the Graiken' (1913) and would urge any reader who has not done so, to investigate the other works by this marvellous writer of sea mysteries.

I

WHEN A YEAR had passed, and still there was no news of the full-rigged ship Graiken, even the most sanguine of my old chum's friends had ceased to hope perchance, somewhere, she might be above water.

Yet Ned Barlow, in his inmost thoughts, I knew, still hugged to himself the hope that she would win home. Poor, dear old fellow, how my heart did go out towards him in his sorrow!

For it was in the Graiken that his sweetheart had sailed on that dull January day some twelve months previously.

The voyage had been taken for the sake of her health; yet since then – save for a distant signal recorded at the Azores – there had been from all the mystery of ocean no voice; the ship and they within her had vanished utterly.

And still Barlow hoped. He said nothing actually, but at times his deeper thoughts would float up and show through the sea of his usual talk, and thus I would know in an indirect way of the thing that his heart was thinking.

Nor was time a healer.

It was later that my present good fortune came to me. My uncle died, and I – hitherto poor – was now a rich man. In a breath, it seemed, I had become possessor of houses, lands, and money; also – in my eyes almost more important – a fine fore-and-aft-rigged yacht of some two hundred tons register.

It seemed scarcely believable that the thing was mine, and I was all in a scutter to run away down to Falmouth and get to sea.

In old times, when my uncle had been more than usually gracious, he had invited me to accompany him for a trip round the coast or elsewhere, as the fit might take him; yet never, even in my most hopeful moments, had it occurred to me that ever she might be mine.

And now I was hurrying my preparations for a good long sea trip – for to me the sea is, and always has been, a comrade.

Still, with all the prospects before me, I was by no means completely satisfied, for I wanted Ned Barlow with me, and yet was afraid to ask him.

I had the feeling that, in view of his overwhelming loss, he must positively hate the sea; and yet I could not be happy at the thought of leaving him, and going alone.

He had not been well lately, and a sea voyage would be the very thing for him, if only it were not going to freshen painful memories.

Eventually I decided to suggest it, and this I did a couple of days before the date I had fixed for sailing.

'Ned,' I said, 'you need a change.'

'Yes,' he assented wearily.

'Come with me, old chap,' I went on, growing bolder. 'I'm taking a trip in the yacht. It would be splendid to have – '

To my dismay, he jumped to his feet and came towards me excitedly.

'I've upset him now,' was my thought. 'I *am* a fool!'

'Go to sea!' he said. 'My God! I'd give – ' He broke off short, and stood suppressed opposite to me, his face all of a quiver with suppressed emotion. He was silent a few seconds, getting himself in hand; then he proceeded more quietly: 'Where to?'

'Anywhere,' I replied, watching him keenly, for I was greatly puzzled by his manner. 'I'm not quite clear yet. Somewhere south of here – the West Indies, I have thought. It's all so new, you know – just fancy being able to go just where we like. I can hardly realise it yet.'

I stopped; for he had turned from me and was staring out of the window.

'You'll come, Ned?' I cried, fearful that he was going to refuse me.

He took a pace away, and came back.

'I'll come,' he said, and there was a look of strange excitement in his eyes that set me off on a tack of vague wonder; but I said nothing, just told him how he had pleased me.

II

We had been at sea a couple of weeks, and were alone upon the Atlantic – at least, so much of it as presented itself to our view.

I was leaning over the taffrail, staring down into the boil of the wake; yet I noticed nothing, for I was wrapped in a tissue of somewhat uncomfortable thought. It was about Ned Barlow.

He had been queer, decidedly queer, since leaving port. His whole attitude mentally had been that of a man under the influence of an all-pervading excitement. I had said that he was in need of a change, and had trusted that the splendid tonic of the sea breeze would serve to put him soon to rights mentally and physically; yet here was the poor old chap acting in a manner calculated to cause me anxiety as to his balance.

Scarcely a word had been spoken since leaving the Channel. When I ventured to speak to him, often he would take not the least notice, other times he would answer only by a brief word; but talk – never.

In addition, his whole time was spent on deck among the men, and with some of them he seemed to converse both long and earnestly; yet to me, his chum and true friend, not a word.

Another thing came to me as a surprise – Barlow betrayed the greatest interest in the position of the vessel, and the courses set, all in such a manner as left me no room to doubt but that his knowledge of navigation was considerable.

Once I ventured to express my astonishment at this knowledge, and ask a question or two as to the way in which he had gathered it, but had been treated with such an absurdly stony silence that since then I had not spoken to him.

With all this it may be easily conceived that my thoughts, as I stared down into the wake, were troublesome.

Suddenly I heard a voice at my elbow:

'I should like to have a word with you, sir.' I turned sharply. It was my skipper, and something in his face told me that all was not as it should be.

'Well, Jenkins, fire away.'

He looked round, as if afraid of being overheard; then came closer to me.

'Someone's been messing with the compasses, sir,' he said in a low voice.

'What?' I asked sharply.

'They've been meddled with, sir. The magnets have been shifted, and by someone who's a good idea of what he's doing.'

'What on earth do you mean?' I inquired. 'Why should anyone mess about with them? What good would it do them? You must be mistaken.'

'No, sir, I'm not. They've been touched within the last forty-eight hours, and by someone that understands what he's doing.'

I stared at him. The man was so certain. I felt bewildered.

'But why should they?'

'That's more than I can say, sir; but it's a serious matter, and I want to know what I'm to do. It looks to me as though there were something funny going on. I'd give a month's pay to know just who it was, for certain.'

'Well,' I said, 'if they have been touched, it can only be by one of the officers. You say the chap who has done it must understand what he is doing.'

He shook his head. 'No sir – ' he began, and then stopped abruptly. His gaze met mine. I think the same thought must have come to us simultaneously. I gave a little gasp of amazement.

He wagged his head at me. 'I've had my suspicions for a bit, sir,' he went on; 'but seeing that he's – he's – ' He was fairly struck for the moment.

I took my weight off the rail and stood upright.

'To whom are you referring?' I asked curtly.

'Why, sir, to him – Mr Ned – '

He would have gone on, but I cut him short.

'That will do, Jenkins!' I cried. 'Mr Ned Barlow is my friend. You are forgetting yourself a little. You will accuse me of tampering with the compasses next!'

I turned away, leaving little Captain Jenkins speechless. I had spoken with an almost vehement over-loyalty, to quiet my own suspicions.

All the same, I was horribly bewildered, not knowing what to think or do or say, so that, eventually, I did just nothing.

III

It was early one morning, about a week later, that I opened my eyes abruptly. I was lying on my back in my bunk, and the daylight was beginning to creep wanly in through the ports.

I had a vague consciousness that all was not as it should be, and feeling thus, I made to grasp the edge of my bunk, and sit up, but failed, owing to the fact that my wrists were securely fastened by a pair of heavy steel handcuffs.

Utterly confounded, I let my head fall back upon the pillow; and then, in the midst of my bewilderment, there sounded the sharp report of a pistol-shot somewhere on the decks over my head. There came a second, and the sound of voices and footsteps, and then a long spell of silence.

Into my mind had rushed the single word – mutiny! My temples throbbed a little, but I struggled to keep calm and think, and then, all adrift, I fell to searching round for a reason. Who was it? and why?

Perhaps an hour passed, during which I asked myself ten thousand vain questions. All at once I heard a key inserted in the door. So I had been locked in! It turned, and the steward walked into the cabin. He did not look at me, but went to the arm-rack and began to remove the various weapons.

'What the devil is the meaning of all this, Jones?' I roared, getting up a bit on one elbow. 'What's happening.?'

But the fool answered not a word – just went to and fro carrying out the weapons from my cabin into the next, so that at last I ceased from questioning him, and lay silent, promising myself future vengeance.

When he had removed the arms, the steward began to go through my table drawers, emptying them, so it appeared to me, of everything that could be used as a weapon or tool.

Having completed his task, he vanished, locking the door after him.

Some time passed, and at last, about seven bells, he reappeared, this time bringing a tray with my breakfast. Placing it upon the table, he came across to me and proceeded to unlock the cuffs from off my wrists. Then for the first time he spoke.

'Mr Barlow desires me to say, sir, that you have the liberty of your cabin so long as you will agree not to cause any bother. Should you wish for anything, I am under his orders to supply you.' He retreated hastily toward the door.

On my part, I was almost speechless with astonishment and rage.

'One minute, Jones!' I shouted, just as he was in the act of leaving the cabin. 'Kindly explain what you mean. You said Mr Barlow. Is it to him that I owe all this?' And I waved my hand towards the irons which the man still held.

'It is by his orders,' replied he, and turned once more to leave the cabin.

'I don't understand!' I said, bewildered. 'Mr Barlow is my friend, and this is my yacht! By what right do you dare to take your orders from him? Let me out!'

As I shouted the last command, I leapt from my bunk, and made a dash for the door, but the steward, so far from attempting to bar it, flung it open and stepped quickly through, thus allowing me to see that a couple of the sailors were stationed in the alleyway.

'Get on deck at once!' I said angrily. 'What are you doing down here?'

'Sorry sir,' said one of the men. 'We'd take it kindly if you'd make no trouble. But we ain't lettin' you out, sir. Don't make no bloomin' error.'

I hesitated, then went to the table and sat down. I would, at least, do my best to preserve my dignity.

After an inquiry as to whether he could do anything further, the steward left me to breakfast and my thoughts. As may be imagined, the latter were by no means pleasant.

Here was I prisoner in my own yacht, and by the hand of the very man I had loved and befriended through many years. Oh, it was too incredible and mad!

For a while, leaving the table, I paced the deck of my room; then, growing calmer, I sat down again and attempted to make some sort of a meal.

As I breakfasted, my chief thought was as to *why* my one-time chum was treating me thus; and after that I fell to puzzling *how* he had managed to get the yacht into his own hands.

Many things came back to me – his familiarity with the men, his treatment of me – which I had put down to a temporary want of balance – the fooling with the compasses; for I was certain now that he had been the doer of that piece of mischief. But *why*? That was the great point.

As I turned the matter over in my brain, an incident that had occurred some six days back came to me. It had been on the very day after the captain's report to me of the tampering with the compasses.

Barlow had, for the first time, relinquished his brooding and silence, and had started to talk to me, but in such a wild strain that he had made me feel vaguely uncomfortable about his sanity for he told me some yarn of an idea which he had got into his head. And then, in an overbearing way, he demanded that the navigation of the yacht should be put into his hands.

He had been very incoherent, and was plainly in a state of considerable mental excitement. He had rambled on about some derelict, and then had talked in an extraordinary fashion of a vast world of seaweed.

Once or twice in his bewilderingly disconnected speech he had mentioned the name of his sweetheart, and now it was the memory of her name that gave me the first inkling of what might possibly prove a solution of the whole affair.

I wished now that I had encouraged his incoherent ramble of speech, instead of heading him off; but I had done so because I could not bear to have him talk as he had.

Yet, with the little I remembered, I began to shape out a

theory. It seemed to me that he might be nursing some idea that
had formed – goodness knows how or when – that his sweetheart
(still alive) was aboard some derelict in the midst of an enormous
'world,' he had termed it, of seaweed.

He might have grown more explicit had I not attempted to
reason with him, and so lost the rest.

Yet, remembering back, it seemed to me that he must
undoubtedly have meant the enormous Sargasso Sea – that great
seaweed-laden ocean, vast almost as Continental Europe, and
the final resting-place of the Atlantic's wreckage.

Surely, if he proposed any attempt to search through that,
then there could be no doubt but that he was temporarily
unbalanced. And yet I could do nothing. I was a prisoner and
helpless.

IV

Eight days of variable but strongish winds passed, and still I was
a prisoner in my cabin. From the ports that opened out astern
and on each side – for my cabin runs right across the whole width
of the stern – I was able to command a good view of the
surrounding ocean, which now had commenced to be laden with
great floating patches of Gulf weed – many of them hundreds and
hundreds of yards in length.

And still we held on, apparently towards the nucleus of the
Sargasso Sea. This I was able to assume by means of a chart
which I found in one of the lockers, and the course I had been
able to gather from the 'tell-tale' compass let into the cabin
ceiling.

And so another and another day went by, and now we were
among weed so thick that at times the vessel found difficulty in
forcing her way through, while the surface of the sea had
assumed a curious oily appearance, though the wind was still
quite strong.

It was later in the day that we encountered a bank of weed so
prodigious that we had to up helm and run round it, and after
that the same experience was many times repeated; and so the

night found us.

The following morning found me at the ports, eagerly peering out across the water. From one of those on the starboard side I could discern at a considerable distance a huge bank of weed that seemed to be unending, and to run parallel with our broadside. It appeared to rise in places a couple of feet above the level of the surrounding sea.

For a long while I stared, then went across to the port side. Here I found that a similar bank stretched away on our port beam. It was as though we were sailing up an immense river, the low banks of which were formed of seaweed instead of land.

And so that day passed hour by hour, the weed-banks growing more definite and seeming to be nearer. Towards evening something came into sight – a far, dim hulk, the masts gone, the whole hull covered with growth, an unwholesome green, blotched with brown in the light from the dying sun.

I saw this lonesome craft from a port on the starboard side, and the sight roused a multitude of questions and thoughts.

Evidently we had penetrated into the unknown central portion of the enormous Sargasso, the Great Eddy of the Atlantic, and this was some lonely derelict, lost ages ago perhaps to the outside world.

Just at the going down of the sun, I saw another; she was nearer, and still possessed two of her masts. which stuck up bare and desolate into the darkening sky. She could not have been more than a quarter of a mile in from the edge of the weed. As we passed her I craned out my head through the port to stare at her. As I stared the dusk grew out of the abyss of the air, and she faded presently from sight into the surrounding loneliness.

Through all that night I sat at the port and watched, listening and peering; for the tremendous mystery of that inhuman weed-world was upon me.

In the air there rose no sound; even the wind was scarcely more than a low hum aloft among the sails and gear, and under me the oily water gave no rippling noise. All was silence, supreme and unearthly.

About midnight the moon rose away on our starboard beam, and from then until the dawn I stared out upon a ghostly world of

noiseless weed, fantastic, silent, and unbelievable, under the
moonlight.

On four separate occasions my gaze lit on black hulks that rose
above the surrounding weeds – the hulks of long-lost vessels.
And once, just when the strangeness of dawn was in the sky, a
faint, long-drawn wailing seemed to come floating to me across
the immeasurable waste of weed.

It startled my strung nerves, and I assured myself that it was
the cry of some lone sea bird. Yet, my imagination reached out
for some stranger explanation.

The eastward sky began to flush with the dawn, and the
morning light grew subtly over the breadth of the enormous
ocean of weed until it seemed to me to reach away unbroken on
each beam into the grey horizons. Only astern of us, like a broad
road of oil, ran the strange river-like gulf up which we had sailed.

Now I noticed that the banks of weed were nearer, very much
nearer, and a disagreeable thought came to me. This vast rift that
had allowed us to penetrate into the very nucleus of the Sargasso
Sea – suppose it should close!

It would mean inevitably that there would be one more among
the missing – another unanswered mystery of the inscrutable
ocean. I resisted the thought, and came back more directly into
the present.

Evidently the wind was still dropping, for we were moving
slowly, as a glance at the ever-nearing weed-banks told me. The
hours passed on, and my breakfast, when the steward brought it,
I took to one of the ports, and there ate; for I would lose nothing
of the strange surroundings into which we were so steadily
plunging.

And so the morning passed.

V

It was about an hour after dinner that I observed the open
channel between the weedbanks to be narrowing almost minute
by minute with uncomfortable speed. I could do nothing except
watch and surmise.

At times I felt convinced that the immense masses of weed were closing in upon us, but I fought off the thought with the more hopeful one that we were surely approaching some narrowing outlet of the gulf that yawned so far across the seaweed.

By the time the afternoon was half-through, the weed-banks had approached so close that occasional out-jutting masses scraped the yacht's sides in passing. It was now with the stuff below my face, within a few feet of my eyes, that I discovered the immense amount of life that stirred among all the hideous waste.

Innumerable crabs crawled among the seaweed, and once, indistinctly, something stirred among the depths of a large outlying tuft of weed. What it was I could not tell, though afterwards I had an idea; but all I saw was something dark and glistening. We were past it before I could see more.

The steward was in the act of bringing in my tea, when from above there came a noise of shouting, and almost immediately a slight jolt. The man put down the tray he was carrying, and glanced at me, with startled expression.

'What is it, Jones?' I questioned.

'I don't know sir. I expect it's the weed,' he replied.

I ran to the port, craned out my head, and looked forward. Our bow seemed to be embedded in a mass of weeds, and as I watched it came further aft.

Within the next five minutes we had driven through it into a circle of sea that was free from the weed. Across this we seemed to drift, rather than sail, so slow was our speed.

Upon its opposite margin we brought up the vessel swinging broadside on to the weed, being secured thus with a couple of kedges cast from the bows and stern, though of this I was not aware until later. As we swung, and at last I was able from my port to see ahead, I saw a thing that amazed me.

There, not three hundred feet distant across the quaking weed, a vessel lay embedded. She had been a three-master; but of these only the mizzen was standing. For perhaps a minute I stared, scarcely breathing in my exceeding interest.

All around above her bulwarks to the height of apparently some ten feet, ran a sort of fencing formed, so far as I could make out, from canvas, rope, and spars. Even as I wondered at the use of such a thing, I heard my chum's voice overhead. He was hailing her:

'Graiken, ahoy!' he shouted. 'Graiken, ahoy!'

At that I fairly jumped. Graiken! What could he mean! I stared out of the port. The blaze of the sinking sun flashed redly upon her stern, and showed the lettering of her name and port; yet the distance was too great for me to read.

I ran across to my table to see if there were a pair of binoculars in the drawers. I found one in the first I opened; then I ran back to the port, racking them out as I went. I reached it, and clapped them to my eyes. Yes; I saw it plainly, her name Graiken and her port London.

From her name my gaze moved to that strange fencing about her. There was a movement in the aft part. As I watched a portion of it slid to one side, and a man's head and shoulders appeared.

I nearly yelled with the excitement of that moment. I could scarcely believe the thing I saw. The man waved an arm, and a vague hail reached us across the weed, then he disappeared. A moment later a score of people crowded the opening, and among them I made out distinctly the face and figure of a girl.

'He was right, after all!' I heard myself saying out loud in a voice that was toneless through very amazement.

In a minute, I was at the door, beating it with my fists. 'Let me out, Ned! Let me out!' I shouted.

I felt that I could forgive him all the indignity that I had suffered. Nay, more; in a queer way way I had a feeling that it was I who needed to ask *him* for forgiveness. All my bitterness had gone, and I wanted only to be out and give a hand in the rescue.

Yet though I shouted, no one came, so that at last I returned quickly to the port, to see what further developments there were.

Across the weed I now saw that one man had his hands up to his mouth shouting. His voice reached me only as a faint, hoarse cry; the distance was too great for anyone aboard the yacht to distinguish its import.

From the derelict my attention was drawn abruptly to a scene alongside. A plank was thrown down on to the weed, and the next moment I saw my chum swing himself down the side and leap upon it.

I had opened my mouth to call out to him that I would forgive all were I but freed to lend a hand in this unbelievable rescue.

But even as the words formed they died, for though the weed appeared so dense, it was evidently incapable of bearing any considerable weight, and the plank, with Barlow upon it, sank down into the weed almost to his waist.

He turned and grabbed at the rope with both hands, and in the same moment he gave a loud cry of sheer terror, and commenced to scramble up the yacht's side.

As his feet drew clear of the weed I gave a short cry. Something was curled about his left ankle – something oily, supple and tapered. As I stared another rose up out from the weed and swayed through the air, made a grab at his leg, missed and appeared to wave aimlessly. Others came towards him as he struggled upwards.

Then I saw hands reach down from above and seize Barlow beneath the arms. They lifted him by main force, and with a mass of weed that enfolded something leathery, from which numbers of curling arms writhed.

A hand slashed down with a sheath-knife, and the next instant the hideous thing had fallen back among the weed.

For a couple of seconds longer I remained, my head twisted upwards; then faces appeared once more over our rail, and I saw the men extending arms and fingers, pointing. From above me there rose a hoarse chorus of fear and wonder, and I turned my head swiftly to glance down and across that treacherous extraordinary weedworld.

The whole of the hitherto silent surface was all of a move in one stupendous undulation – as though life had come to all that desolation.

The undulatory movement continued, and abruptly, in a hundred places, the seaweed was tossed up into sudden billowy hillocks. From these burst mighty arms, and in an instant the evening air was full of them, hundreds and hundreds, coming toward the yacht.

'Devil-fishes!' shouted a man's voice from the deck. 'Octopuses! My Gord!'

Then I caught my chum shouting.

'Cut the mooring ropes!' he yelled.

This must have been done almost on the instant, for immediately there showed between us and the nearest weed a broadening gap of scummy water.

'Haul away, lads!' I heard Barlow shouting; and the same instant I caught the splash, splash of something in the water on our port side. I rushed across and looked out. I found that a rope had been carried across to the opposite seaweed, and that the men were now warping us rapidly from those invading horrors.

I raced back to the starboard port, and, lo! as though by magic, there stretched between us and the Graiken only the silent stretch of demure weed and some fifty feet of water. It seemed inconceivable that it was a covering to so much terror.

And then speedily the night was upon us, hiding all; but from the decks above there commenced a sound of hammering that continued long throughout the night – long after I, weary with my previous night's vigil, had passed into a fitful slumber, broken anon by that hammering above.

VI

'Your breakfast, sir,' came respectfully enough in the steward's voice; and I woke with a start. Overhead, there still sounded that persistent hammering, and I turned to the steward for an explanation.

'I don't exactly know, sir,' was his reply. 'It's something the carpenter's doing to one of the lifeboats.' And then he left me.

I ate my breakfast standing at the port, staring at the distant Graiken. The weed was perfectly quiet, and we were lying about the centre of the little lake.

As I watched the derelict, it seemed to me that I saw a movement about her side, and I reached for the glasses. Adjusting them, I made out that there were several of the cuttlefish attached to her in different parts, their arms spread out almost starwise across the lower portions of her hull.

Occasionally a feeler would detached itself and wave aimlessly. This it was that had drawn my attention. The sight of these creatures, in conjunction with that extraordinary scene the previous evening, enabled me to guess the use of the great screen running about the Graiken. It had obviously been erected as a protection against the vile inhabitants of that strange weed-world.

From that my thoughts passed to the problem of reaching and rescuing the crew of the derelict. I could by no means conceive how this was to be effected.

As I stood pondering, whilst I ate, I caught the voices of men chaunteying on deck. For a while this continued; then came Barlow's voice shouting orders, and almost immediately a splash in the water on the starboard side.

I poked my head out through the port, and stared. They had got one of the lifeboats into the water. To the gunnel of the boat they had added a superstructure ending in a roof, the whole somewhat resembling a gigantic dog-kennel.

From under the two sharp ends of the boat rose a couple of planks at an angle or thirty degrees. These appeared to be firmly bolted to the boat and the superstructure. I guessed that their purpose was to enable the boat to over-ride the seaweed, instead of ploughing into it and getting fast.

In the stern of the boat was fixed a strong ringbolt, into which was spliced the end of a coil of one-inch manilla rope. Along the sides of the boat, and high above the gunnel, the superstructure was pierced with holes for oars. In one side of the roof was placed a trapdoor. The idea struck me as wonderfully ingenious, and a very probable solution of the difficulty of rescuing the crew of the Graiken.

A few minutes later one of the men threw over a rope on to the roof of the boat. He opened the trap, and lowered himself into the interior. I noticed that he was armed with one of the yacht's cutlasses and a revolver.

It was evident that my chum fully appreciated the difficulties that were to be overcome. In a few seconds the man was followed by four others of the crew, similarly armed; and then Barlow.

Seeing him, I craned my head as far as possible, and sang out to him.

'Ned! Ned, old man!' I shouted. 'Let me come along with you!'

He appeared never to have heard me. I noticed his face, just before he shut down the trap above him. The expression was fixed and peculiar. It had the uncomfortable remoteness of a sleep-walker.

'Confound it!' I muttered, and after that I said nothing; for it hurt my dignity to supplicate before the men.

From the interior of the boat I heard Barlow's voice, muffled. Immediately four oars were passed out through the holes in the sides, while from slots in the front and rear of the superstructure were thrust a couple of oars with wooden chocks nailed to the blades.

These, I guessed, were intended to assist in steering the boat, that in the bow being primarily for pressing down the weed before the boat, so as to allow her to surmount it the more easily.

Another muffled order came from the interior of the queer-looking craft, and immediately the four oars dipped, and the boat shot towards the weed, the rope trailing out astern as it was paid out from the deck above me.

The board-assisted bow of the lifeboat took the weed with a sort of squashy surge, rose up, and the whole craft appeared to leap from the water down in among the quaking mass.

I saw now the reason why the oar-holes had been placed so high. For of the boat itself nothing could be seen, only the upper portion of the superstructure wallowing amid the weed. Had the holes been lower, there would have been no handling the oars.

I settled myself to watch. There was the probability of a prodigious spectacle, and as I could not help, I would, at least, use my eyes.

Five minutes passed, during which nothing happened, and the boat made slow progress towards the derelict. She had accomplished perhaps some twenty or thirty yards, when suddenly from the Graiken there reached my ears a hoarse shout.

My glance leapt from the boat to the derelict. I saw that the people aboard had the sliding part of the screen to one side, and were waving their arms frantically, as though motioning the boat back.

Amongst them I could see the girlish figure that had attracted my attention the previous evening. For a moment I stared, then my gaze travelled back to the boat. All was quiet.

The boat had now covered a quarter of the distance, and I began to persuade myself that she would get across without being attacked.

Then, as I gazed anxiously, from a point in the weed a little ahead of the boat there came a sudden quaking ripple that shivered through the weed in a sort of queer tremor. The next instant, like a shot from a gun, a huge mass drove up clear through the tangled weed, hurling it in all directions, and almost capsizing the boat.

The creature had driven up rear foremost. It fell back with a mighty splash, and in the same moment its monstrous arms were reached out to the boat. They grasped it, enfolding themselves about it horribly. It was apparently attempting to drag the boat under.

From the boat came a regular volley of revolver shots. Yet, though the brute writhed, it did not relinquish its hold. The shots closed, and I saw the dull flash of cutlass blades. The men were attempting to hack at the thing through the oar holes, but evidently with little effect.

All at once the enormous creature seemed to make an effort to overturn the boat. I saw the half-submerged boat go over to one side, until it seemed to me that nothing could right it, and at the sight I went mad with excitement to help them.

I pulled my head in from the port, and glanced round the cabin. I wanted to break down the door, but there was nothing with which to do this.

Then my sight fell on my bunkboard, which fitted into a sliding groove. It was made of teak wood, and very solid and heavy. I lifted it out, and charged the door with the end of it.

The panels split from top to bottom, for I am a heavy man. Again I struck, and drove the two portions of the door apart. I hove down the bunk-board, and rushed through.

There was no one on guard; evidently they had gone on deck to view the rescue. The gunroom door was to my right, and I had the key in my pocket.

In an instant, I had it open, and was lifting down from its rack a heavy elephant gun. Seizing a box of cartridges, I tore off the lid, and emptied the lot into my pocket; then I leapt up the companionway on the deck.

The steward was standing near. He turned at my step; his face was white and he took a couple of paces towards me doubtfully.

'They're – they're – ' he began; but I never let him finish.

'Get out of my way!' I roared, and swept him to one side. I ran forward.

'Haul in on that rope!' I shouted. 'Tail on to it! Are you going to stand there like a lot of owls and see them drown!'

The men only wanted a leader to show them what to do, and, without showing any thought of insubordination, they tacked on to the rope that was fastened to the stern of the boat, and hauled her back across the weed – cuttle-fish and all.

The strain on the rope had thrown her on an even keel again, so that she took the water safely, though that foul thing was straddled all across her.

''Vast hauling!' I shouted. 'Get the doc's cleavers, some of you – anything that'll cut!'

'This is the sort, sir!' cried the bo'sun; from somewhere he had got hold of a formidable doublebladed whale lance.

The boat, still under the impetus given by our pull, struck the side of the yacht immediately beneath where I was waiting with the gun. Astern of it towed the body of the monster, its two eyes – monstrous orbs of the Profound – staring out vilely from behind its arms.

I leant my elbows on the rail, and aimed full at the right eye. As I pulled on the trigger one of the great arms detached itself from the boat, and swirled up towards me. There was a thunderous bang as the heavy charge drove its way through that vast eye, and at the same instant something swept over my head.

There came a cry from behind: 'Look out, sir!' A flame of steel before my eyes, and a truncated something fell upon my shoulder, and thence to the deck.

Down below, the water was being churned to a froth, and three more arms sprang into the air, and then down among us.

One grasped the bo'sun, lifting him like a child. Two cleavers gleamed, and he fell to the deck from a height of some twelve feet, along with the severed portion of the limb.

I had my weapons reloaded again by now, and ran forward along the deck somewhat, to be clear of the flying arms that flailed on the rails and deck.

I fired again into the hulk of the brute, and then again. At the second shot, the murderous din of the creature ceased, and, with an ineffectual flicker of its remaining tentacles, it sank out of sight beneath the water.

A minute later we had the hatch in the roof of the superstructure open, and the men out, my chum coming last. They had been mightily shaken, but otherwise were none the worse.

As Barlow came over the gangway, I stepped up to him and gripped his shoulder. I was strangely muddled in my feelings. I felt that I had no sure position aboard my own yacht. Yet all I said was:

'Thank God, you're safe, old man!' And I meant it from my heart.

He looked at me in a doubtful, puzzled sort of manner, and passed his hand across his forehead.

'Yes,' he replied; but his voice was strangely toneless, save that some puzzledness seemed to have crept into it. For a couple of moments he stared at me in an unseeing way, and once more I was struck by the immobile, tensed-up expression of his features.

Immediately afterwards he turned away – having shown neither friendliness nor enmity – and commenced to clamber back over the side into the boat.

'Come up, Ned!' I cried. 'It's no good. You'll never manage it that way. Look!' and I stretched out my arm, pointing. Instead of looking, he passed his hand once more across his forehead, with that gesture of puzzled doubt. Then, to my relief, he caught at the rope ladder, and commenced to make his way slowly up the side.

Reaching the deck, he stood for nearly a minute without saying a word, his back turned to the derelict. Then, still wordless, he walked slowly across to the opposite side, and leant his elbows upon the rail, as though looking back along the way the yacht had come.

For my part, I said nothing, dividing my attention between him and the men, with occasional glances at the quaking weed and the – apparently – hopelessly surrounded Graiken.

The men were quiet, occasionally turning towards Barlow, as though for some further order. Of me they appeared to take little notice. In this wise, perhaps a quarter of an hour went by; then abruptly Barlow stood upright, waving his arms and shouting:

'It comes! It comes!' He turned towards us, and his face seemed transfigured, his eyes gleaming almost maniacally.

I ran across the deck to his side, and looked away to port, and now I saw what it was that had excited him. The weed-barrier through which we had come on our inward journey was divided, a slowly broadening river of oil water showing clean across it.

Even as I watched it grew broader, the immense masses of weed being moved by some unseen impulsion.

I was still staring, amazed, when a sudden cry went up from some of the men to starboard. Turning quickly, I saw that the yawning movement was being continued to the mass of weed that lay between us and the Graiken.

Slowly, the weed was divided, surely as though an invisible wedge were being driven through it. The gulf of weed-clear water reached the derelict, and passed beyond. And now there was no longer anything to stop our rescue of the crew of the derelict.

VII

It was Barlow's voice that gave the order for the mooring ropes to be cast off, and then, as the light wind was right against us, a boat was out ahead, and the yacht was towed towards the ship, whilst a dozen of the men stood ready with their rifles on the fo'c's'le head.

As we drew nearer, I began to distinguish the features of the crew, the men strangely grizzled and old looking. And among them, white-faced with emotion, was my chum's lost sweetheart. I never expect to know a more extraordinary moment.

I looked at Barlow; he was staring at the white-faced girl with an extraordinary fixidity of expression that was scarcely the look of a sane man.

The next minute we were alongside, crushing to a pulp between our steel sides one of those remaining monsters of the deep that had continued to cling steadfastly to the Graiken.

Yet of that I was scarcely aware, for I had turned again to look at Ned Barlow. He was swaying slowly to his feet, and just as the two vessels closed he reached up both hands to his head, and fell like a log.

Brandy was brought, and later Barlow carried to his cabin; yet we had won clear of that hideous weed-world before he recovered consciousness.

During his illness I learned from his sweetheart how, on a terrible night a long year previously, the Graiken had been caught in a tremendous storm and dismasted, and how, helpless and driven by the gale, they at last found themselves surrounded by the great banks of floating weed, and finally held fast in the remorseless grip of the dread Sargasso.

She told me of their attempts to free the ship from the weed, and of the attacks of the cuttlefish. And later of various other matters; for all of which I have no room in this story.

In return I told her of our voyage, and her lover's strange behaviour. How he had wanted to undertake the navigation of the yacht, and had talked of a great world of weed. How I had – believing him unhinged – refused to listen to him.

How he had taken matters into his own hands, without which she would most certainly have ended her days surrounded by the quaking weed and those great beasts of the deep waters.

She listened with an evergrowing seriousness, so that I had, time and again, to assure her that I bore my old chum no ill, but rather held myself to be in the wrong. At which she shook her head, but seemed mightily relieved.

It was during Barlow's recovery that I made the astonishing discovery that he remembered no detail of his imprisoning of me.

I am convinced now that for days and weeks he must have lived in a sort of dream in a hyper state, in which I can only imagine that he had possibly been sensitive to more subtle understandings than normal bodily and mental health allows.

One other thing there is in closing. I found that the captain and the two mates had been confined to their cabins by Barlow. The captain was suffering from a pistol-shot in the arm, due to his having attempted to resist Barlow's assumption of authority.

When I released him he vowed vengeance. Yet Ned Barlow being my chum, I found means to slake both the captain's and the two mates' thirst for vengeance, and the slaking thereof is – well, another story.

DAVY JONES'S GIFT

John Masefield

'Gone to Davy Jones' Locker' is, of course, a very familiar term among seamen to describe anyone who is drowned at sea. Davy Jones is supposed to have been a sailor originally, but for generations now he has been thought of as a sea-spirit or devil. Stories about Davy Jones are naturally many and varied, but few writers have treated the legend with greater imagination than former-seaman-turned-author John Masefield (1878–1967).

Masefield was schooled for the Merchant Navy on the training ship Conway, and then served his apprenticeship on a windjammer. There he acquired the intimate knowledge of life at sea under sail which gave such authenticity and atmosphere to his prose and poetry. When ill-health forced him to leave the sea, he turned to verse and scored an immediate hit with his first collection, Salt Water Ballads (1902). Later, he mingled fact and fantasy in outstanding collections such as A Tarpaulin Muster (1907) and A Mainsail Haul (1913).

John Masefield's distinguished contributions to literature were honoured when he was made Poet Laureate in 1930, and then when he was awarded the O.M. in 1935. In the story which follows, 'Davy Jones's Gift' (1907) there is a little of the poetical and a lot of his feeling for the sea combined in a wholly original way.

'Once upon a time,' said the sailor, 'the Devil and Davy Jones came to Cardiff, to a place called Tiger Bay. They put up at Tony Adams's, not far from Pier Head, at the corner of Sunday Lane. And all the time they stayed there they used to be going to the rumshop, where they sat at a table, smoking their cigars, and dicing each other for different persons' souls. Now you must know that the Devil gets landsmen, and Davy Jones gets sailor-folk; and they get tired of having always the same, so then they dice each other for some of another sort.

'One time they were in a place in Mary Street, having some burnt brandy, and playing red and black for the people passing. And while they were looking out on the street and turning the cards, they saw all the people on the pavement breaking their necks to get into the gutter. And they saw all the shop-people running out and kowtowing, and all the carts pulling up, and all the police saluting. "Here comes a big nob," said Davy Jones. "Yes," said the Devil; "it's the Bishop that's stopping with the Mayor." "Red or black?" said Davy Jones, picking up a card. "I don't play for bishops," said the Devil. "I respect the cloth," he said. "Come on, man," said Davy Jones. "I'd give an admiral to have a bishop. Come on, now; make your game. Red or black?" "Well, I say red," said the Devil. "It's the ace of clubs," said Davy Jones; "I win; and it's the first bishop ever I had in my life." The Devil was mighty angry at that – at losing a bishop. "I'll not play any more," he said; "I'm off home. Some people gets too good cards for me. There was some queer shuffling when that pack was cut, that's my belief."

"'Ah, stay and be friends, man," said Davy Jones. "Look at what's coming down the street. I'll give you that for nothing."

'Now, coming down the street there was a reefer – one of those apprentice fellows. And he was brass-bound fit to play music. He stood about six feet, and there were bright brass buttons down his jacket, and on his collar, and on his sleeves. His cap had a big gold badge, with a house-flag in seven different colours in the middle of it, and a gold chain cable of a chinstay twisted round it. He was wearing his cap on three hairs, and he walked on both the pavements and all the road. His trousers were cut like wind-sails round the ankles. He had a fathom of red silk tie rolling out over his chest. He'd a cigarette in a twisted clay holder a foot and a half long. He was chewing tobacco over his shoulders as he walked. He'd a bottle of rum-hot in one hand, a bag of jam tarts in the other, and his pockets were full of love-letters from every port between Rio and Callao, round by the East.

"'You mean to say you'll give me that?" said the Devil. "I will," said Davy Jones, "and a beauty he is. I never see a finer." 'He is, indeed, a beauty," said the Devil. "I take back what I said about the cards. I'm sorry I spoke crusty. What's the matter with some more burnt brandy?" "Burnt brandy be it," said Davy Jones. So then they rang the bell, and ordered a new jug and clean glasses.

'Now the Devil was so proud of what Davy had given him, he couldn't keep away from him. He used to hang about the East Bute Docks, under the red-brick clock-tower, looking at the barque the young man worked aboard. Bill Harker his name was. He was in a West Coast barque, the *Coronel*, loading fuel for Hilo. So at last, when the *Coronel* was sailing, the Devil shipped himself aboard her, as one of the crowd in the fo'c'sle, and away they went down the Channel. At first he was very happy, for Bill Harker was in the same watch, and the two would yarn together. And though he was wise when he shipped, Bill Harker taught him a lot. There was a lot of things Bill Harker knew about. But when they were off the River Plate, they got caught in a pampero, and it blew very hard, and a big green sea began to run. The *Coronel* was a wet ship, and for three days you could stand upon her poop, and look forward and see nothing but a smother of foam from the break of the poop to the jib-boom. The crew had to roost on the poop. The fo'c'sle was flooded out. So while they were like this the flying jib worked loose. "The jib will be gone in half a tick," said the mate. "Out there, one of you, and make it fast, before it blows away." But the boom was dipping under every minute, and the waist was four feet deep, and green water came aboard all along her length. So none of the crowd would go forward. Then Bill Harker shambled out, and away he went forward, with the green seas smashing over him, and he lay out along the jib-boom and made the sail fast, and jolly nearly drowned he was. "That's a brave lad, that Bill Harker," said the Devil. "Ah, come off," said the sailors. "Them reefers, they haven't got souls to be saved." It was that that set the Devil thinking.

'By and by they came up with the Horn; and if it had blown off the Plate, it now blew off the roof. Talk about wind and weather. They got them both for sure aboard the *Coronel*. And it blew all the sails off her, and she rolled all her masts out, and the seas made a breach of her bulwarks, and the ice knocked a hole in her bows. So watch and watch they pumped the old *Coronel*, and the leak gained steadily, and there they were hove to under a weather cloth, five and a half degrees to the south of anything. And while they were like this, just about giving up hope, the old man sent the watch below, and told them they could start prayers. So the Devil crept on to the top of the half-deck, to look through the scuttle, to see what the reefers were doing, and what kind of prayers Bill Harker was putting up. And he saw them all sitting round the table, under the lamp, with Bill Harker at the head. And each of them had a hand of cards, and a length of knotted rope-yarn, and they were playing able-whackets. Each man in turn put down a card, and swore a new blasphemy, and if his swear didn't come as he played the card, then all the others hit him with their teasers. But they never once had a chance to hit Bill Harker. "I think they were right about his soul," said the Devil. And he sighed, like he was sad.

'Shortly after that the *Coronel* went down, and all hands drowned in her, saving only Bill and the Devil. They came up out of the smothering green seas, and saw the stars blinking in the sky, and heard the wind howling like a pack of dogs. They managed to get aboard the *Coronel*'s hen-house, which had come adrift, and floated. The fowls were all drowned inside, so they lived on drowned hens. As for drink, they had to do without, for there was none. When they got thirsty they splashed their faces with salt water; but they were so cold they didn't feel thirsty very bad. They drifted three days and three nights, till their skins were all cracked and salt-caked. And all the Devil thought of was whether Bill Harker had a soul. And Bill kept telling the Devil what a thundering big feed they would have as soon as they fetched to port, and how good a rum-hot would be, with a lump of sugar and a bit of lemon peel.

'And at last the old hen-house came bump on to Tierra Del Fuego, and there were some natives cooking rabbits. So the Devil and Bill made a raid of the whole jing bang, and ate till they were tired. Then they had a drink out of a brook, and a warm by the fire, and a pleasant sleep. "Now," said the Devil, "I will see if he's got a soul. I'll see if he give thanks." So after an hour or two Bill took a turn up and down and came to the Devil. "It's mighty dull on this forgotten continent," he said. "Have you got a ha'penny?" "No," said the Devil. "What in joy d'ye want with a ha'penny?" "I might have played you pitch and toss," said Bill. "It was better fun on the hen-coop than here." "I give you up," said the Devil; "you've no more soul than the inner part of an empty barrel." And with that the Devil vanished in a flame of sulphur.

'Bill stretched himself, and put another shrub on the fire. He picked up a few round shells, and began a game of knucklebones.'

IN THE
ABYSS

H. G. Wells

Speculation as to what might lie in the depths of the world's greatest oceans has absorbed oceanographers for years, as well as giving rise to a number of sea mysteries – the whereabouts of lost Atlantis being perhaps the most famous of these. With the development of deep-sea-diving equipment and the increasing capabilities of submarines, man is certainly getting closer to solving some of these mysteries, but doubtless the sea will preserve many more of them for generations to come.

In the area of speculative scientific writing, few names loom larger than Herbert George Wells (1866–1946): one of the founding fathers of Science Fiction. His works have not only taken readers to the planets (The First Men in the Moon, 1901), but also to the ends of time (The Time Machine, 1888) and even face to face with alien beings (The War of the Worlds, 1898). But Wells was also interested in the mysteries of his own world and in particular the unexplored regions of the globe, as described in novels like The Island of Dr Moreau (1896) and short stories such as 'The Sea Raiders'.

One of his most intriguing pieces of speculation is to be found in this next story, 'In The Abyss'. Back in the 1890s when it was written, the kind of equipment available for undersea exploration was still rather primitive and far from safe. Yet Wells could foresee a time when the deepest places might be reached, and explores the possibility in this strange and challenging adventure . . .

THE LIEUTENANT STOOD in front of the steel sphere and gnawed a piece of pine splinter. 'What do you think of it, Steevens?' he asked.

'It's an idea,' said Steevens, in the tone of one who keeps an open mind.

'I believe it will smash – flat,' said the lieutenant.

'He seems to have calculated it all out pretty well,' said Steevens, still impartial.

'But think of the pressure,' said the lieutenant. 'At the surface of the water it's fourteen pounds to the inch, thirty feet down it's double that; sixty, treble; ninety, four times; nine hundred, forty times; five thousand, three hundred – that's a mile – it's two hundred and forty times fourteen pounds; that's – let's see – thirty hundredweight – a ton and a half, Steevens; *a ton and a half* to the square inch. And the ocean where he's going is five miles deep. That's seven and a half –'

'Sounds a lot,' said Steevens, 'but it's jolly thick steel.'

The lieutenant made no answer, but resumed his pine splinter. The object of their conversation was a huge ball of steel, having an exterior diameter of perhaps nine feet. It looked like the shot for some Titanic piece of artillery. It was elaborately nested in a monstrous scaffolding built into the framework of the vessel, and the gigantic spars that were presently to sling it overboard gave the stern of the ship an appearance that had raised the curiosity of every decent sailor who had sighted it, from the Pool of London to the Tropic of Capricorn. In two places, one above the other, the steel gave place to a couple of circular windows of enormously thick glass, and one of these, set in a steel frame of great solidity, was now partially unscrewed. Both the men had seen the interior of this globe for the first time that morning. It was elaborately padded with air cushions, with little studs sunk between bulging pillows to work the simple mechanism of the affair. Everything was elaborately padded, even the Myers apparatus which was to absorb carbonic acid and replace the oxygen inspired by its tenant, when he had crept in by the glass manhole, and had been screwed in. It was so elaborately padded that a man might have been fired from a gun in it with perfect safety. And it had need to be, for presently a man was to crawl in through that glass manhole, to be screwed up tightly, and to be flung overboard, and to sink down – down – down, for five miles, even as the lieutenant said. It had taken the strongest hold of his imagination; it made him a bore at mess; and he found Steevens, the new arrival aboard, a godsend to talk to about it, over and over again.

'It's my opinion,' said the lieutenant, 'that that glass will simply bend in and bulge and smash, under a pressure of that sort. Daubrée has made rocks run like water under big pressures – and, you mark my words –'

'If the glass did break in,' said Steevens, 'what then?'

'The water would shoot in like a jet of iron. Have you ever felt a straight jet of high-pressure water? It would hit as hard as a bullet. It would simply smash him and flatten him. It would tear down his throat, and into his lungs; it would blow in his ears –'

'What a detailed imagination you have!' protested Steevens, who saw things vividly.

'It's a simple statement of the inevitable,' said the lieutenant.

'And the globe?'

'Would just give out a few little bubbles, and it would settle down comfortably against the day of judgement, among the oozes and the bottom clay – with poor Elstead spread over his own smashed cushions like butter over bread.'

He repeated this sentence as though he liked it very much. 'Like butter over bread,' he said.

'Having a look at the jigger?' said a voice, and Elstead stood behind them, spick and span in white, with a cigarette between his teeth, and his eyes smiling out of the shadow of his ample hat-brim. 'What's that about bread and butter, Weybridge? Grumbling as usual about the insufficient pay of naval officers? It won't be more than a day now before I start. We are to get the slings ready to-day. This clean sky and gentle swell is just the kind of thing for swinging off a dozen tons of lead and iron, isn't it?'

'It won't affect you much,' said Weybridge.

'No. Seventy or eight feet down, and I shall be there in a dozen seconds, there's not a particle moving, though the wind shriek itself hoarse up above, and the water lifts halfway to the clouds. No. Down there –' He moved to the side of the ship and the other two followed him. All three leant forward on their elbows and stared down into the yellow-green water.

'*Peace*,' said Elstead, finishing his thought aloud.

'Are you dead certain that clockwork will act?' asked Weybridge presently.

'It has worked thirty-five times,' said Elstead. 'It's bound to work.'

'But if it doesn't?'

'Why shouldn't it?'

'I wouldn't go down in that confounded thing,' said Weybridge, 'for twenty thousand pounds.'

'Cheerful chap you are,' said Elstead, and spat sociably at a bubble below.

'I don't understand yet how you mean to work the thing,' said Steevens.

'In the first place, I'm screwed into the sphere,' said Elstead, 'and when I've turned the electric light off and on three times to show I'm cheerful, I'm swung out over the stern by the crane, and all those big lead sinkers slung below me. The top lead weight has a roller carrying a hundred fathoms of strong cord rolled up, and that's all that joins the sinkers to the sphere, except the slings that will be cut when the affair is dropped. We use cord rather than wire rope because it's easier to cut and more buoyant – necessary points, as you will see.

'Through each of these lead weights you notice there is a hole, and an iron rod will be run through that and will project six feet on the lower side. If that rod is rammed up from below, it knocks up a lever and sets the clockwork in motion at the side of the cylinder on which the cord winds.

'Very well. The whole affair is lowered gently into the water, and the slings are cut. The sphere floats, – with the air in it, it's lighter than water, – but the lead weights go down straight and the cord runs out. When the cord is all paid out, the sphere will go down, too, pulled down by the cord.'

'But why the cord?' asked Steevens. 'Why not fasten the weights directly to the sphere?'

'Because of the smash down below. The whole affair will go rushing down, mile after mile, at a headlong pace at last. It would be knocked to pieces on the bottom if it wasn't for that cord. But the weights will hit the bottom, and directly they do, the buoyancy of the sphere will come into play. It will go on sinking slower and slower; come to a stop at last, and then begin to float upward again.

'That's where the clockwork comes in. Directly the weights smash against the sea bottom, the rod will be knocked through and will kick up the clockwork, and the cord will be rewound on the reel. I shall be lugged down to the sea bottom. There I shall stay for half an hour, with the electric light on, looking about me. Then the clockwork will release a spring knife, the cord will be cut, and up I shall rush again, like a soda-water bubble. The cord itself will help the flotation.'

'And if you should chance to hit a ship?' said Weybridge.

'I should come up at such a pace, I should go clean through it,' said Elstead, 'like a cannon ball. You needn't worry about that.'

'And suppose some nimble crustacean should wriggle into your clockwork – '

'It would be a pressing sort of invitation for me to stop,' said Elstead, turning his back on the water and staring at the sphere.

They had swung Elstead overboard by eleven o'clock. The day was serenely bright and calm, with the horizon lost in haze. The electric glare in the little upper compartment beamed cheerfully three times. They let him down slowly to the surface of the water, and a sailor in the stern chains hung ready to cut the tackle that held the lead weights and the sphere together. The globe, which had looked so large on deck, looked the smallest thing conceivable under the stern of the ship. It rolled a little, and its two dark windows, which floated uppermost, seemed like eyes turned up in round wonderment at the people who crowded the rail. A voice wondered how Elstead like the rolling. 'Are you ready?' sang out the commander. 'Ay, ay, sir!' 'Then let her go!'

The rope of the tackle tightened against the blade and was cut, and an eddy rolled over the globe in a grotesquely helpless fashion. Someone waved a handkerchief, someone else tried an ineffectual cheer, a middy was counting slowly: 'Eight, nine, ten!' Another roll, then with a jerk and a splash the thing righted itself.

It seemed to be stationary for a moment, to grow rapidly smaller, and then the water closed over it, and it became visible, enlarged by refraction and dimmer, below the surface. Before one could count three it had disappeared. There was a flicker of white light far down in the water, that diminished to a speck and vanished. Then there was nothing but a depth of water going down into blackness, through which a shark was swimming.

Then suddenly the screw of the cruiser began to rotate, the water was crickled, the shark disappeared in a wrinkled confusion, and a torrent of foam rushed across the crystalline clearness that had swallowed up Elstead. 'What's the idea?' said one A.B. to another.

'We're going to lay off about a couple of miles,' fear he should hit us when he comes up,' said his mate.

The ship steamed slowly to her new position. Aboard her almost everyone who was unoccupied remained watching the breathing swell into which the sphere had sunk. For the next half-hour it is doubtful if a word was spoken that did not bear directly or indirectly on Elstead. The December sun was now high in the sky, and the heat very considerable.

'He'll be cold enough down there,' said Weybridge. 'They say that below a certain depth sea water's always just about freezing.'

'Where'll he come up?' asked Steevens. 'I've lost my

bearings.'

'That's the spot,' said the commander, who prided himself on his omniscience. He extended a precise finger south-eastward. 'And this, I reckon, is pretty nearly the moment,' he said. 'He's been thirty-five minutes.'

'How long does it take to reach the bottom of the ocean?' asked Steevens.

'For a depth of five miles, and reckoning – as we did – an acceleration of two feet per second, both ways, is just about three-quarters of a minute.'

'Then he's overdue,' said Weybridge.

'Pretty nearly,' said the commander. 'I suppose it takes a few minutes for that cord of his to wind in.'

'I forgot that,' said Weybridge, evidently relieved.

And then began the suspense. A minute slowly dragged itself out, and no sphere shot out of the water. Another followed, and nothing broke the low oily swell. The sailors explained to one another that little point about the winding-in of the cord. The rigging was dotted with expectant faces. 'Come up, Elstead!' called one hairy-chested salt impatiently, and the others caught it up, and shouted as though they were waiting for the curtain of a theatre to rise.

The commander glanced irritably at them.

'Of course, if the acceleration's less than two,' he said, 'he'll be all the longer. We aren't absolutely certain that was the proper figure. I'm no slavish believer in calculations.'

Steevens agreed concisely. No one on the quarter-deck spoke for a couple of minutes. Then Steevens' watchcase clicked.

When, twenty-one minutes after, the sun reached the zenith, they were still waiting for the globe to reappear, and not a man aboard had dared to whisper that hope was dead. It was Weybridge who first gave expression to that realisation. He spoke while the sound of eight bells still hung in the air. 'I always distrusted that window,' he said quite suddenly to Steevens.

'Good God!' said Steevens; 'you don't think – ?'

'Well!' said Weybridge, and left the rest to his imagination.

'I'm no great believer in calculations myself,' said the commander dubiously, 'so that I'm not altogether hopeless yet.'

And at midnight the gunboat was steaming slowly in a spiral round the spot where the globe had sunk, and the white beam of the electric light fled and halted and swept discontentedly onward again over the waste of phosphorescent waters under the little stars.

'If his window hasn't burst and smashed him,' said Weybridge, 'then it's a cursed sight worse, for his clockwork has gone wrong, and he's alive now, five miles under our feet, down there in the cold and dark, anchored in that little bubble of his, where never a ray of light has shone or a human being lived, since the waters were gathered together. He's there without food, feeling hungry and thirsty and scared, wondering whether he'll starve or stifle. Which will it be? The Myers apparatus is running out, I suppose. How long do they last?'

'Good heavens!' he exclaimed; 'what little things we are! What daring little devils! Down there, miles and miles of water – all water, and all this empty water about us and this sky. Gulfs!' He threw his hands out, and as he did so, a little white streak swept noiselessly up the sky, travelled more slowly, stopped, became a motionless dot, as though a new star had fallen up into the sky. Then it went sliding back again and lost itself amidst the reflections of the stars and the white haze of the sea's phosphorescence.

At the sight he stopped, arm extended and mouth open. He shut his mouth, opened it again, and waved his arms with an impatient gesture. Then he turned, shouted 'El-stead ahoy!' to the first watch, and went at a run to Lindley and the search-light. 'I saw him,' he said. 'Starboard there! His light's on, and he's just shot out of the water. Bring the light around. We ought to see him drifting, when he lifts on the swell.'

But they never picked up the explorer until dawn. Then they almost ran him down. The crane was swung out and a boat's crew hooked the chain to the sphere. When they had shipped the sphere, they unscrewed the manhole and peered into the darkness of the interior (for the electric-light chamber was intended to illuminate the water about the sphere, and was shut off entirely from its general cavity).

The air was very hot within the cavity, and the indiarubber at the lip of the manhole was soft. There was no answer to their eager questions and no sound of movement within. Elstead seemed to be lying motionless, crumpled up in the bottom of the globe. The ship's doctor crawled in and lifted him out to the men outside. For a moment or so they did not know whether Elstead was alive or dead. His face, in the yellow light of the ship's lamps, glistened with perspiration. They carried him down to his own cabin.

He was not dead, they found, but in a state of absolute nervous collapse, and besides cruelly bruised. For some days he had to lie perfectly still. It was a week before he could tell his experiences.

Almost his first words were that he was going down again. The sphere would have to be altered, he said, in order to allow him to throw off the cord if need be, and that was all. He had had the most marvellous experience. 'You thought I should find nothing but ooze,' he said. 'You laughed at my explorations, and I've discovered a new world!' He told his story in disconnected fragments, and chiefly from the wrong end, so that it is impossible to re-tell it in his words. But what follows is the narrative of his experience.

It began atrociously, he said. Before the cord ran out, the thing kept rolling over. He felt like a frog in a football. He could see nothing but the crane and the sky overhead, with an occasional glimpse of the people on the ship's rail. He couldn't tell a bit which way the thing would roll next. Suddenly he would find his feet going up, and try to step, and over he went rolling, head over heels, and just anyhow, on the padding. Any other shape would have been more comfortable, but no other shape was to be relied upon under the huge pressure of the nethermost abyss.

Suddenly the swaying ceased; the globe righted, and when he had picked himself up, he saw the water all about him greeny-blue, with an attenuated light filtering down from above, and a shoal of little floating things went rushing up past him, as it seemed to him, towards the light. And even as he looked, it grew darker and darker, until the water above was as dark as the midnight sky, albeit of a greener shade, and the water below black. And little transparent things in the water developed a faint glint of luminosity, and shot past him in faint greenish streaks.

And the feeling of falling! It was just like the start of a lift, he said, only it kept on. One has to imagine what that means, that keeping on. It was then of all times that Elstead repented of his adventure. He saw the chances against him in an altogether new light. He thought of the big cuttle-fish people knew to exist in the middle waters, the kind of things they find half digested in whales at times, or floating dead and rotten and half eaten by fish. Suppose one caught hold and wouldn't let go. And had the clockwork really been sufficiently tested? But whether he wanted to go on or to go back mattered not the slightest now.

In fifty seconds everything was as black as night outside, except where the beam from his light struck through the waters, and picked out every now and then some fish or scrap of sinking matter. They flashed by too fast for him to see what they were. Once he thinks he passed a shark. And then the sphere began to get hot by friction against the water. They had under-estimated this, it seems.

The first thing he noticed was that he was perspiring, and then he heard a hissing growing louder under his feet, and saw a lot of little bubbles – very little bubbles they were — rushing upward like a fan through the water outside. Steam! He felt the window, and it was hot. He turned on the minute glow-lamp that lit his own cavity, and looked at the padded watch by the studs, and saw he had been travelling now for two minutes. It came into his head that the window would crack through the conflict of temperatures, for he knew the bottom water is very near freezing.

Then suddenly the floor of the sphere seemed to press against his feet, the rush of bubbles outside grew slower and slower, and the hissing diminished. The sphere rolled a little. The window had not cracked, nothing had given, and he knew that the dangers of sinking, at any rate, were over.

In another minute or so he would be on the floor of the abyss. He thought, he said, of Steevens and Weybridge and the rest of them five miles overhead, higher to him than the very highest clouds that ever floated over land are to us, steaming slowly and staring down and wondering what had happened to him.

He peered out of the window. There were no more bubbles now, and the hissing had stopped. Outside there was a heavy blackness – as black as black velvet – except where the electric light pierced the empty water and showed the colour of it – a yellow-green. Then three things like shapes of fire swam into sight, following each other through the water. Whether they were little and near or big and far off he could not tell.

Each was outlined in a bluish light almost as bright as the lights of a fishing smack, a light which seemed to be smoking greatly, and all along the sides of them were specks of this, like the lighter portholes of a ship. Their phosphorescence seemed to go out as they came into the radiance of his lamp, and he saw then that they were little fish of some strange sort, with huge heads, vast eyes, and dwindling bodies and tails. Their eyes were turned towards him, and he judged they were following him down. He supposed they were attracted by his glare.

Presently others of the same sort joined them. As he went on down, he noticed that the water became of a pallid colour, and that little specks twinkled in his ray like motes in a sunbeam. This was probably due to the clouds of ooze and mud that the impact of his leaden sinkers had disturbed.

By the time he was drawn down to the lead weights he was in a dense fog of white that his electric light failed altogether to pierce for more than a few yards, and many minutes elapsed before the hanging sheets of sediment subsided to any extent. Then, lit by his light and by the transient phosphoresence of a distant shoal of fishes, he was able to see under the huge blackness of the super-incumbent water an undulating expanse of greyish-white ooze, broken here and there by tangled thickets of a growth of sea lilies, waving hungry tentacles about.

Farther away were the graceful, translucent outlines of a group of gigantic sponges. About this floor there were scattered a number of bristling flattish tufts of rich purple and black, which he decided must be some sort of sea-urchin, and small, large-eyed or blind things having a curious resemblance, some to woodlice, others to lobsters, crawled sluggishly across the track of the light and vanished into the obscurity again, leaving furrowed trails behind them.

Then suddenly the hovering swarm of little fishes veered about and came towards him as a flight of starlings might do. They passed over him like a phosphorescent snow, and then he saw behind them some larger creature advancing towards the sphere.

At first he could see it only dimly, a faintly moving figure remotely suggestive of a walking man, and then it came into the spray of light that the lamp shot out. As the glare struck it, it shut its eyes, dazzled. He stared in rigid astonishment.

It was a strange vertebrated animal. Its dark purple head was dimly suggestive of a chameleon, but it had such a high forehead and such a braincase as no reptile ever displayed before; the vertical pitch of its face gave it a most extraordinary resemblance to a human being.

Two large and protruding eyes projected from sockets in chameleon fashion, and it had a broad reptilian mouth with horny lips beneath its little nostrils. In the position of the ears were two huge gill-covers, and out of these floated a branching tree of coralline filaments, almost like the tree-like gills that very young rays and sharks possess.

But the humanity of the face was not the most extraordinary thing about the creature. It was a biped; its almost globular body was poised on a tripod of two frog-like legs and a long thick tail, and its fore limbs, which grotesquely caricatured the human hand, much as a frog's do, carried a long shaft of bone, tipped with copper. The colour of the creature was variegated; its head, hands, and legs were purple; but its skin, which hung loosely upon it, even as clothes might do, was a phosphorescent grey. And it stood there blinded by the light.

At last this unknown creature of the abyss blinked its eyes open, and, shading them with a disengaged hand, opened its mouth and gave vent to a shouting noise, articulate almost as speech might be, that penetrated even the steel case and padded jacket of the sphere. How a shouting may be accomplished without lungs Elstead does not profess to explain. It then moved sideways out of the glare into the mystery of shadow that bordered it on either side, and Elstead felt rather than saw that it was coming towards him. Fancying the light had attracted it, he turned the switch that cut off the current. In another moment something soft dabbed upon the steel, and the globe swayed.

Then the shouting was repeated, and it seemed to him that a distant echo answered it. The dabbing recurred, and the globe swayed and ground against a spindle over which the wire was rolled. He stood in the blackness and peered out into the everlasting night of the abyss. And presently he saw, very faint and remote, other phosphorescent quasi-human forms hurrying towards him.

Hardly knowing what he did, he felt about in his swaying prison for the stud of the exterior light, and came by accident against his own small glow-lamp in its padded recess. The sphere twisted, and then threw him down; he heard shouts like shouts of surprise, and when he rose to his feet, he saw two pairs of stalked eyes peering into the lower window and reflecting his light.

In another moment hands were dabbing vigorously at his steel casing, and there was a sound, horrible enough in his position, of the metal protection of the clockwork being vigorously hammered. That, indeed, sent his heart into his mouth, for if these strange creatures succeeded in stopping that, his release would never occur. Scarcely had he thought as much when he felt the sphere sway violently, and the floor of it press hard against his feet. He turned off the small glow-lamp that lit the interior, and sent the ray of the large light in the separate compartment out into the water. The sea-floor and the man-like creatures had disappeared, and a couple of fish chasing each other dropped suddenly by the window.

He thought at once that these strange denizens of the deep sea had broken the rope, and that he had escaped. He drove up faster and faster, and then stopped with a jerk that sent him flying against the padded roof of his prison. For half a minute, perhaps, he was too astonished to think.

Then he felt that the sphere was spinning slowly, and rocking, and it seemed to him that it was also being drawn through the water. By crouching close to the window, he managed to make his weight effective and roll that part of the sphere downward, but he could see nothing save that pale ray of his light striking down ineffectively into the darkness. It occurred to him that he would see more if he turned the lamp off, and allowed his eyes to grow accustomed to the profound obscurity.

In this he was wise. After some minutes the velvety blackness became a translucent blackness, and then, far away, and as faint as the zodiacal light of an English summer evening, he saw shapes moving below. He judged these creatures had detached his cable, and were towing him along the sea bottom.

And then he saw something faint and remote across the undulations of the submarine plain, a broad horizon of pale luminosity that extended this way and that way as far as the range of his little window permitted him to see. To this he was being towed, as a balloon might be towed by men out of the open country into a town. He approached it very slowly, and very slowly the dim irradiation was gathered together into more definite shapes.

It was nearly five o'clock before he came over this luminous area, and by that time he could make out an arrangement suggestive of streets and houses grouped about a vast roofless erection that was grotesquely suggestive of a ruined abbey. It was spread out like a map below him. The houses were all roofless enclosures of walls, and their substance being, as he afterwards saw, of phosphorescent bones, gave the place an appearance as if it were built of drowned moonshine.

Among the inner caves of the place waving trees of crinoid stretched their tentacles, and tall, slender, glassy sponges shot like shining minarets and lilies of filmy light out of the general glow of the city. In the open spaces of the place he could see a stirring movement as of crowds of people, but he was too many fathoms above them to distinguish the individuals in those crowds.

Then slowly they pulled him down, and as they did so, the details of the place crept slowly upon his apprehension. He saw that the courses of the cloudy buildings were marked out with beaded lines of round objects, and then he perceived that at several points below him, in broad open spaces, were forms like the encrusted shapes of ships.

Slowly and surely, he was drawn down, and the forms below him became brighter, clearer, more distinct. He was being pulled down, he perceived, towards the large building in the centre of the town, and he could catch a glimpse ever and again of the multitudinous forms that were lugging at his cord. He was astonished to see that the rigging of one of the ships, which formed such a prominent feature of the place, was crowded with a host of gesticulating figures regarding him, and then the walls of the great building rose about him silently, and hid the city from his eyes.

And such walls they were, of water-logged wood, and twisted wire-rope, and iron spars, and copper, and the bones and skulls of dead men. The skulls ran in zigzag lines and spirals and fantastic curves over the building; and in and out of their eye-sockets, and over the whole surface of the place, lurked and played a multitude of silvery little fishes.

Suddenly his ears were filled with a low shouting and a noise like the violent blowing of horns, and this gave place to a fantastic chant. Down the sphere sank, past the huge pointed windows, through which he saw vaguely a great number of these strange, ghostlike people regarding him, and at last he came to rest, as it seemed, on a kind of altar that stood in the centre of the place.

And now he was at such a level that he could see these strange people of the abyss plainly once more. To his astonishment, he perceived that they were prostrating themselves before him, all save one, dressed as it seemed in a robe of placoid scales, and crowned with a luminous diadem, who stood with his reptilian mouth opening and shutting, as though he led the chanting of the worshippers.

A curious impulse made Elstead turn on his small glow-lamp again, so that he became visible to these creatures of the abyss, albeit the glare made them disappear forthwith into night. At this sudden sight of him, the chanting gave place to a tumult of exultant shouts; and Elstead, being anxious to watch them, turned his light off again, and vanished from before their eyes. But for a time he was too blind to make out what they were doing, and when at last he could distinguish them, they were kneeling

again. And thus they continued worshipping him, without rest
or intermission, for a space of three hours.

Most circumstantial was Elstead's account of this astounding
city and its people, these people of perpetual night, who have
never seen sun or moon or stars, green vegetation, nor any living,
air-breathing creatures, who know nothing of fire, nor any light
but the phosphorescent light of living things.

Startling as is his story, it is yet more startling to find that
scientific men, of such eminence as Adams and Jenkins, find
nothing incredible in it. They tell me they see no reason why
intelligent, water-breathing, vertebrated creatures, inured to a
low temperature and enormous pressure, and of such a heavy
structure, that neither alive nor dead would they float, might not
live upon the bottom of the deep sea, and quite unsuspected by
us, descendants like ourselves of the great Theriomorpha of the
New Red Sandstone age.

We should be known to them, however, as strange, meteoric
creatures, wont to fall catastrophically dead out of the
mysterious blackness of their watery sky. And not only we
ourselves, but our ships, our metals, our appliances, would
come raining down out of the night. Sometimes sinking things
would smite down and crush them, as if it were the judgment of
some unseen power above, and sometimes would come things of
the utmost rarity or utility, or shapes of inspiring suggestion.
One can understand, perhaps, something of their behaviour at
the descent of a living man, if one thinks what a barbaric people
might do, to whom an enhaloed, shining creature came suddenly
out of the sky.

At one time or another Elstead probably told the officers of the
Ptarmigan every detail of his strange twelve hours in the abyss.
That he also intended to write them down is certain, but he never
did, and so unhappily we have to piece together the discrepant
fragments of his story from the reminiscences of Commander
Simmons, Weybridge, Steevens, Lindley, and the others.

We see the thing darkly in fragmentary glimpses – the huge
ghostly building, the bowing, chanting people, with their dark
chameleon-like heads and faintly luminous clothing, and
Elstead, with his light turned on again, vainly trying to convey to

their minds that the cord by which the sphere was held was to be severed. Minute after minute slipped away, and Elstead, looking at his watch, was horrified to find that he had oxygen only for four hours more. But the chant in his honour kept on as remorselessly as if it was the marching song of his approaching death.

The manner of his release he does not understand, but to judge by the end of cord that hung from the sphere, it had been cut through by rubbing against the edge of the altar. Abruptly the sphere rolled over, and he swept up, out of their world, as an ethereal creature clothed in a vacuum would sweep through our own atmosphere back to its native ether again. He must have torn out of their sight as a hydrogen bubble hastens upward from our air. A strange ascension it must have seemed to them.

The sphere rushed up with even greater velocity than, when weighted with the lead sinkers, it had rushed down. It became exceedingly hot. It drove up with the windows uppermost, and he remembers the torrent of bubbles frothing against the glass. Every moment he expected this to fly. Then suddenly something like a huge wheel seemed to be released in his head, the padded compartment began spinning about him, and he fainted. His next recollection was of his cabin, and of the doctor's voice.

But that is the substance of the extraordinary story that Elstead related in fragments to the officers of the *Ptarmigan*. He promised to write it all down at a later date. His mind was chiefly occupied with the improvement of his apparatus, which was effected at Rio.

It remains only to tell that on February 2, 1896, he made his second descent into the ocean abyss, with the improvements his first experience suggested. What happened we shall probably never know. He never returned. The *Ptarmigan* beat over the point of his submersion, seeking him in vain for thirteen days. Then she returned to Rio, and the news was telegraphed to his friends. So the matter remains for the present. But it is hardly probable that no further attempt will be made to verify his strange story of these hitherto unsuspected cities of the deep sea.

UNDERSEA GUARDIANS

Ray Bradbury

Ray Bradbury (1920–) is one of the heirs to the mantle of H. G. Wells. As a master of speculative fiction his work ranges from pure Science Fiction to delightful fantasy which shows great inventiveness and a brilliant use of language. Though only a small percentage of his work has any direct relationship to the sea, such is his feeling for it that two highlights in his career are directly associated with the maritime world.

The first of these occurred in 1953 when Warner Brothers bought the screen rights to his short story, 'The Foghorn', about a sea monster that is attracted from its deep-sea lair by the sound of a warning horn for shipping. The movie which was made, directed by Eugene Lourie and starring Paul Christian and Paula Raymond, was released as The Beast from 20,000 Fathoms *and has since become something of a cult favourite. Three years later, Bradbury himself was signed by John Huston to write the screenplay for a new version of Herman Melville's classic,* Moby Dick, *with Gregory Peck as Captain Ahab. The book had long been one of his favourites and he transferred its high drama and philosophical complexities to the screen with considerable skill.*

One of his other stories to deal with the sea is 'Undersea Guardians', a rather neglected tale not yet included in any of his collections. It was written back in 1944 and not surprisingly takes the Second World War as its theme. It is an imaginative and memorable story introducing us to another of the sea's strange mysteries – mermaids.

THE OCEAN SLEPT quietly. There was little movement in its deep green silence. Along the floor of a watery valley some bright flecks of orange colour swam: tiny arrow-shaped fish. A shark prowled by, gaping its mouth. An octopus reached up lazily with a tentacle, wiggled it at nothing, and settled back dark and quiet.

Fish swam in and around the rusting, torn hulk of a submerged cargo ship, in and out of gaping holes and ripped ports. The legend on the prow said: *USS Atlantic*.

It was quite soundless. The water formed around the ship like green gelatin.

And then Conda came, with his recruits.

They were swimming like dream-motes through the wide dark-watered valleys of the ocean; Conda at the head of the school with his red shock of hair flurried upright in a current, and his red bush beard trailed down over the massive ribs of his chest. He put out his great arms, clutched water, pulled back, and his long body shot ahead.

The others imitated Conda, and it was very quietly done. The ripple of white arms, cupped hands, the glimmer of quick moving feet, was like the movement of motion pictures from which the sound-track has been cut. Just deep water silence and the mute moves of Conda and his swarm.

Alita came close at his kicking heels. She swam with her sea-green eyes wide-fixed and dark hair spilling back over her naked body. Her mouth twisted with some sort of agony to which she could give no words.

Alita felt something moving at her side. Another, smaller, woman, very thin in her nakedness, with gray hair and a shrivelled husk of face that held nothing but weariness. She swam too, and would keep on swimming.

And then there was Helene, flashing by over their heads like an instantaneous charge of lightning. Helene with her hot angry eyes and her long platinum hair and her strange laughter.

'How much longer, Conda?' The old woman's thought reached through the waters, touching the brains of them all as they swam.

'An hour. Perhaps only forty minutes!' came Conda's blunt retort. It had the depth of fathoms in it; dark like the tides in the sunken water lands.

'Watch out!' somebody cried.

Down through the green waters overhead something tumbled. A shadow crossed the ocean surface, quick, like a gigantic sea-gull.

'Depth-charge!' shouted Conda. 'Get away from it!'

Like so many frightened fish the twenty of them scattered instantly, with a flurry of legs, a spreading of arms, a diving of heads.

The depth-charge ripped water into gouts and shreds, spread terrific vibrations down to kick the sandy bottom, up to ram the surface like a geyser!

Alita screamed to herself as she sank, stunned, to the sea-floor, a queer strange pain going through her limbs. If only this were over, if only the real death came. If only it were over.

A shivering went through her. Quite suddenly the water was icy cold, and she was alone in the green emptiness. So very alone. Alone, staring at a dark ring on her left hand.

'Richard, I want to see you again so very much. Oh, Richard, if we could only be together.'

'Daughter.' The gentle thought husked at her as the old woman glided up, white hair misting around her wrinkled face. 'Don't. Don't think. Come along. There's work. Work to be done. Much of it. Work for you and me and the ships on the surface, and for – for Richard.'

Alita didn't move. 'I don't want to swim. I'd rather just sit here on the sand and . . . wait.'

'You know you can't do that.'

The old woman touched her. 'You'd be all the unhappier. You have a reason to swim or you wouldn't be swimming. Come along. We're almost there!'

The effects of the depth-charge, dropped from a low-flying airplane, had dispersed. Mud-streaks boiled up fogging the water, and there were a million air bubbles dancing toward the outer world like laughing diamonds. Alita let the old woman take her hand and tug her up from the sand floor. Together they progressed toward Conda, who was the nucleus of a growing congregation.

'Submarine!' somebody thought, in a tense whisper. 'Over that crop of coral ahead. That's why the airplane dropped the depth-charge!'

'What kind of submarine?' someone else asked.

'German,' said Conda grimly. His red beard wavered in the water and the red-rimmed eyes stared out with iron fury. Helene flicked by them all, swiftly, laughing. 'A German submarine lying on the bottom, sleeping quietly – waiting for the *convoy!*'

Their minds swirled at the words of Conda, like so many warm-cold currents intermixing with fear and apprehension.

'And the convoy will pass this spot in how long?'

'Half an hour at most, now.'

'Then there isn't much time, is there?'

'Not much.'

'Isn't it dangerous for us to be near it? What if the airplane returns with more depth-charges?'

Conda growled. 'This is the limit to the plane range. That plane won't be back. He's out of bombs and out of gas. It's our job now. And what of it? You afraid?'

Silence.

The ring of faces looked to Conda for the plan. Alita among them; fourteen men, six women. Men with beards grown out for, five months; hair long and unshorn about their ears. Pallid watery faces with determined bone under the skin, set jaws and tightened fists. All gathered like fragments of some oceanic nightmare. The pallid undead, breathing water, and thinking mute thoughts about the stormy night when the USS *Atlantic* had been torpedoed and sent to the bottom, with all of them trapped, screaming, inside her.

'We never had our chance,' said Conda, grimly, 'to get where we were going to do what we had to do. But we'll go on doing it until the war's over because that's all that's worth while doing. I don't know how we live or what makes us live except the will to fight, the will to vengeance, wanting to win – not wanting to lie on the coral shelves like so much meat for the sharks – '

Alita listened and shuddered. Why was she still alive and swimming forty fathoms under?

And then she knew. It was like sudden flame in her. She lived because she loved Richard Jameson. She lived simply because his ship might pass this way some day soon again, like it had three weeks ago, returning from England. And she might see him leaning on the rail, smoking his pipe and trying to smile, still alive.

She lived for that. She lived to keep him safe on every trip. Like the others, she had a purpose, a hot, constricting, unquenchable purpose to prevent more victims from coming down to join her in the same nightmare fashion as the USS *Atlantic*. She guessed that explained everything. There was good reason for her still to be moving, and somehow God had motivated them all in the green sea-weed plateaus and gullies.

'Now,' came Conda's heavy thought, 'we've this German submarine to consider. We have to knock it out of action completely. We can't have it lying here when the convoy comes. Alita – '

Alita jerked. She came out of her thoughts, and her pale lips moved. 'Yes?'

'You know what to do, Alita? And . . . Helene?'

Helene drifted down dreamily, laughing in answer, and opened white fingers to clench them tight.

'It's up to you, Alita and Helene. The rest of us will deploy around the submarine. Jones, you and Merrith try to jam the torpedo openings somehow. Acton, you work on the induction valves. Simpson, see what you can do to the guns on deck; and

Haines, you and the other men try your damnedest with the periscope and conning tower.'

'Yes, sir.'

'Good enough, sir.'

'If we do it, this'll be the sixth sub for us –'

'*If* we do it,' said Conda.

'Alita'll do it for us, won't you Alita?'

'What? Oh, yes. Yes! I'll do it.' She tried to smile.

'All right then.' Conda swung about. 'Spread out and go in toward the submarine under a smoke-screen. Deploy!'

Silently the congregation split into twos and threes and swam toward the coral shelf, around it, then sank to the bottom, scooped up great handfuls of mud and darkened the water with it. Alita followed, cold, tired, unhappy.

The submarine squatted on the bottom like a metal shark, dark and wary and not making a sound. Sea-weed waved drowsy fronds around it, and several curious blue-fish eyed it and fluttered past. Sunshine slanted down through water, touching the gray bulk, making it look prehistoric, primeval.

A veil of mud sprang up as the cordon of Conda's people closed in around the U-boat. Through this veil their pasty bodies twisted, naked and quick.

Alita's heart spasmed its cold grave-flesh inside her. It beat salt water through her arteries, it beat agony through her veins. There, just a few feet from her through the mud-veil lay an iron-womb, and inside it grown-up children stirred, living. And out here in the cold deeps nothing lived but the fish.

Conda and Alita and the others didn't count.

The submarine, a metal womb, nurturing those men, keeping the choking, hungry waters from them. What a difference a few inches of metal made between pink flesh and her own white flesh, between living and not living, between laughing and crying. All of that *air* inside the submarine. What would it be like to gasp it in again, like the old days just a few scant weeks ago? What would it be like to suck it in and mouth it out with talked words on it? To *talk* again!

Alita grimaced. She kicked her legs. Plunging to the U-boat, she beat her fists against it, screaming, 'Let me in! Let me in! I'm out here and I want to live! Let me in!'

'Alita!' The old woman's voice cried in her mind. A shadow drew across her lined face, softening it. 'No, no, my child, do not think of it! Think only of what must be done!'

Alita's handsome face was ugly with torture.

'Just one breath! Just one song!'

'Time shortens, Alita. And the convoy comes! The submarine must be smashed – now!'

'Yes,' said Alita wearily. 'Yes. I must think of Richard – if he should happen to be in this next convoy –' Her dark hair surged in her face. She brushed it back with white fingers and stopped thinking about living again. It was needless torture.

She heard Helene's laughter from somewhere. It made her shiver. She saw Helene's nude body flash by above her like a silver fish, magnificent and graceful as a wind-borne thistle. Her laughter swam with her. 'Open the U-boat up! Open it up and let them out and I'll make love to a German boy!'

There were lights in the submarine. Dim lights. Alita pressed her pale face against the port and stared into a crew's quarters. Two German men lay on small bunks, looking at the iron ceiling doing nothing. After a while one puckered his lips, whistled, and rolled out of the bunk to disappear through a small iron door. Alita nodded. This was the way she wanted it. The other man was very young and very nervous, his eyes were erratic in a tired face, and his hair was corn-yellow and clipped tight to his head. He twisted his hands together, again and again, and a muscle in his cheek kept jerking.

Light and life, a matter of inches away. Alita felt the cold press of the ocean all around her, the beckoning urge of the cold swells. Oh, just to be inside, living and talking like them . . .

She raised her tiny fist, the one with Richard's thick ring on it, from Annapolis, and struck at the port. She struck four times.

No effect.

She tried again, and knew that Helene would be doing the same on the opposite side of the sub.

The Annapolis ring clicked against thick port glass.

Jerking, the German lad pulled his head up half an inch and stared at the port, and looked away again, went back to twisting his fingers and wetting his lips with his tongue.

'I'm out here!' Alita struck again and again. 'Listen to me! Listen! I'm out here!'

The German sat up so violently he cracked his head against metal. Holding his forehead with one hand he slipped out of the bunk and stepped to the port.

He squinted out, cupping hands over eyes to see better.

Alita smiled. She didn't feel like smiling, but she smiled. Sunlight sprang down upon her dark smoke-spirals of hair dancing on the water. Sunlight stroked her naked white body. She beckoned with her hands, laughing.

For one unbelieving, stricken instant, it was as if hands strangled the German lad. His eyes grew out from his face like unhealthy gray things. His mouth stopped retching and froze. Something crumbled inside him. It seemed to be the one last thing to strike his mind once and for all insane.

One moment there, the next he was gone. Alita watched him fling himself back from the port, screaming words she couldn't hear. Her heart pounded. He fought to the door, staggering out. She swam to the next port in time to see him shout into the midst of a sweating trio of mechanics. He stopped, swayed, swallowed, pointed back to the bunk room, and while the others turned to stare in the designated direction, the young German ran on, his mouth wide, to the entrance rungs of the conning tower.

Alita knew what he was yelling. She spoke little German; she heard nothing; but faintly the waves of his mind impinged on hers, a screaming insanity:

'God! Oh God! She's outside. And she is swimming! And alive!'

The sub captain saw him coming. He dragged out a revolver and fired, point-blank. The shot missed and the two grappled.

'God! Oh God! I can't stand it longer! Months of sleeping under the sea! Let me out of this god-damned nightmare! Let me out!'

'Stop! Stop it, Schmidt! Stop!'

The captain fell under a blow. The younger man wrested the

gun from him, shot him three times. Then he jumped on the rungs to the conning tower, and twisted at mechanisms.

Alita warned the others. 'Be ready! One is coming out! He's coming out! He's opening the inner door!'

Instantly, breathlessly, passionately, Helene's voice rang: 'To hell with the inner door! It's the outer door we want open!'

'God in heaven, let me out! I can't stay below!'

'Stop him!'

The crew scrambled. Ringing down, the inner door peeled open. Three Germanic faces betrayed the biting fear in their bellies. They grabbed instruments and threw them at Schmidt's vanishing legs jumping up the rungs!

Conda's voice clashed like a thrust gong in the deep sunlit waters. 'Ready, everyone? If he gets the outer door open, we must force in to stop the others from ever closing it!'

Helen laughed her knifing laughter. 'I'm ready!'

The submarine stirred and rolled to a strange gurgling sound. Young Schmidt was babbling and crying. To Alita, he was now out of sight. The other men were pouring pistol shots up into the conning tower where he'd vanished, to no effect. They climbed after him, shouting.

A gout of water hammered down, crushed them!

'It's open!' Helene exulted. 'It's open! The outer seal is free!'

'Don't let them slam it again!' roared Conda. White bodies shot by, flashing green in the sunlight. Thoughts darkened, veiling like unsettled mud.

Inside the machine-room, the crew staggered in a sloshing, belching nightmare of thrusting water. There was churning and thrashing and shaking like the interior of a gigantic washing machine. Two or three crew-men struggled up the rungs to the inner lock and beat at the closing mechanism.

'I'm inside!' Helene's voice was high, excited. 'I've got him – the German boy! Oh, this is a new kind of love, this is!'

There was a terrific mental scream from the German, and then silence. A moment later his dangling legs appeared half in, half out of the lock as the door started to seal! Now it couldn't seal. Yanking desperately, the crew beneath tried to free him of the lock, but Helene laughed dimly and said, 'Oh, no, I've got him and I'm keeping him here where he'll do the most good! He's mine. Very much mine. You can't have him back!'

Water thundered, spewed. The Germans floundered. Schmidt's limbs kicked wildly, with no life, in the steadily descending torrent. Something happened to release him. The lock rapped open and he fell face down into the rising waters.

Something came with him. Something white and quick and naked. Helene.

Alita watched in a numbed sort of feeling that was too weary to be horror.

She watched until there were three Germans left, swimming about, keeping their heads over the water, yelling to God to save them. And Helene was in among them, invisible and stroking and moving quickly. Her white hands flickered up, grasped one officer by the shoulders and pulled him steadily under.

'This is a different kind of love! Make love to me! Make love! Don't you like my cold lips?'

Alita swam off, shuddering, away from the fury and yelling and corruption. The submarine was dying, shaking its prehistoric bulk with metal agony. In another moment it would be drowned and the job done. Silence would come down again and sunlight would strike on the dead, quiet U-boat and another attack would be successful.

Sobbing, Alita swam up toward the sun in the green silence. It was late afternoon, and the water became warmer as she neared the surface. Late afternoon. Back in Forest Hills they'd be playing tennis now on the hot courts, drinking cool cocktails, talking about dancing tonight at the Indigo Club. Back in Forest Hills they'd be deciding what formal to wear tonight to that dance, what show to see. Oh, that was so long ago in the sanity of living, in the time before torpedoes crushed the hull of the *USS Atlantic* and took her down.

Richard, where are you now? Will you be here in a few minutes, Richard, with the convoy? Will you be thinking of us and the day we kissed goodbye in New York at the harbour, when I was on my way to nursing service in London? Will you remember how we kissed and held tight, and how you never saw me again?

I saw *you*, Richard. Three weeks ago. When you passed by on Destroyer 242, oblivious to me floating a few feet under the water!

If only we could be together. But I wouldn't want you to be like this, white and sodden and not alive. I want to keep you from all this, darling. And I shall. That's why I stay moving, I guess. Because I know I can help keep you living. We just killed a submarine, Richard. It won't have a chance to harm you. You'll have a chance to go to Britain, to do the things *we* wanted to do *together*.

There was a gentle movement in the water, and the old woman was at her side.

Alita's white shoulders jerked. 'It – it was awful.'

The old woman looked at the sun caught in the liquid. 'It always is – this kind of death. It always has been – always will be as long as men are at war. We had to do it. We didn't take lives, we saved lives — hundreds of them.'

Alita closed her eyes and opened them again. 'I've been wondering about us. Why is it that just you and I and Conda and Helene and a few others survived the sinking? Why didn't some of the hundreds of others join us? What are we?'

The old woman moved her feet slowly, rippling the currents.

'We're Guardians, that's what you'd call us. A thousand people drowned when the *Atlantic* went down, but twenty of us came out, half-dead, because we have somebody to guard. You have a lover on the convoy routes. I have four sons in the Navy. The others have similar obligations. Conda has sons too. And Helene – well, her lover was drowned inside the *Atlantic* and never came half-alive like us, so she's vindictive, motivated by a great vengeance. She can't ever really be killed.

'We all have a stake in the convoys that cross and recross the ocean. We're not the only ones. Maybe there are thousands of others who cannot and will not rest between here and England, breaking seams in German cargo boats, darkening Nazi periscopes and frightening German crewmen, sinking their gun-boats when the chance comes.

'But we're all the same. Our love for our husbands and sons

and daughters and fathers makes us go on when we should be meat for fish, make us go on being Guardians of the Convoy, gives us the ability to swim faster than any human ever swam while living, as fast as any fish ever swam. Invisible guardians nobody'll ever know about or appreciate. Our urge to do our bit was so great we wouldn't let dying put us out of action . . .'

'I'm so tired, though,' said Alita. 'So very tired.'

'When the war is over – we'll rest. In the meanwhile –'

'The convoy is coming!'

It was Conda's deep voice of authority. Used to giving captain's orders for years aboard the *Atlantic*, he appeared below them now, about a hundred yards away, striving up in the watered sunlight, his red hair aflame around his big-nosed, thick-lipped face. His beard was like so many living tentacles, writhing.

The convoy!

The Guardians stopped whatever they were doing and hung suspended like insects in some green primordial amber, listening to the deeps.

From far, far off it came: the voice of the convoy. First a dim note, a lazy drifting of sound, like trumpets blown into eternity and lost in the wind. A dim vibration of propellers beating water, a bulking of much weight on the sun-sparkled Atlantic tides.

The convoy!

Destroyers, cruisers, corvettes, and cargo ships. The great bulking convoy!

Richard! Richard! Are *you* with them?

Alita breached water in her nostrils, down her throat, in her lungs. She hung like a pearl against a green velvet gown that rose and fell under the breathing of the sea.

Richard!

The echo of ships became more than a suggestion. The water began to hum and dance and tremble with the advancing armada. Bearing munitions and food and planes, bearing hopes and prayers and people, the convoy churned for England.

Richard Jameson!

The ships would come by like so many heavy blue shadows over their heads and pass on and be lost soon in the night-time, and tomorrow there would be another and another stream of them.

Alita would swim with them for a way. Until she was tired of swimming, perhaps, and then she'd drop down, come floating back here to this spot on a deep water tide she knew and utilized for the purpose.

Now, excitedly, she shot upward.

She went as near to the surface as she could, hearing Conda's thunder-voice commands.

'Spread out! One of you to each major ship! Report any hostile activity to me instantly! We'll trail with them until after sunset! Spread!'

The others obeyed, rising to position, ready. Not near enough to the surface so the sun could get at their flesh.

They waited. The hammer-hammer, churn-churn of ships folded and grew upon itself. The sea brimmed with its bellow going down to kick the sand and striking up in reflected quivers of sound. Hammer-hammer-churn!

Richard Jameson!

Alita dared raise her head above the water. The sun hit her like a dull hammer. Her eyes flicked, searching, and as she sank down again she cried, 'Richard. It's his ship. The first destroyer. I recognize the number. He's here again!'

'Alita, please,' cautioned the old woman. 'Control yourself. *My* boy too. He's on one of the cargo ships. I know its propeller voice well. I recognize the sound. One of my boys is here, near me. And it feels so very good.'

The whole score of them swam to meet the convoy. Only Helene stayed behind. Swimming around and around the German U-boat, swimming swiftly and laughing her strange high laugh that wasn't sane.

Alita felt something like elation rising in her. It was good, just to be this close to Richard, even if she couldn't speak or show herself or kiss him ever again. She'd watch him every time he came by this way. Perhaps she'd swim all night, now, and part of the next day, until she couldn't keep up with him any longer, and then she'd whisper goodbye and let him sail on alone.

The destroyer cut close to her. She saw its number on the prow in the sun. And the sea sprang aside as the destroyer cut it like a glittering knife.

There was a moment of exhilaration, and then Conda shouted it deep and loud and excited:

'*Submarine!* Submarine coming from north, cutting across convoy! German!'

Richard!

Alita's body twisted fearfully as she heard the under-water vibration that meant a submarine was coming in toward them, fast. A dark long shadow pulsed underwater.

There was nothing you could do to stop a moving submarine, unless you were lucky. You could try stopping it by jamming its propellers, but there wasn't time for that.

Conda yelled, 'Close in on the sub! Try to stop it somehow! Block the periscope. Do anything!'

But the German U-boat gnashed in like a mercurial monster. In three breaths it was lined up with the convoy, unseen, and squaring off to release its torpedoes.

Down below, like some dim-moving fantasy, Helene swam in eccentric circles, but as the sub shadow trailed over her she snapped her face up, her hot eyes pulled wide and she launched herself with terrific energy up at it, her face blazing with fury!

The ships of the convoy moved on, all unaware of the poisoned waters they churned. Their great valvular hearts pounding, their screws thrashing a wild water song.

'Conda, do something! Conda!' Alita shivered as her mind thrust the thoughts out at the red-bearded giant. Conda moved like a magnificent shark up toward the propellers of the U-boat, swift and angry.

Squirting, bubbling, jolting, the sub expelled a child of force, a streamlined torpedo that kicked out of its metal womb, trailed by a second, launched with terrific impetus – at the destroyer.

Alita kicked with her feet. She grasped at the veils of water with helpless fingers, blew all the water from her lungs in a stifled scream.

Things happened swiftly. She had to swim at incredible speed just to keep pace with submarine and convoy. And – spinning a bubbled trail of web – the torpedoes coursed at the destroyer as Alita swam her frantic way.

'It missed! Both torps missed!' someone cried; it sounded like the old woman.

Oh, Richard, Richard, don't you know the sub is near you. Don't let it bring you down to . . . *this*, Richard! Drop the depth charges! Drop them now!

Nothing.

Conda clung to the conning tower of the U-boat, cursing with elemental rage, striving uselessly.

Two more torpedoes issued from the mouths of the sub and went surging on their trajectories. Maybe –

'Missed again!'

Alita was gaining. Gaining. Getting closer to the destroyer. If only she could leap from the waters, shouting. If only she were something else but this dead white flesh . . .

Another torpedo. The last one, probably, in the sub.

It was going to hit!

Alita knew that before she'd taken three strokes more. She swam exactly alongside the destroyer now, the submarine was many many yards ahead when it let loose its last explosive. She saw it come, shining like some new kind of fish, and she knew the range was correct this time.

In an instant she knew what there was to be done. In an instant she knew the whole purpose and destiny of her swimming and being only half-dead. It meant the end of swimming forever, now, the end of thinking about Richard and never having him for herself ever again. It meant –

She kicked her heels in the face of water, stroked ahead, clean, quick. The torpedo came directly at her with its blunt, ugly nose.'

Alita coasted, spread her arms wide, waited to embrace it, take it to her breast like a long-lost lover.

She shouted it out in her mind:

'Helene! Helene! From now on – from now on – take care of Richard for me! Watch over him for me! Take care of Richard – !'

'Submarine off starboard!'

'Ready depth-charges!'

'Torpedo traces! Four of them! Missed us!'

'Here comes another one! They've got our range this time, Jameson! Watch it!'

To the men on the bridge it was the last moment before hell. Richard Jameson stood there with his teeth clenched, yelling, 'Hard over!' but it was no use; that torp was coming on, not caring, not looking where it was going. It would hit them amidship! Jameson's face went white all over and he breathed under his breath and clutched the rail.

The torpedo never reached the destroyer.

It exploded about one hundred feet from the destroyer's hull. Jameson fell to the deck, swearing. He waited. He staggered up moments later, helped by his junior officer.

'That was a close one, sir!'

'What happened?'

'That torp had our range, sir. But they must have put a faulty mechanism in her. She exploded short of her goal. Struck a submerged log or something.'

Jameson stood there with salt spraying his face. 'I thought I saw something just before the explosion. It looked like a . . . log. Yeah. That was it. A log.'

'Lucky for us, eh, sir?'

'Yeah. Damn lucky.'

'Depth-charge! Toss 'em!'

Depth-charges were dropped. Moments later a subwater explosion tore up the water. Oil bubbled up to colour the waves, with bits of wreckage mixed in it.

'We got the sub,' someone said.

'Yeah. And the sub almost got us!'

The destroyer ran in the wave channels, in the free wind, under a darkening sky.

'Full speed ahead!'

The ocean slept quiet as the convoy moved on in the twilight. There was little movement in its deep green silence. Except for some things that may have been a swarm of silver fish gathered below, just under the waters where the convoy had passed; pale things stirring, flashing a flash of white, and swimming off silently, strangely, into the deep green soundlessness of the undersea valleys . . .

The ocean slept again.

THE TURNING
OF THE TIDE

C. S. Forester

It is perhaps only right after spending so much of this collection far out on the vastness of the oceans, to return to the shore for this final contribution. It is also most appropriately by the Twentieth Century's best-known writer of sea stories, C. S. Forester (1899–1966), creator of the immortal Horatio Hornblower series which ran from 1937 to his death.

Forester was born in Egypt, and spent much of his childhood travelling in Europe, before coming to England to study medicine. However, the urge to write caused him to neglect his studies and before long they had been abandoned altogether. The sea featured in his work almost from the start, and in 1926 he described the voyage he and his wife made for their honeymoon in a dinghy called the Annie Marble.

The first Hornblower story, The Happy Return *appeared in 1937 and with success following success Forester was attracted to Hollywood. There he scored another major hit with the film based on his book,* The African Queen, *which appeared in 1952 starring the inimitable Humphrey Bogart.*

A number of his short stories likewise took their inspiration from the sea, the most notable being 'The Turn of the Tide' (1960). It is a grim little mystery, and like the sea itself there is something almost inevitable about what happens in the dramatic climax. For mystery and the sea have always been inextricably entwined – as this collection has clearly shown. And I have litle doubt they always will be.

'WHAT ALWAYS beats them in the end,' said Dr Matthews, 'is how to dispose of the body. But, of course, you know that as well as I do.'

'Yes,' said Slade. He had, in fact, been devoting far more thought to what Dr Matthews believed to be this accidental subject of conversation than Dr Matthews could ever guess.

'As a matter of fact,' went on Dr Matthews, warming to the subject to which Slade had so tactfully led him, 'it's a terribly knotty problem. It's so difficult, in fact, that I always wonder why anyone is fool enough to commit murder.'

All very well for you, thought Slade, but he did not allow his thoughts to alter his expression. *You smug, self-satisfied old ass! You don't know the sort of difficulties a man can be up against.*

'I've often thought the same,' he said.

'Yes,' went on Dr Matthews, 'it's the body that does it, every time. To use poison calls for special facilities, which are good enough to hang you as soon as suspicion is roused. And that suspicion – well, of course, part of my job is to detect poisoning. I don't think anyone can get away with it, nowadays, even with the most dunderheaded general practitioner.'

'I quite agree with you,' said Slade. He had no intention of using poison.

'Well,' went on Dr Matthews, developing his logical argument, 'if you rule out poison, you rule out the chance of getting the body disposed of under the impression that the victim died a natural death. The only other way, if a man cares to .

237

stand the racket of having the body to give evidence against him, is to fake things to look like suicide. But you know, and I know, that it just can't be done.

'The mere fact of suicide calls for a close examination, and no one has ever been able to fix things so well as to get away with it. You're a lawyer. You've probably read a lot of reports on trials where the murderer has tried it on. And you know what's happened to them.'

'Yes,' said Slade.

He certainly had given a great deal of consideration to the matter. It was only after long thought that he had, finally, put aside the notion of disposing of young Spalding and concealing his guilt by a sham suicide.

'That brings us to where we started, then,' said Dr Matthews. 'The only other thing left is to try and conceal the body. And that's more difficult still.'

'Yes,' said Slade. But he had a perfect plan for disposing of the body.

'A human body,' said Dr Matthews, 'is a most difficult thing to get rid of. That chap Oscar Wilde, in that book of his – *Dorian Gray*, isn't it? – gets rid of one by the use of chemicals. Well, I'm a chemist as well as a doctor, and *I* wouldn't like the job.'

'No?' said Slade, politely.

Dr Matthews was not nearly as clever a man as himself, he thought.

'There's altogether too much of it,' said Dr Matthews. 'It's heavy, and it's bulky, and it's bound to undergo corruption. Think of all those poor devils who've tried it. Bodies in trunks, and bodies in coal-cellars, and bodies in chicken-runs. You can't hide the thing, try as you will.'

Can't I? That's all you know, thought Slade, but aloud he said: 'You're quite right. I've never thought about it before.'

'Of course, you haven't,' agreed Dr Matthews. 'Sensible people don't, unless it's an incident of their profession, as in my case.

'And yet, you know,' he went on, meditatively, 'there's one decided advantage about getting rid of the body altogether. You're much safer, then. It's a point which ought to interest you, as a lawyer, more than me. It's rather an obscure point of law, but I fancy there are very definite rulings on it. You know what I'm referring to?'

'No, I don't,' said Slade, genuinely puzzled.

'You can't have a trial for murder unless you can prove there's a victim,' said Dr Matthews. 'There's got to be a *corpus delicti*, as you lawyers say in your horrible dog-Latin. A corpse, in other words, even if it's only a bit of one, like that which hanged Crippen. No corpse, no trial. I think that's good law, isn't it?'

'By jove, you're right!' said Slade. 'I wonder why that hadn't occurred to me before?'

No sooner were the words out of his mouth than he regretted having said them. He did his best to make his face immobile again; he was afraid lest his expression might have hinted at his pleasure in discovering another very reassuring factor in this problem of killing young Spalding. But Dr Matthews had noticed nothing.

'Well, as I said, people only think about these things if they're incidental to their profession,' he said. 'And, all the same, it's only a theoretical piece of law. The entire destruction of a body is practically impossible. But, I suppose, if a man could achieve it, he would be all right. However strong the suspicion was against him, the police couldn't get him without a corpse. There might be a story in that, Slade, if you or I were writers.'

'Yes,' assented Slade, and laughed harshly.

There never would be any story about the killing of young Spalding, the insolent pup.

'Well,' said Dr Matthews, 'we've had a pretty gruesome conversation, haven't we? And I seem to have done all the talking, somehow. That's the result, I suppose, Slade, of the very excellent dinner you gave me. I'd better push off now. Not that the weather is very inviting.'

Nor was it. As Slade saw Dr Matthews into his car, the rain was driving down in a real winter storm, and there was a bitter wind blowing.

'Shouldn't be surprised if this turned to snow before morning,' were Dr Matthews's last words before he drove off.

Slade was glad it was such a tempestuous night. It meant that, more certainly than ever, there would be no one out in the lanes, no one out on the sands when he disposed of young Spalding's body.

Back in his drawing-room Slade looked at the clock. There was still an hour to spare; he could spend it making sure that his plans were all correct.

He looked up the tide tables. Yes, that was right enough. Spring tides. The lowest of low water on the sands. There was not so much luck about that. Young Spalding came back on the midnight train every Wednesday night, and it was not surprising that, sooner or later, the Wednesday night would coincide with a Spring tide. But it was lucky that this particular Wednesday night should be one of tempest; luckier still that low water should be at one-thirty, the best time for him.

He opened the drawing-room door and listened carefully. He could not hear a sound. Mrs Dumbleton, his housekeeper, must have been in bed some time now. She was as deaf as a post, anyway, and would not hear his departure. Nor his return, when Spalding had been killed and disposed of.

The hands of the clock seemed to be moving very fast. He must make sure everything was correct. The plough chain and the other iron weights were already in the back seat of the car; he had put them there before old Matthews arrived to dine. He slipped on his overcoat.

From his desk, Slade took a curious little bit of apparatus; eighteen inches of strong cord, tied at each end to a six-inch length of wood so as to make a ring. He made a last close examination to see that the knots were quite firm, and then he put it in his pocket; as he did so, he ran through in his mind, the words – he knew them by heart – of the passage in the book about the Thugs of India, describing the method of strangulation employed by them.

He could think quite coldly about all this. Young Spalding was a pestilent busybody. A word from him, now, could bring ruin upon Slade, could send him to prison, could have him struck off the rolls.

Slade thought of other defaulting solicitors he had heard of, even one or two with whom he had come into contact professionally. He remembered his brother-solicitors' remarks about them, pitying or contemptuous. He thought of having to beg his bread in the streets on his release from prison, of cold and misery and starvation. The shudder which shook him was succeeded by a hot wave of resentment. Never, never, would he endure it.

What right had young Spalding, who had barely been qualified two years, to condemn a grey-haired man twenty years his senior to such a fate? If nothing but death would stop him, then he deserved to die. He clenched his hand on the cord in his pocket.

A glance at the clock told him he had better be moving. He turned out the lights and tiptoed out of the house, shutting the door quietly. The bitter wind flung icy rain into his face, but he did not notice it.

He pushed the car out of the garage by hand, and, contrary to his wont, he locked the garage doors, as a precaution against the infinitesimal chance that, on a night like this, someone should notice that his car was out.

He drove cautiously down the road. Of course, there was not a soul about in a quiet place like this. The few street-lamps were already extinguished.

There were lights in the station as he drove over the bridge; they were awaiting there the arrival of the twelve-thirty train. Spalding would be on that. Every Wednesday he went over to his subsidiary office, sixty miles away. Slade turned into the lane a quarter of a mile beyond the station, and then reversed his car so that it pointed towards the road. He put out the sidelights, and settled himself to wait; his hand fumbled with the cord in his pocket.

The train was a little late. Slade had been waiting a quarter of an hour when he saw the lights of the train emerge from the cutting and come to a standstill in the station. So wild was the night that he could hear nothing of it. Then the train moved slowly out again. As soon as it was gone, the lights in the station began to go out, one by one; Hobson, the porter, was making ready to go home, his turn of duty completed.

Next, Slade's straining ears heard footsteps.

Young Spalding was striding down the road. With his head bent before the storm, he did not notice the dark mass of the motor car in the lane, and he walked past it.

Slade counted up to two hundred, slowly, and then he switched on his lights, started the engine, and drove the car out into the road in pursuit. He saw Spalding in the light of the headlamps and drew up alongside.

'Is that Spalding?' he said, striving to make the tone of his voice as natural as possible. 'I'd better give you a lift, old man, hadn't I?'

'Thanks very much,' said Spalding. 'This isn't the sort of night to walk two miles in.'

He climbed in and shut the door. No one had seen. No one would know. Slade let his clutch out, drove slowly down the road.

'Bit of luck, seeing you,' he said. 'I was just on my way home from bridge at Mrs Clay's when I saw the train come in and remembered it was Wednesday and you'd be walking home. So I thought I'd turn a bit out of my way to take you along.'

'Very good of you, I'm sure,' said Spalding.

'As a matter of fact,' said Slade, speaking slowly and driving slowly, 'it wasn't altogether disinterested. I wanted to talk business to you, as it happened.'

'Rather an odd time to talk business,' said Spalding. 'Can't it wait till tomorrow?'

'No, it cannot,' said Slade. 'It's about the Lady Vere trust.'

'Oh, yes. I wrote to remind you last week that you had to make delivery?'

'Yes, you did. And I told you, long before that, that it would be inconvenient, with Hammond abroad.'

'I don't see that,' said Spalding. 'I don't see that Hammond's got anything to do with it. Why can't you just hand over and have done with it? I can't do anything to straighten things up until you do.'

'As I said, it would be inconvenient.'

Slade brought the car to a standstill at the side of the road.

'Look here, Spalding,' he said desperately, 'I've never asked a favour of you before. But now I ask you, as a favour, to forgo delivery for a bit. Just for three months, Spalding.'

But Slade had small hope that his request would be granted. So little hope, in fact, that he brought his left hand out of his pocket holding the piece of wood, with the loop of cord dangling from its ends. He put his arm round the back of Spalding's seat.

'No, I can't, really I can't,' said Spalding. 'I've got my duty to my clients to consider. I'm sorry to insist, but you're quite well aware of what my duty is.'

'Yes,' said Slade, 'but I beg of you to wait. I implore you to wait, Spalding. There! Perhaps you can guess why, now.'

'I see,' said Spalding, after a long pause.

'I only want three months,' pressed Slade. 'Just three months. I can get straight again in three months.'

Spalding had known other men who had had the same belief in their ability to get straight in three months. It was unfortunate for Slade – and for Spalding – that Slade had used those words. Spalding hardened his heart.

'No,' he said. 'I can't promise anything like that. I don't think it's any use continuing this discussion. Perhaps I'd better walk home from here.'

He put his hand to the latch of the door, and as he did so, Slade jerked the loop of cord over his head. A single turn of Slade's wrist – a thin, bony, old man's wrist, but as strong as steel in that wild moment – tightened the cord about Spalding's throat.

Slade swung round in his seat, getting both hands to the piece of wood, twisting madly. His breath hissed between his teeth with the effort, but Spalding never drew breath at all. He lost consciousness long before he was dead. Only Slade's grip of the cord round his throat prevented the dead body from falling forward, doubled up.

Nobody had seen, nobody would know. And what that book had stated about the method of assassination practised by Thugs was perfectly correct.

Slade had gained, now, the time in which he could get his affairs in order. With all the promise of his current speculations, with all his financial ability, he would be able to recoup himself for his past losses. It only remained to dispose of Spalding's body, and he had planned to do that very satisfactorily. Just for a moment Slade felt as if all this were only some heated dream, some nightmare, but then he came back to reality and went on with the plan he had in mind.

He pulled the dead man's knees forward so that the corpse lay back in the seat, against the side of the car. He put the car in gear, let in his clutch, and drove rapidly down the road – much faster than when he had been arguing with Spalding. Low water was in three-quarters of an hour's time, and the sands were ten miles away.

Slade drove fast through the wild night. There was not a soul about in those lonely lanes. He knew the way by heart, for he had driven repeatedly over that route recently in order to memorize it.

The car bumped down the last bit of lane, and Slade drew up on the edge of the sands.

It was pitch dark, and the bitter wind was howling about him, under the black sky. Despite the noise of the wind, he could hear the surf breaking far away, two miles away, across the level sands. He climbed out of the driver's seat and walked round to the other door. When he opened it the dead man fell sideways, into his arms.

With an effort, Slade held him up, while he groped into the back of the car for the plough chain and the iron weights. He crammed the weights into the dead man's pockets, and he wound the chain round the dead man's body, tucking in the ends to make it all secure. With that mass of iron to hold it down, the body would never be found again when dropped into the sea at the lowest ebb of the Spring tide.

Slade tried now to lift the body in his arms, to carry it over the sands. He reeled and strained, but he was not strong enough – Slade was a man of slight figure, and past his prime. The sweat on his forehead was icy in the cold wind.

For a second, doubt overwhelmed him, lest all his plans should fail for want of bodily strength. But he forced himself into thinking clearly – forced his frail body into obeying the vehement commands of his brain.

He turned round, still holding the dead man upright. Stooping he got the heavy burden on his shoulders. He drew the arms round his neck, and, with a convulsive effort, he got the legs up round his hips. The dead man now rode him pig-a-back. Bending nearly double, he was able to carry the heavy weight in that fashion, the arms tight round his neck, the legs tight round his waist.

He set off, staggering, down the imperceptible slope of the sands towards the sound of the surf. The sands were soft beneath his feet. It was because of this softness that he had not driven the car down to the water's edge. He could afford to take no chances of being embogged.

The icy wind shrieked round him all that long way. The tide was nearly two miles out. That was why Slade had chosen this place. In the depth of winter, no one would go to the water's edge at low tide for months to come.

He staggered on over the sands, clasping the limbs of the body close about him. Desperately, he forced himself forward, not stopping to rest, for he only had time now to reach the water's edge before the flow began. He went on and on, driving his exhausted body with fierce urgings from his frightened brain.

Then, at last, he saw it: a line of white in the darkness which indicated the water's edge. Farther out, the waves were breaking in an inferno of noise. Here, the fragments of the rollers were only just sufficient to move the surface a little.

He was going to make quite sure of things. Steadying himself he stepped into the water, wading in farther and farther so as to be able to drop the body into comparatively deep water. He held to his resolve, staggering through the icy water, knee deep, thigh deep, until it was nearly at his waist. This was far enough. He stopped, gasping in the darkness.

He leaned over to one side, to roll the body off his back. It did not move. He pulled at its arms. They were obstinate. He could not loosen them. He shook himself, wildly. He tore at the legs round his waist. Still the thing clung to him. Wild with panic and fear, he flung himself about in a mad effort to rid himself of the burden. It clung on as though it were alive. He could not break its grip, no matter how hard he tried.

Then another breaker came in. It splashed about him, wetting him far above his waist. The tide had begun to turn now, and the tide on those sands comes in like a race-horse.

He made another effort to cast off the load, and, when it still held him fast, he lost his nerve and tried to struggle out of the sea. but it was too much for his exhausted body. The weight of the corpse and the iron with which it was loaded overbore him. He fell.

He struggled up again in the foam-streaked, dark sea, staggering a few steps, fell again – and did not rise. The dead man's arms were round his neck, throttling him, strangling him. Rigor mortis had set in and Spalding's muscles had refused to relax.

ACKNOWLEDGEMENTS

The editor wishes to thank the following authors, their agents or executors, for permission to include copyright material in this collection:

Popular Publications Inc. for 'The Benevolent Ghost and Captain Lowrie' by Richard Sale © 1940.

Macmillan London for 'A Matter of Fact' by Rudyard Kipling © 1935.

William Heinemann for 'Davy Jones's Gift' by John Masefield © 1907.

A. P. Watt Ltd for 'In The Abyss' by H. G. Wells © 1946.

A. D. Peters Literary Agency for 'Undersea Guardians' by Ray Bradbury © 1944; and 'The Turning of the Tide' by C. S. Forester © 1952.

Every effort has been made to trace the copyright holders of the stories in this book. The editor offers his apologies in the event of any acknowledgement being accidentally omitted.